ALSO BY MATT FORBECK

MOJANG

MINECRAFT DUNGEONS

THE RISE OF THE ARCH-ILLAGER

MATT FORBECK

DEL REY

NEW YORK

Copyright © 2020 by by Mojang AB and Mojang Synergies AB.
All rights reserved.

Published in the United States by Del Rey,
an imprint of Random House, a division of
Penguin Random House LLC, New York.

Del Rey is a registered trademark and the
Circle colophon is a trademark of Penguin Random House LLC.

Hardback ISBN 978-0-399-18081-1
International edition ISBN 978-0-593-15964-4
Ebook ISBN 978-0-399-18082-8

Printed in the United States of America on acid-free paper

randomhousebooks.com

2 4 6 8 9 7 5 3 1

First Edition

Book design by Elizabeth A. D. Eno

For my kids—Marty, Pat, Nick, Ken, and Helen—who taught me the wonders of playing Minecraft back when it was still in public alpha. And for my wife, Ann, who loved watching us all play.

PROLOGUE

Karl wasn't sure why a bunch of undead mobs had decided to attack the raiding party of Illagers who'd been roaming through the lands outside of the village he'd adopted, but he didn't question his good fortune. He'd been spoiling for a fight all week. Now, on this otherwise dreary and rainy day, he finally had one on his hands.

A smarter hero might have found a comfortable place to sit—any clear stretch of grass or even a convenient tree stump would do—and might have watched the entire battle unfold in the clearing below the hill on which he stood. It would have been easy to just let the two sides fight it out, wasting all their energy on each other. In the end, there might only have been a few foes left over to take care of, or maybe just to run off.

But Karl was a man of action. A hero in his own mind, if not in the minds of others. So help him, the fight looked like fun, and he wasn't about to let all those fools down there have all of it.

Bellowing a loud, wordless battle cry, Karl drew his jagged iron sword and charged down into the fray. A wide and reckless grin creased his face.

The undead mobs were too focused on their current foes to

notice the screaming hero racing toward them, but the Illagers spotted him and began to break off from the fight. Karl cackled with delight at their reaction. Clearly his reputation as a mighty warrior had preceded him.

He could understand why the Illagers would flee before him. They had lives they valued. The undead—who weren't burdened with such treasures—continued to ignore him though. They chased after the Illagers instead.

Karl knew it wasn't terribly fair to attack foes from behind, but he'd never worried about such things. After all, the undead were mobs, right? And there were so many of them, it only seemed wise.

He waded into the skeletons and the zombies, swinging at them from behind. *Thwack-a-wack-wack!*

He mowed them down like fresh grass, his blade singing a metallic song of death. "Death to the undead!" he shouted as he struck again and again.

If he stopped to think about it—which he wouldn't—those words wouldn't make any sense, but he didn't care. The undead weren't about to correct him.

Karl smacked a nearby skeleton, knocking it into a pile of bones with a single swing of his sword. He stopped to shade his eyes from the rain and watch as its bleached skull arced high over the fleeing Illagers and landed in front of them. They skidded to a halt before it, horrified at what its sudden appearance might mean for them.

Karl threw back his head to laugh at their reaction, but when he was through he saw that the remaining skeletons and zombies had finally figured out that he was the bigger threat and had turned on him. The skeletons spread out to flank him, already peppering him with arrows from their bows. Meanwhile, the pack of zombies lunged toward him, filling the air with their wordless groans.

Karl's smile grew even wider. "Bring it on!" he shouted as he plunged into the crowd of zombies and slung his blade back and forth, smashing down foes with every strike.

There were downsides to being a hero. It was a lonely job in a strange land where you couldn't make a bit of sense out of the local language. You wound up saving the place over and over, and no one ever bothered to say thank you. The only people who really got him were other heroes, and they didn't always want to have much to do with him, either.

But Karl didn't care about any of that. *This* was what he lived for. He never felt more alive than when he was beating down mobs and taking their loot.

The zombies crowded so thick around Karl that they couldn't all get at him. Despite this, the skeletons kept shooting at him, planting arrows in the backs of their zombie pals.

Karl spun about like a top, hacking away with his sword in every direction. Zombies fell away from him, toppling like saplings before an axe. Few of them managed to lay a rotting finger on him, and even those glanced off his armor, leaving him unharmed.

As the crowd of groaning zombies around him thinned, an arrow finally made its way through the melee and caught him on the shoulder. It stuck in his armor as if it had been fired into a tree. The tip of it had punctured the iron and stabbed into his skin, although not much farther.

The magnitude of the injury didn't matter to Karl. The fact that he'd been damaged at all made him see red.

"Hey!" he shouted at the skeletons. "That hurt!"

Furious, Karl put down the last of the zombies with a few quick blows and then turned his attention to the skeletons. "You'll pay for that," he told them. "With your bones!"

He flanked the skinny monsters, moving to line them up in a rough row so they couldn't all shoot at him at once. Then he began chopping his way through them like a farmer taking down grains at the harvest.

The creatures peppered him with arrows, sticking several more into his armor, but all they did was make him angrier. Fighting skeletons was supposed to be fun for him, not dangerous!

As the last bony beast fell before his mighty blade, Karl let loose a howl of triumph and spun about to see who else might want a piece of him. His eyes fell upon the hapless Illagers, who had turned to face him, their weapons out and ready. Apparently they'd found their courage in the defeat of the undead.

They were too witless to shiver at his approach. Foes with any brains in their heads would have fallen to their knees and begged for mercy, but these nomadic raiders actually charged at him as if they stood a chance.

The ridiculousness of the moment brought a laugh to Karl's lips once again. The anger he'd felt at the skeletons faded away, and he roared with delight as he threw himself and his sword against the oncoming Illagers.

Before he could reach them, though, one of the Illagers—a particularly short one with a massive nose—raced forward, spun about, and shouted something at his compatriots. He seemed to be pleading with them to show some sense, something that Karl had long decided wasn't worth bothering with when it came to such people.

"They won't listen," Karl said to the little Illager, even though he knew no one could understand him. "They never do."

Out of morbid curiosity, he held up and let the tiny guy speak. If the imp wanted to keep his buddies from trying to take off Karl's head, well, he wasn't going to stop him.

But he wasn't going to lower his sword either.

The little guy gibbered along in his barbaric language, begging the others to see reason. To be swayed by the power of his logic, emotion, and words.

Karl marveled at it the way he would have if he'd spotted a two-headed pig roaming around the village. Amazing but really beside the point. It didn't matter how crazy it looked, it wasn't going to make a difference. In the end, he was still going to whack it with his sword.

Probably.

The other Illagers listened to the little guy for a moment, but they steamed at him, clearly unhappy with whatever he was blathering about. The little guy's voice rose almost to a squeak as he reduced himself to what Karl could only interpret as actual begging.

It ended when the Illager standing right in front of the little guy reached out and smacked him on the side of the head with the flat of his sword. That put a sudden end to the squeaking, and the little guy toppled right over, senseless before he hit the ground.

Before the bigger Illager could even call for an attack, Karl took him out with a sharp snap of his blade. He recognized a fight starting when he saw one, and he wasn't going to get caught flat-footed.

"It's on!" he shouted at the Illagers as he barreled into them, knocking them over like bowling pins. *"It's on!"*

Over the course of the next few minutes, Karl systematically took down each and every one of the Illagers. Some of them fought well. Most of them didn't.

Some of them tried to flee. He didn't let them.

In his experience, if he allowed them to get away, they'd only come back to bother him later, or torch the village, or annoy him in some other way. The only way to make sure that didn't happen was to get rid of them for good.

He might have felt bad about it, but they were the ones who'd attacked him. Even after he'd saved them from all those undead mobs.

"Not an ounce of gratitude from any of you," he said as he surveyed the tattered battlefield and the utter absence of anyone to stand against him. "So that's what you get."

A high-pitched groan sounded from across the field, and Karl perked up his ears and squinted around to see if he could detect where it had come from. It stumped him at first, but after a moment he spotted an Illager stirring on the far side of the field.

"Hm," he said as he strolled over to check out the one survivor. "Thought I got them all . . ."

When he reached the softly groaning Illager, he realized his mistake. This one was much smaller than all the rest.

"Ah," Karl said as he recognized the Illager who'd tried to talk some sense into the others. "The little guy with the big mouth."

He knelt down next to the creature and turned him over onto his back. "Nice try there, fella," he said with a chuckle. "I mean, it was worthless, but I respect the effort."

The sawed-off Illager gazed up at him with dismay and then tried to retreat. Since he was already on the ground, all he could do was worm away on his butt, right up until he bumped into a tree stump behind him.

Karl got up, put away his sword, and dusted off his hands. "I'm not going to hurt you," he told the little guy. "You did me a solid by distracting that big fella anyway. Once I took him out, the rest of your little band of misfits went down easy."

The body the little guy had run into let out a low moan. Karl edged up to the fallen Illager and leaned over to get a better look at him. Was that the one he'd stabbed to start the battle with them? Honestly, he had a hard time telling the bandits apart.

"That's all right," he told the little guy, who goggled at him with fear-struck eyes. "He doesn't look like much of a threat to anyone at the moment."

Karl backed off a few steps and smirked down at the little guy. "Neither do you."

He was feeling magnanimous at the moment. All he'd wanted to do was keep the mobs away from the village, and he'd managed that. Mopping up the last injured Illagers just didn't seem worth the bother.

An idea struck Karl then, something that would make him seem clever rather than lazy. At least in his own estimation.

"Tell you what," he said to the little guy, as the other Illager seemed too miserable to manage to listen. "This is your lucky day. I'm going to let you and your groaning pal there go. You know why?"

The little guy couldn't possibly have understood Karl's words, but maybe he got the gist of them from his tone. Either way, he shook his big-nosed head in terror at just the right time.

Karl flashed a wide smile. "Because you're going to go back to whatever you rotten, scummy Illagers call a home, and you're going to tell the rest of your kind not to come around here any-more. This village is under my protection, you get it? And when your people ask you what happened to you and all your friends, I want you to tell them one thing."

Karl held up his index finger to emphasize this particular point. "One thing, right?"

The little guy gaped at him while he tried to parse what to do. Maybe he gave up, or maybe he finally got it. In any case, he nodded so hard in agreement it looked like his head might fall off.

"Tell them my name." Karl pointed at himself. "Tell them, 'Karl.'"

CHAPTER ONE

Archie couldn't stand it anymore. The so-called "hero" who had taken down the rest of his raiding party strolled off, leaving him there among the ruin of the failed battle, and he hadn't been able to do a thing to stop it. All Archie could manage was to seethe in frustration and fury.

Sure, technically he could have picked up a sword and chased after the man, but what good would that have done? The only way that venture could end would be with Archie utterly defeated, and he'd had a rotten enough day already. He didn't want to cap it off with that.

Instead, Archie pushed himself to his feet and surveyed the complete disaster that surrounded him. As the runt of his band of Illagers, he was used to having bad days, but this topped them all.

It was awful enough that Archie had been roped into joining the patrol designated to defend the rest of the Illagers from that marauding mob of undead that had been wandering too close to their lands, but to wind up as the only survivor? He didn't think he could return to the rest of the Illagers if he had to bring home news like that. Enough of them already hated him that they'd probably kick him out of the tribe, and if that happened, he didn't have anywhere else to go.

Archie had fully expected to meet his end today at the clawing hands and teeth of a zombie or a skeleton's arrow. The irony that he had failed at even that made him struggle to choose between laughing and crying. He decided to do both.

As he stood there, racked with sobbing guffaws, someone smacked him on the back of the head.

Archie spun about, figuring the hero had changed his mind and decided to come back and finish off the job. He almost welcomed that. At least it would put his misery to a quick end.

Instead, he found himself face-to-face with something even worse: Thord.

Thord had been Archie's nemesis since childhood. The vicious Illager had picked on Archie relentlessly for as long back as either one of them could remember. The simple sight of Archie skulking around the dark forest in which they lived often spurred Thord to torture Archie with terrible taunts and even magical spells.

Of course, Thord usually spent whatever spare time he had plotting against someone. It didn't take much to encourage him to ruin someone's day. The elders in the Illagers' woodland mansion had tried to clamp down on his tendency toward violence over the years, which perhaps explained why Archie had somehow managed to survive to this day, but they'd failed often enough that Archie flinched every time he encountered his old foe.

Unfortunately, he hadn't scurried away fast enough that morning when the elders had called for volunteers to join the raiding party. Thord had pointed out Archie trying to slink off unseen and had insisted on dragging him along instead. "Just so I can keep an eye on you."

The one bit of good news about everyone else in the raiding party being taken down was that Archie wouldn't have to worry about Thord picking on him anymore. It might have been a small consolation, but he had clung to it.

But somehow Thord had survived too.

Of course.

Thord snarled at Archie and staggered over toward the smaller Illager, nearly tripping over the hem of the long, dark robes that marked him as an evoker, a dangerous Illager spellcaster. Archie could see how the hero had thought he'd taken care of the Illager. He looked more than half-dead. If he'd stayed on the ground, Archie would never have suspected he was still breathing.

"Don't just stand there gawking at me," Thord said, his voice curdled with humiliation and disgust. "Help me out!"

Archie wanted to mock Thord in the evoker's moment of weakness, but he worried that Thord might still have enough energy to attack him with a spell. He leaped forward to try to support the evoker, who was wobbling precariously on his feet. Weak as he was, Thord smacked Archie away with the back of his hand. The smaller Illager tumbled to the ground, clutching at his stinging cheek.

"As if a weakling like you could hold me up," Thord said with a shaky, frustrated sneer. "Find me a staff—or at least a sword!"

"But the undead are all destroyed, and that hero's gone too," Archie said, both uncertain and suspicious about Thord's intentions.

"Lucky for him!" Thord said as he staggered forward. "And for you. Now get me that sword!"

Archie glanced around frantically and found the weapon Thord was pointing at. It was battered and notched, but at least still in one piece. He snatched it up and handed it to the evoker without bothering to clean it off.

Thord didn't seem to care a bit about how battered it was. He just grabbed the weapon by the hilt, stabbed it into the ground, and used it as a crutch. Then, finally stabilized, he gazed out over the battlefield and frowned.

Archie didn't say a word. He knew from experience that anything he did could send Thord into a fit of rage, and he didn't want to trigger that. Not now for sure.

After a long moment, Thord spoke, his voice rough and low. "So, it's just you and me then, is it?"

Archie nodded.

Thord sucked at his teeth and grimaced. "You're going to pay for this."

Archie's jaw dropped. "But I didn't have anything to do with this! I barely fought at all!"

"Exactly," Thord said. "When your people needed you most, you curled up in a ball and ignored them while they screamed for help. They fought on valiantly while you sat there and let them be defeated."

"I-I-I . . ." Archie couldn't believe what Thord was saying. How could anyone think that of him? He hadn't wanted his people to lose! True, he hadn't done much to prevent that, but that was beyond his control. As Thord and the others had taught him over and over throughout his life, he was a weak creature who couldn't make a difference in anything, no matter how hard he might try. And now Thord was going to hold him responsible for that?

Archie cringed in fear. "I'm worthless! I always have been. I didn't even want to be here in the first place!"

"And that's my point! You would have happily allowed that hero to defeat us all—the entire tribe if you'd had your choice. You don't care about any of us. You let that hero destroy us, and don't think I'm going to let you get away with it."

Archie collapsed to the ground, unable to bear the horrors of the accusation. If Thord managed to limp back to the tribe and tell them such awful things about him, they'd probably destroy him on the spot. The best he'd be able to hope for would be eternal banishment.

"Oh, please no!" Archie gawked at Thord in dismay. "I knew this would go wrong. I just knew it! I told you!"

Thord scoffed at him. "Like mere words ever helped with anything."

It pained Archie to hear a sentiment like that. As weak as he was—and as little as he knew of magic—a sword was useless to him. All he had was words.

"I knew exactly what was going to happen as soon as that hero arrived, and I tried to warn you," Archie said, trying to explain. "I wanted to save you. I wanted to save us all!"

Thord snorted at Archie as if the pathetic Illager had just fallen into an outhouse and crawled out of the filth on his hands and knees. "You go ahead and try to tell that to the others. See what they have to say." He started staggering back in the direction of the Illager mansion, deep in the nearby dark forest.

"Wait!" Archie said as he scampered after Thord. "Why torture me? I'm no threat to you. It's that horrible hero you should be angry at."

Thord didn't bother glancing over his shoulder at Archie. "He's not at fault here. Can you really blame a hero for being a hero?"

"It wasn't me who destroyed the others." Archie scrambled to catch up. "I'm no hero! Haven't you had enough of them pushing us all around?"

"Illagers never run from a fight. Never!"

"We ran from the hero."

"We were *regrouping*!"

Archie ignored the lie. "But we couldn't have beaten one of them with a single patrol like that. We didn't have a chance. That was my whole and entire point!"

Archie grabbed Thord by the elbow. Thord ground to a halt with a painful wince and glared down at him. "You coward." He spat at him, striking him square on the side of his face.

Archie wiped his cheek clean. "We should have gone for help. We could have rallied the entire tribe together to take care of him. Think what that would mean!"

Thord rubbed his chin while he considered this. "Mobilizing the entire tribe to gang up on a single hero?"

"Exactly!" Hope leaped in Archie's chest. "Think about it! Think about how many Illagers there are compared to the heroes. If we could just gather every Illager we can find and pit them against the heroes, nothing could stop us!"

Thord snorted in disgust. "You really are the most worthless Illager I've ever known."

"Imagine five patrols working together. Or ten! Or twenty!"

"I'm in charge here! If we brought all those Illagers together, who would be in charge then?"

Archie knew that it was all about power for Thord—much as it was for most Illagers. If only he weren't so shortsighted! "But we fight heroes all the time! And how often do we win?"

Thord shook his head at Archie like he was an especially stupid child who'd been struck in the head far too many times. "We don't hunt *heroes*. We just *hunt*, and we take down whatever we can. That's our way, and it always has been. There's no reason to change it."

Archie pointed back at the battlefield where they'd suffered such a terrible loss. "Isn't that reason enough?"

Thord grunted. "What would you have us do? Start farming? Build villages? Become civilized and weak?" He sneered down at the smaller Illager. "I suppose you're already halfway there."

"We have to try something new," Archie said. "What we've been doing clearly isn't working. New heroes arrive here every day. It won't be too long until they build a village of their own. Maybe a city, even."

"You're a fool."

"And when that happens, they'll be unstoppable. We won't just lose a raiding party to them. We'll lose our entire tribe."

"That's coward's talk!"

"Instead of the hunters, we'll be the prey. They'll track us down and destroy every last Illager in the land!"

Even as injured as he was, Thord moved faster than Archie could see. One instant he was leaning on his sword as a crutch, and the next the flat of the blade smacked into the side of Archie's head.

The impact knocked Archie sprawling backward, stars spinning in his eyes. It took him a terrifying moment to recover his senses, during which he fully expected Thord to finish him off.

When he finally regained himself, though, Archie saw that Thord hadn't bothered to keep at him. He'd just started off toward the dark forest once more without uttering a single new word.

If anything, that terrified Archie even more.

CHAPTER TWO

"You can't tell everyone this is my fault!" Archie said. "You can't!"

He'd snatched up a blade of his own, one too heavy for him to wield properly, although there wasn't much to be done about that. The entire way back to the Illager mansion, he'd kept well behind Thord, making sure to stay far out of range of the bigger Illager's spells.

He'd paid the price for being too careless around Thord once today already. He didn't care to make that mistake again.

For his part, Thord ignored Archie's pleas, with the exception of the occasional smug chuckle. Archie knew the evoker would sell him out the moment they got back to the Illager mansion, but he didn't see what he could do about it. He kept begging until his voice grew hoarse, and then he finally gave up.

When they came within a bowshot of the mansion—a large, three-story building that housed most of the tribe—the other Illagers rushed out to greet them, and Archie's stomach twisted in his guts. He knew exactly how they were going to take the news of the raiding party's defeat and who they were going to blame—if he let them.

An idea blazing in his head, Archie set his jaw, braced himself, and raced out in front of Thord. The evoker growled at him as he passed him by, but with his injuries, he couldn't keep up. He barely even seemed to try.

The Illager leader—a tall, skinny one by the name of Walda—stepped forward from the pack of anxious people who had gathered for news of the raiding party. Archie could tell by the disgusted looks on their faces that they already suspected how awful the raid had gone. No one ever came back alone from such a venture with good news.

"A hero did it," Archie told Walda. "He came up while we were fighting the undead mobs—and beating them—and stole our victory!"

A few of the Illagers in the back of the crowd growled in contempt. While every Illager knew the risks involved in being part of a raiding party, they took any such loss personally.

"And how did this happen?" Walda asked, a deep frown creasing her face.

Archie pointed back toward Thord. "It was all because that worthless fool thought he could take on a hero all by himself. It's all his fault!"

It worried Archie to do this—to openly turn against a fellow Illager as powerful and conniving as the evoker—but Thord had announced his intentions to do the very same thing to him. The only way Archie could prevent being banished was to start his campaign of lies first. It was a long shot—one that he might suffer for—but he didn't see that he had any other choice.

A gasp went up in the crowd. The people here knew Thord well. They understood he was a braggart and a bully—but they also held him up as one of their most powerful evokers. The idea that he would make such a horrible mistake that would cost them an entire raiding party horrified them.

Archie realized he was going to have to sell his story hard—and fast. Thord was getting closer every second. "Thord was our designated leader," he told Walda. "You appointed him yourself."

She hesitated then nodded. "That I did."

"Then he bears the ultimate blame for our failure, doesn't he?"

Walda's shoulders wobbled at this as she tried to absorb the implications of Archie's words. "Perhaps. By that logic, you might be able to say the blame is mine."

Archie gasped in dismay, sensing that he'd perhaps gone too far. "I would never—"

Walda dismissed his impending apology with an impatient wave, and he continued. "It's more than that. He didn't set a watch to look for troubles like a hero. He just plunged straight into the battle against the undead without taking any precautions at all."

Walda didn't seem moved by that, and the others nearby had begun staring at Archie as if he'd gone mad. "I mean, wouldn't that seem wise? To set a watch to make sure we didn't get ambushed by someone else while we were in battle? That's exactly how the last raiding party we lost died!"

"That was many years ago," Walda said with a pitying look.

She clearly remembered that both of Archie's parents had perished in that incident.

"And we still haven't learned any lessons from that! We still charge into the fight without figuring out what other dangers might lie in wait for us. And we're still paying the worst price!"

"And it's all your fault," Thord said from right behind him.

Archie spun around and realized that he'd gotten so caught up with complaining to Walda that he hadn't heard Thord arrive. On top of that, he'd wasted all the advance time for which he'd run so hard.

"What?" Archie put a hand to his chest as if his heart might pop out of it in shock. "How is it my fault?"

Walda raised a hand to silence Archie and then turned toward Thord. "Word from our little friend here is that this disaster is actually your fault."

Thord smirked down at the little Illager. "Of course he would say that. Trying to cover his own butt. After he failed to spot that hero coming our way—"

"And how would I have managed that? I was in the middle of that battle against the undead mobs, just like you. Just like everyone else! Just like you ordered us to do!"

Thord looked down at Archie and gave him a sad shake of his head. "I understand what you're trying to do here. After all, why wouldn't you? What do you have to lose?"

Archie stared at him. "What are you talking about?"

"The lying. All the lies. Just listen to yourself. You can't bear to think about what you did, so you're blaming anyone else but yourself."

"What I did?" Archie almost fell over in shock. "Are you out of your tiny mind?"

"See?" Thord said to the crowd hovering around them, but especially to Walda. "The denial runs so deep, I almost wonder if he believes the lies himself."

Archie actually gaped at Thord, unable to summon any words to complain.

"The fact is," Thord continued, "that I did set a watch over our battlefield, and I gave Archie the job."

The little Illager struggled to find his voice. "That's not true!"

Thord ignored the interruption. "As you know, he doesn't much care for fighting, and he complained about having to come along with us and do his duty for the tribe the entire time. By now, we're all used to that, right? And he's not much use on the battle-field anyway."

A few in the crowd chuckled at that. Archie glared at them, but his naked fury didn't seem to sting them at all.

"I figured he at least could lend us his eyes." Thord peered down at Archie with scathing contempt. "But he couldn't even manage that."

Thord turned fully toward Archie now. "Where were you when the hero showed up? That's what I can't figure out. I know you weren't in the battle. You're never in a battle if you can help it."

There was some truth to that. Archie hated fighting and would have done anything to get out of being part of that patrol if he could have managed it. Now, though, he saw why Thord had brought him along.

"You knew this was going to go wrong," Archie said to him, seething. "And when it did, you knew you were going to need a scapegoat. That's why you chose me."

"It's the duty—actually, the privilege—of every Illager to take their turns in the raiding parties," Walda said.

Archie's heart dropped. The moment she opened her mouth to defend Thord, he knew he was ruined. If he couldn't convince her of what Thord had done to the raiding party—and especially to him—he was doomed.

"I didn't deny that. I went along on the raid. I even brought my own sword."

"If you can call that a sword," Thord said with a barely concealed sneer.

"And Thord here never assigned me to watch over the battle. He was in charge. That should have been his job. This is all his fault!"

The crowd of Illagers surrounding Archie and Thord seemed to hold their collective breath. No one said a word, apparently waiting on Walda to render a verdict.

Eventually she opened her mouth to speak. "It horrifies me that you would accuse each other of such terrible things. Illagers must stick together, even on the field of battle. *Especially* on the field of battle. Otherwise, we stand no chance against our foes."

She gazed at both Archie and Thord. The evoker met her steely eyes, but Archie couldn't help but wither beneath her glare.

"Do you remember what it was like when we roamed the lands, each to ourselves? The mobs picked us off one by one, destroying us at their will. It was only when we united—when we became a tribe—that we stood any chance against them at all."

Walda spread the arms of her robe wide to encompass every person in the tribe, and the other Illagers all muttered in agreement with her. They all knew exactly what she was talking about, as did Archie. While life among the tribe wasn't always wonderful, it was far better than any time he'd spent wandering alone. He shuddered at the memories that still haunted his sleep.

"And now you two come to us, still bickering with each other after having suffered such a horrible and complete loss? You complain about each other while the rest of your raiding party is defeated and gone? Clearly you care not about the tribe but about yourselves."

"No," Archie whispered to himself. He could see what was coming next, but he felt powerless to stop it. He racked his brain, trying to come up with something—anything—he could say to bring it all to a screeching halt, to keep Walda from making a decision that would condemn him to the worst fate he could possibly contemplate.

He looked over to Thord for help. That's how desperate he was. And the larger Illager reached out and put a comforting hand on his shoulder.

Then he gave Archie a nasty yet expectant frown. "Why don't you explain yourself?" he said, enjoying every moment of it. "Tell everyone here how you let the rest of us die."

Archie's jaw dropped. For a moment, he'd let hope creep back into his heart, but just like always, Thord had ripped it clear out of his chest again.

"You won't get away with this!" he shouted as he launched himself at Thord. He swung at him wildly with his fists, intending to bash the injured evoker about the head and shoulders.

To Archie's utter shock, Thord dropped to the ground the instant one of Archie's fists made contact with him. Archie had landed only a glancing blow, but the evoker toppled backward and sprawled across the open ground as if he'd been punched by a giant.

The people around Archie gasped in horror. Archie stared down at Thord and then at his fist. He had barely made contact.

There was no way he'd knocked him down. That could only mean one thing.

"Get up, you faker!" Archie shouted at Thord. "Quit pretending to be hurt, and get up!"

Thord squirmed away from Archie, still on his backside, clutching his wounded leg. Archie stomped over and kicked him in the thigh.

The Illagers prized strength over anything. To show a sign of weakness before others could be lethal. If Thord was going to fake being injured, then Archie was willing to fake triumphing over him.

"Get up!"

Thord howled in agony and curled up into a ball. As he did, the other Illagers surged forward, and several of them grabbed Archie by the arms and hauled him back, away from where Thord lay writhing in pain.

"What are you doing?" Walda demanded. "Kicking an Illager leader after a battle? Are you out of your mind?"

"I'm not going to put up with him anymore!" Archie said. "It's bad enough he's bullied me my entire life! Now he's lying about me too! I've had it!"

Walda stood there before Archie and waited for him to fall silent, even if he couldn't quite calm down. "Are you finished?" she asked softly, but with enough command in her voice that everyone in that part of the forest could hear her, even over Thord's groans.

Archie glanced down at Thord and caught him grinning up at him. The downed evoker wiped the smile from his face before anyone else could catch him, though.

Archie drew in a deep breath and let it out slowly as he struggled to calm himself. "I suppose I am."

Walda nodded at him. "I'd like to thank you," she said. "I had thought this was going to be a hard decision, but you just made it far easier on me."

Archie cocked his head to one side, not quite clear on what Walda was heading toward. Despite that, he kept his mouth shut and waited for her to continue.

She motioned to both Thord and Archie. "Obviously, this kind of behavior can't go on. In a way, I blame myself. I should have put a stop to it a long time ago."

Archie imagined being able to be a part of a tribe that didn't have Thord in it, and he felt a huge surge of relief. "I would have truly appreciated that."

"The tension was always between keeping on someone who already contributed greatly to the tribe's might, or keeping on a weakling who had potential."

Archie suddenly didn't like the turn the conversation had taken. "Wait, what?"

"But your actions today have made the choice clear."

Archie put up his hands to plead with Walda to stop. "Hey, no, I didn't betray the raiding party. He's lying!"

He stabbed a finger down at Thord, who rolled over and groaned in pain, pretending to be only half conscious.

"That may be true," Walda said. "I cannot prove or disprove that. But the manner in which you attacked him in front of the rest of the tribe . . . The way you kicked a wounded Illager nearly to death . . ."

"He was already halfway there!" Archie shouted, both desperate and indignant.

"That's enough!" Walda said. Her calm facade had finally cracked, and the naked rage on her face hit Archie like a diamond blade. "You're not only worthless and weak, you've done actual harm to the leadership of the tribe. You need to leave. *NOW!*"

"But that's not fair!" Archie protested, although he knew it would do him no good.

Walda pointed toward the lands beyond the camp, into the dark and foreboding forest that sprawled all around them. "You have been banished forever. Go, and never come back!"

CHAPTER THREE

Archie wandered lost in the plains, distraught over being kicked out of the only tribe—the only family, really—he'd ever known. His entire life he'd worried that no one actually liked him much. That the only ones who even seemed like they might tolerate him had only been doing so out of politeness.

And now he had proof.

When the tribe had been given a choice between Thord and him, they'd thrown Archie to the mercy of the mobs. Given how Illagers prized strength over anything, he'd been expecting it to happen forever, but he'd still hoped for something better. Without the protection of the tribe, he'd probably be dead within a week.

He wondered how he'd go. Would a zombie take him down? Would a skeleton skewer him with an arrow? Or would a creeper come hissing up behind him and blast him to nothing?

As night fell, Archie did what he'd been trained to do if he was ever caught out alone in the open after dark, something that had rarely happened to him before. It was supposed to be the only way to protect yourself from the roaming hordes of undead mobs that came out at night to claw and tear at the living.

So, Archie found a hole in the ground—a bit of a depression, really—and jumped into it. Then he buried himself under the earth.

He knew he'd done a bad job of it right away. It wasn't like he'd carved out a proper space in the ground below himself and then sealed himself in. He'd just done the best he could, which came down to covering himself with as much loose dirt as he could manage.

It didn't take Archie long to realize he couldn't breathe—or at least that the fear that gripped him made it feel that way. Maybe that was the kind of thing that people with proper tools and discipline could manage by making themselves a well-protected space, but Archie had neither such implements nor the know-how to use them.

Terrified by the tight confines and gasping for air, Archie clawed his way back up out of the dirt and stood there exposed under the night sky. It was a big world, he knew, and he was a tiny Illager. Maybe the mobs would just miss him?

He looked around the woods through which he had wandered, hoping perhaps that they could offer him some shelter. In the day, the trees had kept the sun off his head, but now, in the darkness, they seemed like they only gave cover in which all sorts of nameless nightmares could hide. He peered around them in every direction, fully expecting death to leap out from behind them.

That's when he heard the groans, and he knew just how much trouble he was in.

Somewhere there in the woods, a zombie was staggering around, looking for something living on which to feast. Archie knew that he would be at the top of the mob's menu. He began to edge away from it, hoping that maybe its ears had rotted off enough that it wouldn't be able to hear him rustling around in the dark.

As he did, he heard another moan, this time coming from the opposite direction. Archie nearly leaped out of his skin. He spun about, staring into the utter blackness of the night, trying to see how far away the zombie might be.

He must have made too much noise as he moved around. The first zombie moaned louder this time, having come even closer.

Archie knew then, without any doubt in his mind, that if he stayed in those dark woods, he would surely die. The only hope he had was to leave as soon as possible. To get away before the zombies cornered him among the trees and made a screaming meal out of him.

Unfortunately, he didn't have anywhere to get away to. He could try to worm his way back into the tribe, but he knew that wouldn't work. His people were not known for their pity, and Walda had been extremely clear about expelling him. The best result he could hope for from them was to be killed by someone he knew rather than by a zombie, and he didn't think that would be all that comforting.

Waiting around in the woods for someone to murder him didn't appeal much more though. If he lay down to sleep there, he was sure to wake up with an undead mob attacking him— if he was lucky enough to wake up at all. The only solution was to stay awake, alert, and on the move, so he decided to do just that.

Archie made his way through the woods as quietly as he could manage, moving away from the two zombies he'd already heard roaming nearby in the dark. He was far from a good sneak, but he figured if he could just stay quieter than a zombie's moaning, he might be all right.

The same went for creepers. They always started hissing before they exploded. All he had to do was keep his ears sharp for them and be ready to bolt if they got too close.

Skeletons had no lungs to breathe with and therefore couldn't groan at him. Fortunately, their bleached-white bones rattled as they walked, and stood out a bit better in the darkness. He kept his eyes wide in the hopes that he'd see them before they put an arrow into his heart.

Perhaps that was why he spotted the torch flickering in the distance. If he hadn't been so anxious about threatening mobs, he might have missed it entirely. As it was, even its faint illumination seemed like a blazing lighthouse beam reaching out for him in the darkest part of the night.

Archie moved toward the light carefully. He feared it might be a trap of some sort, meant to draw in weary travelers so that whoever built it could attack them as they came near. Even if it wasn't meant that way, whoever had set the torch burning probably wouldn't be happy to find a lone, lost Illager approaching in the middle of the night.

Unless, of course, they were another tribe of Illagers. Sometimes other tribes roamed into the area—often by accident, occasionally with bad intentions. If that's what this was, as improbable as that sounded, Archie thought that he might be able to plead with them to take him in. They wouldn't have the awful history with him that his old tribe had. Perhaps he could step in new and start fresh for the first time in his life.

Still, that was a long shot at best. If he'd had a camp to return to, Archie would have opted for that. As it was, he could either approach the torch or take his chances with the creatures in the night.

The torch got his vote.

As Archie got closer, he saw more than one torch. First one more appeared behind it, off to one side, and then another and another. Soon he saw a whole array of torches spread out before him, and he realized he'd not stumbled upon a camp.

It was a village.

Archie's heart constricted in his chest. He wanted both to dash forward and to run away.

Villagers were the sort of people that Illagers liked to raid best. Sure, they often just hid inside their houses where they were relatively safe, but they usually did that at night. During the day, you could find them just wandering around, tending to their gardens and their domesticated animals: cows, pigs, and sheep.

Best of all, they never came chasing after you once the raid was over. Maybe it was because they had more important things to do—or perhaps because they simply weren't warriors at heart— but once the Illagers wrapped up a raid, the Villagers always let them be.

That meant, of course, that the only time Archie had ever had anything to do with a Villager was during a raid that Walda had ordered him into. He only knew about Villagers as targets, not as people—and certainly not as saviors.

But then Archie didn't really need a savior. He needed a host, someone who would let him into the village without running him off. He was so hard-pressed, he'd have settled for being allowed to sleep near a lit torch—anything that would keep the mobs off him, if only for a little bit.

He creeped closer to the village and peered around, looking for anyone who happened to be wandering about. At this time of night, he wouldn't have blamed all the Villagers for simply hunkering down inside their homes, but he didn't want to startle someone into ringing the village's alarm before he got the chance to at least plead his case with them.

That's when he spotted the iron golem wandering through the edge of the line of torches that encircled the town. It stood nearly three times as tall as Archie and almost three times as wide as well. It was an artificial person that had been fashioned out of raw metals and then imbued with a semblance of life by some arcane magic.

Having grown up around evokers like Thord—and even Walda—Archie knew that magic existed and that it could do all sorts of inexplicable things, but he had no real notion about how it worked. Walda had tested him for any aptitude with magic years ago, and to his disappointment, he'd utterly failed. So, while he didn't really get how a person made of iron could be made to patrol and protect a village, he could see that it had happened, and now he had to deal with the consequences.

He wasn't sure if he should stride right into town and present himself openly or not. It seemed like the most honest and straightforward thing to do—but it also was the most likely to cause him to wind up being smashed flat by an iron fist.

Instead, Archie watched the golem lumber through the outskirts of the village until it disappeared behind the corner of one of its houses. As soon as it was out of sight, he scurried toward the village, hoping that it wouldn't somehow turn around and spot him. As he reached the front door of the nearest building, he stopped and cocked his head to listen for the iron golem's earth-thumping stride.

He heard nothing but his own shallow breaths. While his success emboldened him, he knew that he had to act before the iron golem's patrol brought it around again. If the thing saw him, it might attack him on sight, and he knew how badly that would go.

He steeled himself with a deep breath, raised his fist, and knocked firmly on the front door before him. The inside of the place was dark, but someone in there started moving about and lit a torch to see by. A moment later, a curious face peered out through the window in the front door at him.

The person was a clean-faced woman with sandy skin—something that marked her as a Villager rather than an Illager, for sure. As she looked at Archie, her eyes grew wide, and she gasped in surprise.

Eager to keep the woman from screaming, Archie ginned up the best, most harmless smile he could manage and gave her an innocent little wave. "Sorry to bother you," he said, "but I'm stuck outside tonight."

"You don't belong here," she said, confused by more than simply having her sleep disturbed. "You must be lost."

Archie braced himself for the conversation to take a bad turn. As it was, he felt delighted that the woman hadn't started screaming in horror at the very sight of him. He hoped she wouldn't come to her senses and change her mind about him anytime soon.

"I *am* lost," he said to her. "I don't have any idea where I am."

The woman squinted at him as if she was unsure if she was still asleep and dreaming this whole encounter. "We're in a village on the Squid Coast. Where are you from?"

Archie didn't know how to explain that, so he shrugged at her. "I was kicked out of my tribe. I don't have anywhere to go."

"You poor thing. Hold on just a moment." The Villager hesitated and then the door to her home swung open.

She burst straight past Archie and dashed for the alarm bell that stood in the little square just beyond her home. He gasped in horror as she reached up to grab the rope hanging from the bell.

He let loose a pitiful whimper, which elicited an angry snarl from the Villager. "Just how stupid do you think I am?"

CHAPTER FOUR

"**H**elp!" the Villager hollered at the top of her lungs as she hauled on the bell's rope, ringing it loud and clear. "Help!"

Until that moment, Archie had held out some insane sort of hope that he'd be able to talk with the woman and get her to see his point of view. He'd planned to just turn around and run like a herd of creepers was after him the moment anything went wrong. But when he went to do just that, an iron golem appeared out of the darkness, cutting off his clearest avenue of escape.

The golem reached out to grab Archie, and he squealed in terror. Before the massive creature could crush him, though, the Villager signaled for it to stop, and she stormed up to interrogate him instead.

"Where are the rest of them?" she demanded. "What's your trick here?"

"No trick!" Archie put his hands up in a way that he hoped would calm the Villager down and show her that he meant absolutely no harm. "I'm here alone!"

"Liar! Illagers like you never come around here for anything but looting and pillaging!"

Archie took heart from the fact that the Villager hadn't let the iron golem smash him flat. He knew that the Illagers probably wouldn't have been so patient if she'd shown up in their camp.

The woman turned her head for an instant to call for help again. Archie didn't want to run away—he wanted to have the chance to explain himself and plead his case—but he knew that this would probably be the only chance he would have. His sense of self-preservation took hold of his feet, and before he knew it, he tried to bolt away from both her and the iron golem.

He wasn't nearly fast enough. The iron golem snagged him before he got even a full step away. Archie tried to squirm out of its grasp, but the iron golem's grip was as strong as steel.

"Where do you think you're going?" the Villager said with a snarl as she got right back into his face again

"Don't kill me!" Archie screeched, now in raw panic. "I just— I don't want to die!"

"Then you shouldn't have come here, Illager scum," a deeper voice said from off to Archie's right.

Archie wrenched his head around to see who had joined them and he spied a Villager standing there, brandishing a garden hoe. He wore a wide-brimmed hat and clothing streaked with sweat and dirt. The sight of him made Archie scream in terror.

"Put that thing down, Salah!" the woman said. "I've got this under control."

"Doesn't quite look like you do, Yumi." The man didn't drop

his hoe. In fact, he came closer with it, waving it in Archie's face. "He's a squirmy sort! Just back off and let the iron golem take care of him!"

"This isn't your standard sort of Illager here. He seems smarter than the average ones." Yumi leaned over and hissed in Archie's ear. "And if he's *actually* smart, he'll stop squirming around so the iron golem doesn't *accidentally* hurt him."

Archie froze.

A handful of other people appeared behind Salah, all wearing looks of fear mixed with anger. They were upset about being woken up in the middle of the night, and they were ready to run whoever had caused that out of town.

Archie glanced back over his shoulder, slowly enough not to make anyone think he was trying to escape—or so he hoped. The iron golem loomed over him with its unblinking eyes, and Archie realized exactly how much trouble he'd gotten himself into.

Archie slumped to his knees. "I'm sorry," he said meekly to Yumi. "I didn't mean to cause any trouble."

The woman knelt down so she could see his face. She wasn't a big woman, but Archie was an even smaller Illager.

"Get away from that creature, Yumi," Salah said, gruff and angry still. "The iron golem can take care of it."

Despite himself, Archie reached up and grabbed Yumi by the arms. "Please, no," he said, his voice barely above a whimper. "Don't let it hurt me."

The woman looked at him, and the fury in her face melted. "You're not much of a threat to anyone, are you?"

Archie shook his head, slow and sad. Then he closed his eyes, braced himself, and waited for the end.

He supposed it might be better this way. After all, his tribe had kicked him out, and he had nowhere to go. If the undead had caught him, it would surely have been worse.

Yumi stood up, leaving Archie alone on the ground. Although he tried not to, he began to silently weep. Tears leaked from his eyes and ran straight down his face to drip on the ground beneath him.

"Yumi!" Salah said. "Get clear."

"Shut up, Salah," Yumi said as she stood up. "This little guy hasn't done anything wrong here today."

Archie blinked open his eyes, astonished that he was still unharmed. He wondered how much longer that might go on, but he didn't dare get his hopes up. Not yet.

"He woke up the entire village!" Salah said, frustrated and spluttering. "He was going to burn the whole place to the ground!"

Yumi snorted at that. "Do you see a torch in his hand?"

Salah hesitated. He peered down at Archie and at the path he'd made from Yumi's place to where the iron golem had grabbed him. He pointed to a torch burning just outside her door. "Is that not a torch?"

"Nice try," Yumi said. "That one's mine."

Salah frowned. "So he would have taken it and burned down your home!"

Yumi barked an outright laugh this time. "From me?" She pointed down at Archie. "That little thing. How well do you think that would go for him? He practically ran at the sight of me."

"He's an Illager!" Salah said. "They're like mice in a house. Where there's one, there's always more!"

Yumi spread her arms wide and gazed out into the night. "They must be hiding awfully well then. Far out of sight. Maybe many miles from here. How clever of them."

Salah pulled back his hoe and set the end of the handle in the grass. "Well, what are we supposed to do with him then? We can't just let him go."

Yumi pursed her lips at the man. "And why not?"

Salah gestured out into the dark at the imaginary horde of Illagers waiting to pounce on and pulverize the village. "Because he'll bring them all back here to kill us!"

Yumi rolled her eyes so hard that Archie feared she might fall over backward. "Do you think the Illagers don't already know where to find us?"

"You know they do! They used to come and raid our little village all the time!"

"So our location isn't exactly a secret then, is it?"

"They could do it again!"

"They've barely even tried since the heroes started making regular stops through here," Yumi said.

Salah let out a dramatic groan. "Do you see any heroes around here now?"

Yumi stared straight at him and shook her head. "Not a one."

Salah's face flushed red. "Now, Yumi—"

"Don't 'Now, Yumi' me, Salah. You might be in charge of the village, but you're not in charge of me."

He opened his mouth to protest, to say something like "But you're part of the village." Before he could actually say any words, though, he thought better of it and clammed his lips up tight.

Satisfied, at least for now, Yumi peered down at Archie again. "Are you going to hurt anyone here?"

Archie shook his head violently.

"Are you going to bring anyone else to hurt us?"

Archie shook his head again.

"What are you going to do if I let you stand up?"

Archie's mind went blank. He had no idea how to answer that question. He'd been so absolutely convinced the end was here that his brain hadn't allowed him to think any further ahead than that.

"I—I don't know." His voice barely edged above a whisper, but she could hear him just fine.

She put out her hand to him to help him up. "Well," she said. "Let's find out."

Archie stared at her hand for a long moment and then reached up and took it. She hauled him to his feet, and he stood there shaking.

He glanced around to see that a crowd of Villagers had now assembled around him, including a couple more iron golems. At a gesture from Yumi, the one holding Archie by the collar set him free. After a moment's reflection, Archie realized why.

They were giving him a way out. If he wanted to, he could spin on his heels and flee into the darkness.

That would have been the easy answer for everyone involved. Archie would disappear into the night, supposedly returning to wherever he'd come from, and the Villagers could all go back to sleep, safe and warm in their beds. In the morning, he'd be nothing but a memory to them, something they'd grumble or crack jokes about over breakfast—and forget soon enough.

Archie shuddered as he stared into the darkness. When he turned back toward the Villagers, he saw everyone there gazing at him, waiting expectantly. Some glared at him with hatred in their eyes. Others watched him in wonder, not sure what to expect from him.

Yumi, though, wore a wry smile on her face. She held a hand out to him, low but open, her palm up.

He reached for it. "I have nowhere else to go," he told her. "Can I please stay?"

"Forget it!" Salah thundered loud enough to make Archie cringe. "I forbid it!"

Yumi drew Archie next to her and put an arm around his shoulders as she turned to face Salah and the rest of the Villagers alongside him. "I'm welcoming this little fellow into my home. He can stay in my spare room."

Salah opened his mouth to protest, but Yumi shut him down with a withering glare. With that, she guided Archie back toward her front door. As she reached her home, she turned the little Illager around to face the crowd again.

Some of the people there—including Salah—gaped at her in stunned silence. Others chuckled at the way she'd defied Salah's will. A couple children who had crept out of their beds to see what was happening gawked at Archie in curious delight. They'd probably never seen an Illager before, especially not this close, and the sight of him amazed them.

"I realize some of you may not be happy about my decision here," Yumi said. "That's your problem, not mine."

"Now listen here," Salah started.

Yumi cut him off, clearly not caring about anything he might have to say. "This little fellow—" She glanced down at the Illager. "What's your name?"

Surprised to be addressed, he cleared his throat before he answered. "Archie."

She tried the name out for herself. "Archie." Seeming to approve how it felt on her tongue, she picked up where she'd left off.

"Archie here is my guest. As such, I expect you all to treat him with the same respect you give to Salah's cousins when they visit."

A few of the people laughed at that. Apparently Salah's extended family had a bit of a reputation in the village.

She looked back down at Archie and gave him a little shake. "And just like with Salah's cousins, I expect you to behave. That means respecting the people here and their property. Can you do that?"

Archie couldn't believe how well she was treating him—especially compared to being defeated or, at the very least, run out of town—and he found himself eager to agree to do anything she wanted. "Of course I can!"

She gave him a firm nod of appreciation and then gazed back out at the others. "And if he can't manage that, we'll treat them exactly like we did Salah's cousins. Sound fair?"

The people in the crowd all murmured in rough agreement. Salah himself flushed a bit in embarrassment, and when Yumi stared directly at him, he shook his head at her. "When this all goes wrong—and it will—this is on your head," he told her. "It's not a question of *if* that little monster will cause a disaster here. It's only a question of *when*."

"Don't listen to him," Yumi whispered to Archie out of the side of her mouth. "He's professionally wrong about everything."

She raised her voice again to speak to the crowd. "Now that that's settled, I suggest the rest of you go back home and get some sleep. That's what I plan to do myself."

She turned around and escorted Archie into her home and shut the door behind her. Once inside, she placed her back against the door and slid down it until she was sitting on the floor. This placed her just below Archie's eye level.

Yumi took a moment to rub her face with her hands before she regarded Archie again. "You're one lucky beast," she told him.

"Thank you," he said, feeling truly grateful to her. "I really didn't have anywhere else to go. If you'd sent me back into the woods . . ."

"You'd probably have been finished off by morning," she finished for him. "Of course, that's exactly what Salah and maybe half the town was hoping for."

Archie nodded. He couldn't blame any of them for that. He knew that Illagers sometimes tried to raid villages. It didn't seem to succeed all that often—just when the Villagers grew careless about protecting their homes—but he could see how that would make the Villagers hate his people.

"I'm not too fond of other Illagers myself," Archie said.

Yumi marveled at him for a moment. "What in the world did you do to get them to kick you out?"

Archie's shoulders slumped. The last thing he wanted to do was relive all that, even for someone who'd taken such a huge risk on him.

"Don't worry about it," she said as she pushed herself to her feet. "That story can wait for another day."

CHAPTER FIVE

Despite the Villagers' initial reservations about him, Archie managed to find a way to fit in well in relatively little time. The morning after he arrived, Yumi sat him down and listened to the tale of how he'd been banished from his tribe. Later that day, she took him around and introduced him to everyone in the village, one home at a time.

In the naked light of day, Archie must have seemed much less threatening to the Villagers. Yumi had found an old set of clothes to dress him in. They were simple but serviceable for Villager clothing, or so she told him. Even so, they were nicer than just about anything he'd ever worn as part of his Illager tribe.

Most of the Villagers Archie met seemed kind and happy now. Even ones who'd scowled at him last night. A few of them actually said "Welcome to our village," to him.

The only real exception was Salah. He refused to speak to Archie at all. Instead, he tried to pretend the Illager wasn't there as he growled at Yumi. "That thing you dressed up like a doll is vermin," he told her. "It doesn't belong here, and every minute you keep it here, you put the entire village in danger."

Yumi scoffed at him and gestured at Archie. "Look at him. Does he look like a threat to you?"

Salah pointedly didn't take his eyes off Yumi's face. "That's an Illager, not a Villager. Only Villagers belong in the village. *It's in the name.*"

With that, he slammed the door of his house in Yumi's face. She narrowed her eyes at it for a moment, as if she was considering kicking it down. Instead, she turned and escorted Archie away.

"Don't worry about him," she said as they headed back to her place. "He'll come around eventually."

"What if he doesn't?" Archie couldn't help but worry that the man would do anything in his power to get rid of him.

"Then it'll make him miserable—not you—but there's nothing you can do about that."

Over the next couple of weeks, Archie did his best to make himself useful. He accompanied Yumi out of her house whenever she went out, mostly because he didn't want to be left there alone. Anytime she asked him to do something, he jumped to comply. He wanted nothing more than to please her and to—as Yumi often commented with a gentle smile—earn his keep.

Archie wasn't always good at doing what he was asked, but he put every bit of effort into it that he could muster. Terrified that Yumi's mercy toward him could expire any moment, he made up his mind that he wasn't going to give her any excuse to let the rest of the people kick him out of the village. At least, not if he could help it.

Everything seemed to be going smoothly. Archie actually felt more useful than he ever had at any other point in his life, and even appreciated. While the people of the village didn't completely trust him—*yet*, he told himself—they treated him better than almost all of his fellow Illagers ever had.

Where the Illagers valued cunning, viciousness, and might, the Villagers placed importance on harmony, teamwork, and community instead. There hadn't been a place for Archie among the Illagers, but the Villagers seemed to be willing to make room for him—as long as he could prove himself worthy of that space. He set himself to doing exactly that.

He got to know the people in the village: their names, their occupations, the things they cared about, and the people they loved. That included Xu (the baker), Wendy (the farmer), Farouk (the tailor), Chandra (the smith), Zuri (the shepherd), Nanuq (a cowhand), and Liam (the cook), as well as many more.

At first, many of them were reluctant to share things with him, but he was so insistent about being allowed to help out that they eventually relented on that front, if only to shut him up. During the time he spent with them after that, they would while away moments by chatting with him, answering his questions, and telling him stories about their land and their lives in it.

In his early days in the village, Archie wasn't really trying to make friends. His life as an Illager hadn't prepared him to do anything but assume the worst of anyone, so he was only trying to see how he could make himself useful to the Villagers so they wouldn't hurt him or kick him out. Back at the Illager mansion, Archie—and apparently all of the other Illagers—had long ago decided he wasn't much use to anyone, so he'd just spent his time trying to avoid everyone else. In the village, though, that just wasn't possible.

First, Archie stuck out. Even in Villager clothes, he didn't look anything like them. His gray skin gave him away.

Second, the Villagers had a well-earned distrust of Illagers, so they always kept at least one eye on him no matter where he was. He didn't have any chance to blend in.

Third, and maybe most important, Archie discovered that he liked the attention. As an outsider, he was an oddity, sure, but not in the way he'd been with the Illagers. Once the Villagers got over their initial wariness of him, they showed actual curiosity about him, his Illager culture, and how he fit into it.

Salah, for example, took to asking Archie all sorts of questions about Illager life. Archie knew that he was only—at least at first— trying to pick apart his story so that he could out the Illager as some sort of spy. As they conversed, usually with Yumi at Archie's side to ensure he felt safe to speak, Salah's questions became less probing and more philosophical. He wanted to know not just *if* the Illagers would attack the village but *why*.

Many of the things the Villagers learned about the Illager way of life earned Archie their pity—or that was how he saw it at first. It took him a long time to realize it wasn't the kind of pity an Illager would show him: condescending and scathing, filled with disgust. Instead, it came from a place of real sympathy and understanding based in compassion.

As the Villagers began to care about Archie as a person, he began to see them not as foolishly benevolent souls from whom he could beg shelter and protection but as folks who might someday come to care for him and maybe even trust him.

Every evening, Yumi brought Archie back to her place, fed him a hot and delicious dinner, and let him sleep in a warm and comfortable bed in her spare room. She called it *hospi-*

tality, something he'd never experienced before as an Illager. Back at the mansion, people had what they could take from others—which meant Archie rarely had much of anything—and if they had any extra, they hoarded it rather than sharing it. The idea that Yumi would give things to Archie freely, and that he could accept them without compunction disturbed him at first.

It took him a long while to get used to it. To let it feel like home.

In their off hours, Archie and Yumi would chat endlessly about their different experiences with the world and their places in it. Over time, they opened up to each other, and Archie realized that he was no longer trying to help out in the village simply to prove his worth. He'd come to care about the place and the Villagers who lived in it—especially Yumi, who'd showed him so much kindness.

Yumi's hobby in the village, it turned out, was watching over the iron golems that protected the place. The Villagers were a peaceful people, so much so that they usually kept their hands hidden inside the sleeves of their clothes to indicate their lack of aggression. But the world wasn't always as kind as they were, so they needed something to protect them from it. That's where the golems came in.

Archie didn't like to spend much time around the golems, as he worried that they would see him as a threat and attack him, but since he was living in Yumi's home, he couldn't entirely avoid them. Yumi soon showed him the error of his ways by introducing him to the village's protectors. It turned out that the iron golems were entirely peaceful—at least until someone attacked one of the Villagers. Instead of preparing for a fight, they spent most of their time just strolling around the village and keeping an eye on it. Sometimes they stood staring at things for so long that they seemed like little more than metal statues.

One afternoon one of the golems—Yumi's favorite, who spent lots of time near her home—approached Archie directly. The little Illager's first instinct had been to scramble away from it and find someplace to hide. Yumi caught him, though, before he could slip into the house.

"Don't be shy," she told him with a laugh. "It has something for you."

"What?" Archie said, surprised. He suspected that something involved causing him pain, and he steeled himself for whatever came next.

Yumi smiled at him. "Stick out your hand."

In spite of his reservations, Archie decided to trust Yumi, who hadn't steered him wrong so far, and he did as she said. In response, the iron golem held out its own hand, in which it held a pretty flower, which it presented to Archie.

"Go ahead," Yumi said with a warm giggle. "Take it."

Archie reached out and gingerly took the flower from the iron golem's outstretched hand. Apparently satisfied, the creature turned around and went back to its duties. The Illager marveled at the beauty of its gift as it left.

The village, as Archie came to know it, had been built by the people who lived there—or at least the people who came before them—with their bare hands. They'd harvested and mined the resources they needed, and crafted them into the homes and buildings that dotted the area they'd carved out of the Squid Coast. People like them had originally settled far from one another, staking out their own separate portions of the land, but the ever-present threat of undead mobs and Illager raids had driven them to band together, for their own safety if nothing else.

"I'm sorry about that," Archie told Yumi one night. "About the Illager raids, I mean."

She snorted at him. "Did you ever take part in any of them?"

He lowered his eyes. "Only the ones I was forced to—but yes."

"Did you ever hurt anyone?"

He hesitated before he answered. They'd been enjoying a quiet dinner, and he was loath to ruin it. "Not for lack of trying," he finally said. "But I was fortunately awful at it."

"That's good," she replied with a chuckle. "Good that you're so awful at being bad."

He nodded in agreement. "I'm trying hard to get better at being good instead."

"Just keep practicing," Yumi said as she started to clear the dishes. "You'll get the hang of it."

Soon, Archie didn't feel like he was a guest in the village anymore. It became more of a home to him than any other place he'd known. He actually began to relax. Just a little. Enough that he wasn't waking up in the middle of the night ready to scream at an insect scratching against the glass in the window in his bedroom.

Inevitably, something ruined it for him. If he'd had to guess beforehand, he would have bet that it would have been the fault of Salah, who sometimes was still rude and mean to him—although not every chance he got.

But Salah wasn't the one who shattered Archie's dreams of becoming a part of the village community. Of becoming at least an honorary Villager himself.

That was all due to the hero.

Well, heroes.

Archie was working in the garden in the center of the village when the heroes arrived. He'd already helped feed the cows and pigs that morning and had spent the afternoon assisting people who actually knew what they were doing when shearing the village's pen full of sheep. He was looking forward to another peaceful dinner with Yumi when he heard the commotion at the edge of the village.

The sun was drawing lower in the sky when the heroes arrived. In contrast to the Villagers, the newcomers were loud and boisterous. As they chattered with one another, their voices carried throughout the entire place, almost like alarms set to let the Villagers know that they were coming.

The heroes spoke in some kind of odd language that Archie had never been able to understand. He'd only heard it before from the hero who had defeated his entire raiding party, and then he'd only been able to guess at the meaning from the tones of the hero's exclamations. They'd mostly been expressions of surprise and triumph, sprinkled with cursing about the rare injury anyone had been able to inflict upon him.

Now, though, the tones had the rhythm of a pleasant conversation among people who were at least casual acquaintances, if not actual friends. Still, their words made no sense to Archie or, as far as he could tell, anyone around him.

As the voices grew closer, Yumi appeared at Archie's side and put a gentle hand on his shoulder. "We should get you inside," she said, her voice all hurried business.

Archie considered telling her that he wasn't afraid of the heroes—but it turned out he was. He nodded at her and then followed her from the garden and headed toward her home.

"Can you understand them?" she asked him as they strode

along at a brisk pace, fast enough to make progress but hopefully not enough to draw too much attention to themselves.

He shook his head. "I was hoping you might be able to."

Yumi shook her head as she glanced back over her shoulder in the direction from which the loud, strange conversation rolled toward them. "We manage to barter with them, mostly by grunts and hand signals, but they're not from around here. They don't feel the need to learn our language or to teach any of us theirs. I don't think anyone's ever been able to have a proper, civilized chat with them, but it's been that way forever."

Archie glanced backward with her, hoping that he wouldn't spy the heroes chasing after them. That's how he didn't see Salah stepping straight in front of them. Not until he slammed right into the Villager's chest.

"Hey!" Yumi snapped at Salah. Her strides had sent her straight past him while he'd knocked down Archie, and she had to spin back around to return to them. "What do you think you're doing?"

"Where are you off to in such a hurry?" Salah asked, as if he didn't already know exactly where they were headed.

He pointed down at the still-prone Archie. "We have new guests in the village. I thought our current guest might want to meet them."

Yumi swung around Salah and helped Archie to his feet. "And why would he want that?"

Salah gave her an exaggerated shrug. "They have so much in common, don't you think? For one thing, no one really wants any of them here. Not permanently."

"And why is that?" Yumi jutted her chin out, defiant.

Salah stabbed a finger at the ground. "Because they don't be-long here."

"That's not really for you to say, is it?" Yumi took Archie by the hand and led him around Salah.

Salah matched her move, sidestepping in front of her and blocking her way. He replied to her loudly, "I suppose when someone brings an *Illager* into the *village*, it's every good Villager's concern."

Yumi hissed at the man as if she might strike him down right there. "Get out of our way."

"It's strange, isn't it?" Salah's voice rose with each word until he was actually shouting. "I mean, Villagers live in a village, right? *But Illagers? THEY DON'T LIVE IN AN ILLAGE, DO THEY?*"

Archie didn't understand what Salah was doing. Not then anyhow. But when he heard the people chattering in their nonsense tongue behind him, he finally got it.

He turned around slowly, hoping not to find what he knew he was doomed to see.

The heroes had strolled up right behind him, and now they were staring straight down at him.

There were five of them. At first, that was all that Archie could take in.

He'd never seen more than one hero at a time before, and one of them had been enough to take on a whole raiding party and destroy it. That's why the Illagers generally gave them a wide berth.

But here were five of them together. Archie couldn't imagine what force could stand before them.

Not his Illager tribe. Certainly not the entirety of the Villagers. And definitely not Yumi and him.

The heroes gazed down at him with curious eyes, as if they'd never seen anything like him before. *At least they haven't attacked me*, Archie thought. *Yet.*

Somewhere behind him, Salah started laughing. Archie wanted to turn around and kick him in the shins, but he didn't dare take his eyes off the heroes. He feared if he did so he'd wind up with a sword jabbed into his back.

The heroes looked so different from even the Villagers. There was something ephemeral about them that set them apart. They were stronger, faster, and just . . . sharper.

They each wore a suit of armor, although each suit was made out of different materials and fashioned in different colors. They each carried a sword in their hands, sharp and ready. Some of them carried shields too, while others bore mighty bows and quivers stuffed full of arrows instead. All of them simply gazed down at Archie as if he were a mystery waiting to be solved.

"That's him!" Salah pointed at Archie as he walked out from behind him in a wide circle, making sure that Yumi couldn't intervene. "That's the one you're looking for!"

"Shut up!" Yumi barked at Salah. "They couldn't possibly be looking for him!"

Archie gasped and gaped at Salah. Had the Villager somehow managed to tell the heroes of his presence here? Had he figured out a way to communicate with them? Would they do his bidding?

And what would that be? Would they run him out of town? Or would they simply end him then and there?

Archie's head swam from the horrible possibilities. He felt like passing out on the spot. At least that would put an end to all the speculation. He'd either wake up, or he wouldn't—and it would all be outside of his control.

Yumi reached out and steadied him with a hand on his shoulder. "It's all right," she told him. "I won't let them hurt you."

Archie tried his best to believe her, but he just couldn't manage it.

One of the heroes stepped forward and peered down at Archie. Curiosity narrowed his gaze. He seemed confused, as if Archie's presence presented an unwelcome puzzle the hero needed to solve.

Archie tried to turn away, but the hero reached out and grabbed him by the chin and forced Archie to look into his eyes. It was then that Archie finally recognized him.

He was the hero who'd destroyed his raiding party.

CHAPTER SIX

Archie's knees gave out, and his legs folded beneath him. The hero who was holding him up by the chin released him and watched him collapse into a boneless puddle on the ground.

Archie tried to will his legs to work, to stand him up and put one foot in front of the other as fast as they could, and to carry him far and fast away, but they felt like raw rubber. No matter how hard he tried, he couldn't get them to move. They just wobbled there beneath him, like his whole body, trembling in fear.

Yumi knelt down next to him and tried to rouse him. "Archie," she said. "It's okay. I'm here. You don't need to be afraid."

Archie believed her even less now than he had before. He'd watched that so-called hero defeat many of the most powerful Il-lagers he'd known. It was a miracle of sorts that he'd survived witnessing those acts, and now he knew in his heart that—given the slightest chance—the hero would finish the job.

He looked up past Yumi's shoulder and saw the hero staring down at him. In fact, all of the heroes were staring at him. Salah was too, with a vicious sneer on his lips.

Despite that, the heroes seemed not just mystified but perhaps actually concerned for Archie's welfare. None of them had reached for their swords yet. In fact, one of them had actually pulled a glass bottle filled with a glowing pink fluid from her backpack and was holding it out to Archie for him to take.

The Illagers had never been able to fashion healing potions of their own, but they'd occasionally find or steal one from someone else or barter with a witch for one. Walda had always kept them in her tent, ready to be dispensed only in case of emergency. Archie had never needed one. In fact, he'd rarely ever seen one.

But this bottle, he knew, contained a magic healing potion of the greatest potency.

He didn't know if it would do anything for him. Although he'd fallen, he wasn't physically hurt, so there wasn't anything about him that needed healing. But he didn't know enough about magic to argue with the hero, so he reached up to accept the bottle being offered to him.

Before he could lay a finger on it, though, the first hero shoved his hand right between Archie and the other hero. His open palm faced out, right toward the other hero, and he said something Archie could only interpret as, "Stop!"

Archie cringed back, a little yelp of terror escaping from between his lips.

The other heroes seemed surprised and began to argue with the angry hero, who Archie began to think of as Smacker. He was the one, after all, who'd smacked Archie into unconsciousness on the field of battle, and here he was, smacking a healing potion away from him. It was at least, Archie thought, a kinder name than Ender of Illagers.

Archie couldn't really tell the difference between the other heroes. He hadn't had a traumatic experience with any of them, and they all were just so dazzlingly superior that they seemed to blend together in their awesomeness, like looking at the brightest stars sparkling in a clear night sky. Even among them, though, Smacker stood out.

It wasn't that he was stronger, smarter, or better than any of them. It was more that he was louder and meaner. That and the fact that he usually reached for a blade to solve any problem he faced set him apart.

Smacker stood between Archie and the others and began shouting at him. Archie couldn't understand the words, but he got the gist of it. The hero had recognized him as an Illager. Maybe he even knew him from the fight in which he'd destroyed Archie's raiding party.

That detail didn't matter, Archie knew. Smacker was bound to hate him either way. And he wasn't alone in that.

"I knew it!" Salah flung an accusatory index finger at Archie. "You brought nothing but trouble to our village. That's the only thing an Illager can ever bring!"

"Shut up, and stay out of this," Yumi snapped at Salah, so hard that the Villager flinched. "You've caused enough trouble already."

Smacker began to snicker at the trouble he was causing between the two Villagers. He couldn't tell exactly what they were saying, of course, but the fact that they were bickering at all seemed to cause him no end of delight. He pointed at the two of them and laughed out loud to the other heroes.

Yumi ignored Smacker's antics and snarled at Salah. "I've put up with you picking on Archie and causing him trouble and generally being a jerk, but that ends now. It's one thing to give the little guy a hard time. It's another to put his life in danger."

Salah didn't back down an inch. "I'm the one putting his life in danger? He's an *Illager*. His people regularly try to hurt us. And I don't care how pretty you dress him up, he's still always going to be one of them!"

Yumi stepped right up into Salah's face and pointed her finger so close between his eyes that he had to cross them to be able to see it. "You think he's the biggest threat around here? He hasn't even said a cross word to you or anyone else the entire time he's been here. Me, though, I'm sick and tired of the grief you're causing us all."

The words might have been harsh, but Yumi spoke in an even tone, so nonchalant that she could have just been discussing the weather or the state of the sheep in the village's central pen. The heroes who were watching the entire conversation seemed confused about why Salah was so clearly frightened of Yumi. When he looked to them for some kind of support, they shrugged at him, unsure what he could possibly need help with when the lady chatting with him was being so kind.

It seemed to Archie, though, that Smacker could tell what was going on, but he didn't clue the others in. Instead, he just laughed out loud once again, his unrestrained mirth growing to knee-slapping guffaws.

Salah's face grew redder every second Smacker kept laughing. Soon he was as ruddy as a pig and as angry as a next-door creeper.

He clenched his jaw so tight it seemed like it might crack, but only Archie seemed to notice.

No one else seemed to recognize the threat. Not even Yumi, who was still too focused on Salah's face to pay attention to what he was doing with his hands.

The moment Salah opened his mouth to snarl at Yumi, though, Archie couldn't stand there and watch any longer. He launched himself straight at the Villager and punched him in the crotch.

Salah folded over like he'd been cut in half. He fell to his knees, groaning in pain.

Proud of himself for defending Yumi, Archie gave Salah a solid kick for good measure. As he did, the people all around him gasped in horror.

It took Archie a moment to understand what they were upset about. In his mind, he'd just saved Yumi from being hurt by a cheap, underhanded attack by Salah. If anything, the people around them ought to hoist him up on their shoulders and parade him around the village as a hero.

Well, not a *hero* hero, but at least as someone who'd saved a friend. Someone who'd done a good thing. Even in the Illager mansion, he would have been cheered. More for taking someone out than for defending someone else, but still.

Archie soon realized, though, that no one had recognized that Salah had been about to attack Yumi. All they'd seen was him attacking the Villager—apparently without cause.

Archie stared up at them all for a moment before he figured it out. Then he gaped at his still-clenched fist.

The other heroes stared at Archie. Maybe they were just astonished to see how violent the conversation had turned. Maybe they wanted to see how the scene played out before they rendered a judgment as to who was in the right or wrong. Or maybe they were waiting for Smacker to take charge—because no matter the truth of the situation, that's what happened.

Spurred into action, Smacker backhanded Archie across the cheek. The blow sent the little Illager sprawling onto the grass behind him.

Archie's face felt so odd that for an instant he wondered if he'd been defeated. It seemed entirely numb at first, as if his face had been somehow removed by the attack and replaced with something rubbery and wet. Then the feeling started to return, and it stung like he'd stuck his face into a hive of angry bees.

Archie wanted to curl up into a ball and cry, even though he knew that this might be his final moment. It would have been a terrible way to spend it, but he didn't feel like he had a choice in the matter.

Smacker loomed over him, blocking out the rays of the setting sun, which cast him in an evil, crimson light. Archie braced himself for another blow, which he felt sure would be the end of him.

He wished then that he were strong enough to stand up to Smacker and teach him a lesson. He wished that he was still back with his Illager tribe and that they'd never kicked him out. He wished for the power to not only defend himself—and Yumi—but also to have his revenge.

Smacker drew his sword and raised it over his head. Archie threw up an arm to shield himself, even though he knew it would do him no good.

"Please!" he shouted up at the hero, begging him for unexpected mercy. "No!"

As Smacker's blade came down, Yumi charged out of nowhere

and placed herself between Archie and that glittering sword. This so startled the hero that he fumbled his blade and fell into Yumi, knocking them both to the ground.

Normally, Archie suspected, Yumi wouldn't have stood a chance of knocking over someone like Smacker, but she'd surprised the hero just as he was shifting his feet. They went down together in a ball, and rolled a short bit away before coming to a painful stop.

Smacker sprang to his feet, his sword still in his hand. He roared at Yumi in fury, spurred on by his embarrassment at a Villager having knocked him to the ground. The other heroes laughed about it, which only seemed to make it worse.

Yumi struggled to stand up to him, but Smacker kicked her feet out from under her. Terror grew on her face as she realized that Smacker might actually harm her and would make quick work of her. She didn't stand a chance against him.

The other heroes stood gawking at Smacker, stunned into inaction by the ferocity of his reaction. They couldn't seem to believe that one of them could suddenly turn so violent against such a minor threat. It wasn't like a Villager could hurt one of them, right?

To his credit, Salah actually did step forward to defend Yumi. While they certainly had their differences—including, most important, how to treat Archie—he couldn't just watch while Smacker hurt her.

"Hey!" he shouted at Smacker. "Leave her alone!"

Despite this last-second display of bravery and loyalty to one of his fellow Villagers, Salah had even less of a chance against Smacker than Yumi did. Smacker whipped back his sword and caught Salah on the chin with the flat of his blade.

The Villager tumbled back senseless. His legs gave out beneath him, and he crumpled into a pile next to Archie, unconscious but still breathing.

The heroes finally yelped in protest, no longer able to deny the fact that Smacker had lost his temper.

Fearful that the hero might attack Yumi next, Archie moved without thinking. If he'd given his action any consideration—if he'd actually formed a plan of any kind—he would have dithered about it until it was too late. And *too late*—in his mind, at least— meant that Yumi would meet her end.

Instead, Archie darted forward and punched the hero right in the stomach with everything he had.

It should have glanced off Smacker's armor. Then it wouldn't have hurt him any more than a hurled insult, and Archie would have bruised his knuckles.

But Smacker had raised his arms high to argue with the other heroes, which had raised the bottom of his armor shirt just enough to expose a thin strip of flesh, right at Archie's level. Archie's knuckles plowed straight into Smacker's unprotected gut.

CHAPTER SEVEN

Smacker yelped and dropped his sword, less in pain than in shock. His blade clattered to the ground near his feet, and his hands darted to his stomach, right where he'd been struck.

Archie staggered backward, as surprised as anyone that his insane, doomed-to-fail attempt to save Yumi from Smacker's rage had actually succeeded. He looked down at his fist as if it had suddenly appeared at the end of his arm by magic.

In all the times Archie had joined an Illager raiding party, he'd never once managed to defeat anything. A few times, he'd broken the bone of a skeleton or knocked an arm off a zombie, but despite his best attempts, he'd never harmed a living thing.

It wasn't that Archie hadn't wanted to. In fact, he'd wanted more than anything to prove himself a strong Illager, of value to his tribe—someone the others wouldn't constantly taunt. But the other Illagers were faster than he was and invariably got to anything that might have been his victim long before he could manage it himself.

So when he actually punched Smacker, a mixture of horror and pride flooded through him. It flowed up from his arms to his head, clogging his mouth as it went, so that he couldn't muster up a word of either triumph or excuse. All he could do was goggle at his clenched fingers.

Then Smacker shouted something both offensive and dismissive at him, finally breaking the spell.

Archie gaped up at the much taller hero blotting out the sunset's final red rays. Smacker gazed down at the little Illager with wide eyes. As he did, the surprise on his face transformed to righteous rage. He growled something, which Archie could only interpret as a declaration of a vendetta that would inevitably end in Archie's spectacular doom.

Smacker took one step toward Archie before two of the other heroes stopped him, each with a hand on one of Smacker's shoulders. They spoke to him in their odd tongue, but Smacker only tried to shrug them off. They refused to let him go, even when he bent over and reached for the sword he'd dropped.

Archie backed away slowly, unable to take his eyes off the shamefaced hero for even an instant. To his relief and disbelief, the heroes pulled Smacker away from his sword and set him back on his rump. Smacker grimaced in embarrassment as they laughed at him.

One of the heroes lifted the edge of Smacker's armor shirt, confirming that there was no wound there of any kind—not even a mark left on Smacker's skin. Another—the one who'd tried to help Archie earlier—produced a healing potion again and brought it toward Smacker's lips as a joke. Smacker growled at the others, pushing them away while he scrabbled toward his sword. From the way Smacker glared at him, Archie knew he would be the hero's next target.

A hand fell on Archie's shoulder from behind, and he spun about to find Yumi kneeling next to him. "We need to leave," she said. "Now."

He didn't feel the need to argue with her. In fact, he didn't feel much of anything at all. He'd gone numb from his toes straight up to his brain. He let her grab him by the hand and pull him away. His feet moved along as fast as she hauled him, if only to keep himself from being physically dragged on his knees.

"Where are we going?" Archie eventually managed to say. He'd thought that she might haul him right to the edge of the village and eject him into the wilderness, but he'd gotten turned around in the tumult and couldn't tell which direction they were headed.

"Away from there," she said, her voice full of determination, trying to quell a rising panic. They seemed to be heading toward the edge of the village. From there, the whole of the Squid Coast sprawled before them, edging toward the distant Creeper Woods. "Someplace safe."

"There's no place safe," Archie told her. He'd meant those words as a complaint—a comment about the insecurity of the nature of the world around them—but they struck him as painfully true. He couldn't go anywhere that Smacker wouldn't follow. He could chase Archie down to the ends of the land itself.

Yumi hauled up short so fast that Archie bumped into her. For a moment, she stood with her back to him, her shoulders heaving. Then she whirled around to look at him.

Her face was filled with anger and frustration, but it melted away when she saw him. "You're right," she said. "You can't run from them. But that doesn't mean there's no place safe."

She grabbed him by the wrist again and marched back into the village. This time, Archie could tell exactly where they were going.

"No," he said to Yumi. "Why would we go there? They'll just tear it to the ground."

"Do you have a better idea?" she asked.

He considered asking her to cut him loose. To let him run off on his own. He was small, almost unnoticeable. He might be able to hide for long enough, perhaps until Smacker and the other heroes lost interest in looking for him.

But he couldn't muster the courage. When it came to trying to save Yumi in the heat of a fight, he apparently could find the means to do something lethally stupid, but when he had to make a cold decision about it, he couldn't find a way.

Still, he had to try.

"Let me go," he whispered, secretly hoping she wouldn't hear him.

Her ears were sharper than he'd guessed. "Forget it," she told him. "You didn't abandon me, and I sure am not going to abandon you. You're coming with me."

As she spoke, they arrived at the front door of her home. Archie dug in his heels then, refusing to enter. "They'll destroy the place and defeat you!" he told her. "I've seen it happen before."

She stopped yanking on his arm, but she did not let him go. "This place has never been destroyed."

"Heroes don't understand anything but violence," Archie said.

"They swing around swords so much that everything looks to them like something to slash."

"We don't have time to argue this," Yumi said with a scowl. "Just get inside!"

Archie was ready to make a stand against her and force her to hear his argument. She, at least, would listen to him. She was kind and reasonable, unlike Salah—and unlike Smacker.

Before he could open his mouth again, though, he heard Salah shouting, "There he is!"

Archie turned to see the Villager coming straight at him with the heroes in his wake. The idea that Archie should stop and argue with Yumi vanished from his head. Instead, he leaped toward the door to Yumi's home, which she yanked open wide for him.

The moment Archie was inside the house, the door slammed behind him. He spun about to thank Yumi for the kindness of her foolish act, but he saw that she wasn't there. She was standing outside the door instead.

Archie tried to pull the door open so he could join her, but Yumi had a death-grip on the doorknob and held it shut. She gave him a stern look through the window and told him, "Stay there, and be quiet!" Then she turned to face the others.

"What is it you want?" Yumi said to Salah as he approached. She wasn't about to wait for him to start shouting at her.

"You know what we want," he said. "*Who* we want. Give him to us!"

She crossed her arms and set her jaw against him and the heroes who had massed behind him. "So you can defeat him? Forget it."

Salah gave her a self-satisfied snort. "*I* won't touch him. Villagers don't hurt anyone. You know that."

"But it's okay to turn them over to hulking bullies who will do that for you?" She glared at Smacker. "That's the same thing!"

Smacker shoved Salah aside, sending the Villager sprawling along the grass. He pointed at the door to Yumi's home in a vicious way and then at his boot.

The meaning was clear. If Yumi didn't let the hero into her home—or at least bring Archie out of it—Smacker would kick down the door and haul the little Illager out.

Yumi didn't budge. "If you want him, you'll have to go through me."

Smacker drew his sword and raised it to cut Yumi down, but she refused to give him an inch. Before he could do anything to actually harm her, though, the other heroes grabbed Smacker and pulled him away.

Smacker yowled in protest at his assault being foiled, but the other heroes refused to release him. They spoke to him in calm but firm tones, evidently trying to talk some sort of reason into him. He answered them with frustration and anger—all while still flushed red with embarrassment—resolutely refusing to listen to them.

Eventually the four other heroes each grabbed Smacker by a limb and lifted him bodily off of the ground. With him hanging suspended helpless among them, they marched him out of town and into the surrounding darkness.

Archie couldn't help but pump a fist in the air and cheer. He'd been sure that he and Yumi were doomed. The idea that the other heroes might step in to save them had never crossed his mind.

To him—as an Illager—all so-called heroes were actually villains: people who didn't care about the lives of others, only their own interests. To see them corral one of their own and haul him away gave him hope he had never dreamed of. For a moment, he thought he might actually be able to carve out a home for himself in this village, among people who cared about him and his safety.

It was then that he saw the torches and pitchforks.

"No," Yumi told the other Villagers. "Don't do this. Go home."

"We are home," Salah said, with a mournful look on his face as he got up and dusted himself off. "So are you." He pointed to Archie staring at them through the window in the door. "But he is not."

Yumi wasn't about to give in that easily. "We've been over this. You can't just kick him out. He hasn't done anything wrong!"

Salah frowned as if something awful had crawled into his mouth and was actively making him sick. "He punched one of the heroes. You know how we feel about violence."

Yumi scoffed at that, but even Archie could tell the implications of that disturbed her. "Do you really think that little Archie could harm someone like that? The rest of them had a healing potion ready for him before he could even say 'Ouch!' *As a joke!*"

Salah put up his hands, palms out, in what he probably thought was a placating manner. "Look, Yumi, that's not the point."

"Then what is the point, Salah? Answer me that? If we can agree that Archie doesn't have the ability to beat up a hero, then what else is there to discuss?"

Salah glanced out into the darkness. "Hard as it might be to believe, that attack really did disturb that hero. It hurt his pride, if nothing else. And if there's one thing we know about heroes, it's that they have long memories. That hero's friends might have hauled him away tonight, but there is no doubt that he will be back."

Yumi's shoulders sagged as both she and Archie realized that

Salah was right. As long as Archie remained here, the village was in danger. Smacker might come back there at any point and raze the place to the ground out of sheer spite.

"So what?" Yumi said. "Heroes come through here all the time. They take our food, butcher our cattle, and even sleep in our beds. They don't think of us as real people. They never have. How is what happened with Archie going to change that?"

Salah turned toward the other Villagers. They had all massed behind him, carrying their torches and pitchforks. Archie realized that these were all they really had to protect themselves. If the heroes came back—even if just Smacker came back—that wouldn't be enough. They'd be helpless before such an onslaught.

They nodded at Salah in wordless agreement. Some of them wore pained looks on their faces. Others braced themselves with grim determination. But they had all agreed on one thing.

Salah was right. Archie had to go.

Salah gave Yumi a sad shrug. "Honestly, I wish it wasn't so. Up until today, you were right about your little friend there. But now, when it matters most, he showed his true colors."

"He stood up to defend me, just as I defended him."

"That's the problem," Salah said. "Have you ever known a Villager to attempt violence against a hero before? It doesn't happen, because we are a peaceful people, and we know better. Up until he arrived, you knew better too."

Yumi glared at the man. "Are you telling me you're kicking me out of here too?"

"None of us want that to happen," Salah said, choosing his words with care. "That hero might be angry, but his anger seems focused on the Illager. Our hope is that once your friend is gone, he won't care about the rest of the village."

Yumi snorted at him in disgust. "And if that bully comes after me? What are you going to do then?"

Salah squirmed, uncomfortable with the implied accusation. Yumi turned to the rest of the crowd and spoke to them, her voice raw with emotion. "What about the rest of you? Where do you draw the line? If the bully comes for me, what would you do?"

Archie tested the door. In her anger, Yumi had let go of the knob, and it turned freely. He opened the door and stepped out of the house.

"Don't do this, Yumi," he told her as he came to her side. "I won't let you do this. Not for me."

She turned to him, tears glittering in her wide eyes. "No, Archie," she said softly. "Don't *you* do this. Stay here with me. Be safe. Stay."

He shook his head. "Salah is right."

"Salah's a jerk."

Archie chuckled despite the dark moment, as did several people in the crowd. "But he's right about that hero. He'll come back for me, and he might well tear this place down to get to me. We can't let that happen." He gazed deep into her eyes. "*I* can't let that happen."

"What are you going to do?" Yumi's voice cracked a bit as she came to the realization that this was an argument she wasn't going to win.

"Leave," Archie said. "Now."

INTERLUDE

"Are you out of your mind?" one of the heroes asked as they dropped Karl to the ground on a hilltop overlooking the village they'd had to drag him out of. "You could have killed those Villagers!"

"Yeah?" Karl said as he sprang to his feet and dusted himself off. "So what?"

He glared at the other four heroes. He didn't know their names or, really, much of anything else about them. They'd told him at one point, he was pretty sure, but the information hadn't lodged in his brain—mostly because he couldn't be bothered to care about it. He just called them by nicknames he'd come up with for them instead.

From Karl's point of view, other heroes were just people who competed with him for resources. If they got to the emeralds and artifacts and all the other cool stuff the world had to offer before him, that meant there was less for him. He hadn't come to this forsaken world to make friends. He'd come here to make it his playground—and maybe to conquer a bit of it while he was at it—and he didn't care what the other heroes thought about that.

"They're Villagers!" said Stache, who wore a magnificent bit of facial hair that was impossible to forget. "They're innocent! Defenseless! And mostly harmless!"

"Innocent? Ha!" Karl's voice dripped with scorn. "You think those little runts wouldn't do the same thing to us given half a chance? The only reason they don't is that they're too weak!"

"That's an awful way to think about this place and the people who call it home," said Scarface, who bore the mark of a nasty cut on their forehead. "They're not bullies. They're good souls, and we ought to respect that."

Karl couldn't help snorting at that. "We're *heroes*. Don't you get that? We're better than them on every level. We don't need to respect them. They just need to get out of our way."

"That doesn't mean you have to hurt them," said Red, who had crimson hair.

Karl never could stand talking to them. They were always so condescending, going on and on about "obligations" and "doing the right thing." So boring.

And so beside the point.

"You seem to be forgetting that the little rat down there punched me!" He pointed at his stomach for emphasis.

"I don't see anything wrong with you," said Pinky, who had bright pink hair, as they hid their mouth behind a hand.

"Healed rather nicely," said Stache, who almost managed to not roll their eyes.

"I do take pride in my potions," Scarface said with a wry chuckle.

"No harm, no foul," Red said while repressing a laugh.

Karl scowled at them all as they faced him in the moonlight. "Laugh it up! Sure, it didn't hurt, but that's not the point. That little guy attacked me!"

Pinky sighed, clearly already tired of the conversation. "Still, that's hardly a good reason to defeat a Villager much less threaten to lay an entire village to waste."

Karl stared at them in disbelief. "You just let the things out there attack you? Don't I have a right to defend myself?"

"You weren't being too friendly with them, as I recall," said Stache. "Seems to me like they were maybe just defending themselves from you."

Karl grunted as if he'd been expecting just that sort of response. "You're really going to side with them? Against a fellow hero, no less. I guess I shouldn't let that surprise me so much."

Scarface lit a torch to see the rest of them by. "What are you trying to say?"

Karl pointed back at the village. A crowd of people with torches were dispersing from the edge of the place. The Villagers were returning to their homes. Whatever had gone on there after the heroes had left was done.

"I'm saying you're soft and your priorities are messed up. You care more about them than me."

Red screwed up their face, disgusted at the implications of what Karl had said. "Just because they grew up here doesn't mean they're beneath us. Actually, it means we should respect them more."

"How do you figure that?" Karl stuck out his chin.

"They belong here. We're just visitors. Guests, if you will."

Karl blew a raspberry at that thought. "They live in one of the richest lands around, and they don't have any idea how to use it. Doesn't that seem like a waste?"

"It's not our home," Pinky said. "It's theirs. If they want to 'waste' it, whatever that means, that's their business."

"We discovered this place! It's ours to explore!"

"You think we found this place?" Stache shook their head. "The Villagers and Illagers were here long before us. If anyone found it, it was them."

Karl moved toward the edge of the torchlight. "But that's just it! It's such an amazing place. So much to see. So much to do. And they just live here! They just farm! How ridiculous is that?"

"They seem to like it that way," Scarface said. "It seems like the least we can do is leave them to their farming."

Karl groaned in disbelief. "You've borrowed their houses, just like me. You've eaten their food! Slept in their beds! You like to act like you're saints, but you're no better than me!"

Red shrugged. "None of the rest of us have tried to attack a Villager."

"That wasn't a Villager!" Karl's eyes grew wide with his frustration. "That was an *Illager*! They attack us all the time! Don't I have the right to defend myself?"

"Of course, you do," Pinky said in a serene voice. "All we're saying is that you shouldn't have to. Not in a village."

"That little thing wasn't going to hurt you," Stache said with a sad shake of their head. "It's kind of odd it was even there in the first place, but if the Villagers took it in, what's the harm?"

Karl pointed at his stomach once again. "It punched me!"

"Look," Scarface said. "We're not getting anywhere with this. And I don't want to have a fight break out here too." They looked straight at Karl. "If you think you're better than the locals, then start acting like that's true. Be the bigger person here. Let it go."

Karl rubbed the place where the Illager had struck him. It hadn't hurt him at all—except for his pride. He wasn't about to forget the humiliation anytime soon.

Karl was used to getting banged up. As a hero, he faced and

fought all sorts of dangerous creatures: creepers, guardians, golems, zombie pigmen, blazes, ghasts, and endermen. Some of them had hurt him awfully bad, beating, bashing, cutting, slashing, and even burning him within inches of his life. But none of them had embarrassed him as much as that little Illager had—and in front of the other heroes!

It was one thing to take on a mob in battle. When you did that, you expected trouble. The risk was part of your calculations. You balanced the possible rewards against the actual harm you might suffer.

That runt's useless little punch, though, had shaken Karl to his core. Even if it hadn't hurt, the fact that he'd been attacked in a place where he'd felt so safe bothered him. In a village, a place where—until that point—he'd felt invulnerable.

That meant that even a village might not be safe for him anymore. And if that was true, then there was no place in this land where he could relax and feel like nothing could harm him.

That thought made him shiver from head to toe.

"Forget it," Karl said to the others, who had started to set up camp by posting torches around the hilltop. "Maybe you can ignore something like that, but I can't."

"You cannot go hunting for that sad little wretch," Red said. "Leave him alone."

"And why should I do that?" Karl asked, angry and perplexed. "Someone does something like that to a hero, then I need to teach him a lesson."

"What good would that do?" Stache said. "You'd defeat him, right? Can't learn much of a lesson after that."

"I want to make an example out of him. Let the Villagers know what they can expect if any of them tries to hurt one of us!"

Stache cocked their head at Karl. "Has any of them ever tried to hurt any of us before?"

"That's not the point!" Karl protested. "They might now that they've seen someone attack us."

Scarface laughed as they stretched out on the open ground to rest. "They already know we get attacked. Every last one of us has hauled our beaten bodies into that place at one point or another, just to scrounge up a meal or some medicine."

"Well, sure," Karl said. "But that was because something else had hurt us. And usually something we were protecting them from!"

"So they know we can be hurt. This is not news to anyone."

"But till today, no one ever tried to make that happen in a village. And now that it's happened?" Karl let his question hang there in silence, waiting for any of the others to answer. No one took his bait.

"They're going to line up to take their shots at us!" Karl shouted. His voice echoed out into the darkness. In the distant village, a lone straggler still strolling in the central square cocked their head and looked back at the strange noise echoing in the night.

"You think it's bad having to deal with all the mobs?" Karl said in a low voice to the others. "At least you can see them coming. Most of them are afraid of the light. They don't go for you in your beds when you're sleeping at night. They don't step up and attack you while you're talking to someone else.

"When you let Illagers infiltrate villages like that? All bets are off. Those last safe places we thought we had? They're gone. Forever. We'll spend every moment there wondering when one of them is going to sneak up on us in our sleep and put an end to us."

"You're being ridiculous," Red said. "That little guy wasn't a real threat to you. If you'd just left him alone, none of this would have ever happened."

"Hey." Pinky had taken up the first watch—as was the custom—on the edge of the hilltop. They were standing just beyond the ring of torches, to help preserve their night vision, and they were pointing at something in the distance, moving off to the east. "Isn't that him?"

The other heroes—including Karl—all joined Pinky at their position and peered into the night. Sure enough, there on the edge of the Squid Coast, edging toward the Soggy Swamp, a person was trudging northward. They were moving slowly and were hard to pick out in the night, but it was certainly someone.

"You really think that's him?" asked Stache.

"Who else could it be?" said Scarface. "Not too many people desperate enough to be roaming around by themselves in the middle of the night. It's dangerous out there."

"Only one way to find out." Karl drew his sword. "Let's go get him."

"What? No!" Red yelped in surprise and frustration. "Did nothing we said get through that thick head of yours? He's no threat to you or anyone else!"

Karl dismissed the complaint with a "Whatever," and then headed out into the darkness. He didn't get ten steps from the camp before Stache and Scarface raced after him and stopped him.

"You can't do this," Stache told him. "We won't let you."

"I don't recall you being my boss," Karl said as he shrugged off their hands. Still, he didn't start stomping off into the darkness again.

"It's not worth your time," Scarface said. "Are you really going to wander off into the night and try tracking that little Illager down? The mobs will take care of him for you."

Karl frowned. Maybe Scarface was right. It was a long way to the Soggy Swamp from their campsite on the edge of the Creeper Woods, and the hike would be filled with mobs of all sorts. They'd be just as eager to kill him as they would the Illager.

"Maybe we should go after him," Stache said, now unsure too. "He's probably going to need saving." They looked at Karl. "We'd leave you here though."

"You're going to *save* him? You realize that if you'd found him anywhere else, you'd just put a quick end to him, no questions asked." Karl folded his arms across his chest. "Either way, if you're going after that little mob, then I'm coming too. That's the right thing to do. It's not safe for any of us, right?"

He knew he wasn't fooling anyone.

"We'll never find him in the dark," Scarface said. "It's one thing to spot him from a high vantage point like our campsite, but once we get down into the woods or the swamp, we won't be able to see him. On top of that, we don't know where he's going."

"It's insane that he's even out there alone right now," Stache said. "The Villagers must have kicked him out."

Scarface shuddered at the thought. "They must have been furious with him. It's tantamount to a death sentence. They had to have known that."

"Good riddance," Karl said, not bothering to hide his relief. "At least he won't attack anyone else."

CHAPTER EIGHT

Archie had no idea where he was going. He just knew where he was no longer welcome. He couldn't return to the village, and he couldn't go back to his tribe's camp. Other than that, the world stood open to him.

Of course, it was night, which meant the mobs were out and looking for fresh prey. Someone like him—a small person traveling alone at night, without weapons or armor—made for a perfect target for such creatures. It made him wonder exactly when his luck might run out and he would find himself their next victim.

Archie shivered from both fear and the cold as he made his way through the darkness. He'd never learned to navigate by the stars, so without the sun in the sky, he had no idea in which direction he was headed. He only knew that he had to leave the village behind.

He already missed the safety of the village. The torches that warned the mobs away. The walls of the homes that kept the mobs out. The iron golems that served to protect all who behaved within their borders.

He'd felt safer there than he ever had among the Illagers. With the exception of Salah, no one there had picked on him. Some of them, like Yumi, had actually become friends with him. Until then, he'd never had a real friend, and he found that he instantly missed it.

Still, he clung to hope. When he'd been kicked out of the tribe, he'd thought he was dead for sure. He'd been shocked when he'd survived his first night on his own. And that had led him to the village, which had been comparatively wonderful.

Now that he'd lost that, he was still better off than when he'd left the tribe. He was relatively unharmed. He'd eaten well and rested up over the past couple weeks. He wasn't happy to have been forced out of the village, but he was more ready to face the darkness now than he had been beforehand.

Any mobs he ran into weren't going to care about that though. They would just tear him apart.

To keep that from happening, he kept as quiet as he could. He didn't need to attract any trouble. That would probably find him on its own just fine.

A few times, he thought he heard something from high up in the Creeper Woods, and once, he even managed to spot lights flickering way up there. He wondered who might be so brave as to be camping in such a remote and mob-ridden place, and then he thought better of it. It occurred to him that it might be the heroes who'd gotten him ejected from the village. And if it wasn't them there was a good chance it was someone even worse.

Archie had never expected to be treated well in the village. He had Yumi to thank for that. He could only look upon that time as a fluke now, a brief moment of brightness in an otherwise miserable life.

He had no hopes of finding another village. He only wanted to survive. He just had no real idea about how to manage that.

But the next morning came, and he was still alive.

Archie tried to keep moving for a bit longer, until the sun rose fully into the sky, but that was all he could manage. His feet hurt too much, and he was simply too tired to march on.

He made it to the top of a low hill and shaded his eyes with his hand as he scouted around, looking for any kinds of threats that might accidentally stumble upon him. The sun might solve the problem of the mobs while it was up, but it wouldn't do him any good against Villagers, Illagers, or—worst of all—heroes who might find him.

Archie believed himself to be utterly alone. His eyes drooping and legs aching, he found himself a patch of deep grass underneath the shade of some tall trees. There he curled up and went to sleep.

The sun was high in the sky when he finally awakened once again. He stood up and stretched his arms and discovered that a group of giant spiders were crawling up the slope to the south of him. They didn't look too hungry at the moment, but he didn't want to test that out.

Having nowhere else to go, Archie decided that he should head north. The village lay on the Squid Coast, to the south, and beyond that only the open sea tumbled away. If he wanted to keep moving, he had to make sure he didn't get trapped up against it.

Archie had never learned how to swim much less how to build

a boat. Even if he could find something that would let him float on the waves, he didn't know how to sail or row it. It didn't seem all that complicated, but making any mistake in water that would be over his head should he fall into it could easily prove fatal.

Higher ground seemed like the wisest choice. Ideally he'd find someplace from which he could see any threats coming from miles away. There he could carve out a home in which he could finally feel safe.

If that meant he had to be alone, then he would bear up under that. At least that way no one could kick him out ever again.

High mountains ranged to the northwest and northeast, but a wide and easy valley forged its way between them. Archie decided to follow it and see where it would lead him. He didn't have any particular destination in mind, and no well-trodden path presented itself to him. Instead, he navigated by the sound of threats emerging around him. Anytime he heard a zombie's groan, a creeper's hiss, or the clattering of a skeleton's bones, he walked directly away from it. He had no way to know if fate, luck, or something more actively intelligent was steering him, but his path brought him more or less straight north.

At one point, a few days into his journey, Archie decided that he'd made a mistake. He needed to go back south to where the mountains were easier to climb. From there, he could either make his way into them properly, or he could try his luck in the Creeper Woods, as horrifying as that seemed.

It didn't take long, though, for him to hear the groans of zombies and the rattling of skeletons coming from ahead of him. The noises of the mobs seemed to be hemming him in on three sides. The only way that stood clear and open was to the north.

Steeling himself, he began marching south again anyhow.

With every step he took, the groans and rattles grew louder and louder until he felt sure that undead mobs were about to lurch out of the darkness straight at him.

And then they did.

He'd secretly been hoping that the noises had been some kind of trick. A ploy to get him to go north. A bluff without any teeth.

But the crowd of zombies that appeared out of the darkness, groaning and reaching for his living flesh, told him that he was flat-out wrong.

Fortunately, he spotted them before they could surround him. The closest one actually got within arm's reach of him, and Archie had to duck to avoid getting grabbed and pulled toward the rotting mob's busted-up mouth. He threw himself backward and rolled away on the ground before shoving himself to his feet and sprinting away back north again.

The best thing he could say about zombies was that they were slow. If enough of them surrounded you, they could cut you off from escape, but otherwise, he could easily outpace them.

The worst thing about zombies was—unlike the living in general and Archie in particular—they never got tired. They could keep walking all night long, right until the moment the sun came up and turned them into smoking piles of ash.

Skeletons were a bit faster, perhaps because they didn't have all that rotten flesh on their bones slowing them down. And they carried bows, which meant that running from them wasn't always effective. Even if you were much faster than they were, they could put an arrow or two in your back before you managed to race out of their range.

Archie could hear a bunch of skeletons rattling nearby, just behind the groaning zombies. He couldn't see them under the cover of night, but if they spotted him and started firing arrows at him, he had no doubt they would fill him with enough arrows that someone passing by his corpse later might think him to have been not an Illager but a porcupine.

He had no choice but to run north and to keep running until he couldn't hear any pursuit. He set to doing just that, but while the rattling and groans grew fainter and more distant, they never entirely faded away to the kind of silence his hammering heart demanded.

As the night wore on, Archie thought that he saw the sun rising before him, and he wondered how he'd gotten turned that far around. Had he been heading east ever since the zombie attacked him?

It wasn't until Archie topped a low-sloping rise in his path that he realized the crimson light wasn't the product of a rising sun. Instead, it came from a glowing river of lava that stretched before him.

CHAPTER NINE

Despair knocked Archie's knees out from under him.

The lava seemed like it blocked his way entirely, stretching from one side of the canyon he'd been hiking through to the other. This meant that he had no way forward and countless undead mobs behind. He was finished.

Archie sat there and watched the lava flow as he tried to come to terms with his impending doom. He wished once again that he could have lived in peace in the village. Perhaps in time he'd have found a place of his own, maybe even next door to Yumi's. They could have been neighbors, working in the fields and doing chores together.

She'd even started teaching him to read. There had been books in the woodland mansions, but Archie hadn't been granted access to them. Even if he could have swiped one for a moment, he wouldn't have been able to decipher it. But Yumi had shown him how.

That had seemed so magical to him, the idea that you could make shapes on a page — letters — that would put words from your head into other people's heads. That you could store knowledge or feelings or even epic stories on those pages for other people to put into their heads whenever they sat down to read them.

He wished he'd been a better student. He wished he'd had a chance to read more. To learn more. To do more.

To be a better person.

To transform from an Illager into a Villager.

But now he would never have that chance.

Besides which, if the way the heroes and Villagers like Salah had treated him had taught him anything it was that they would never accept him. He could have become the model Villager, and they still would have looked down on him, kicked him, sneered at him.

In the end, they would have found some excuse to kick him out — just as they had. Working so hard to become one of them had been a fool's errand from the start, and Archie now regretted even embarking on it.

A chorus of zombie groans shuffling up behind Archie thrust him to his feet. He had given up hope for survival, but that didn't mean the mobs didn't scare the wits out of him. He was too much of a coward to lie there and let them eat him when he could still try to run.

If it came to it, he wasn't sure if he would run into the lava or let the zombies have him. His brain wouldn't let him think about that. Not yet.

As Archie moved farther north, though, he saw that the cliff face to his right didn't run quite all the way up to the river of lava, as he'd thought. A narrow passage stretched between the side of the canyon and the molten rock, off to the east. Scarcely believing his eyes, he sprinted for the clear and level strip of land and raced along it as fast as he could.

The entire time, he expected the land to end, leaving him trapped between the undead and the lava once again. The land turned from rocky to sandy as Archie went, and hope rose in his heart. If he could just hold out long enough, he might actually survive.

The barest hint of the breaking dawn—the actual dawn, this time—began to show in the east as the strip of land widened and spilled fully out into an expansive desert that sprawled before him. He stopped there for a moment, stunned by the fact that he had somehow managed to escape what he'd thought was certain death. Then he heard the groans of the undead mobs growing closer once again.

Archie walked into the desert. After he got a fair way out into the sand, he turned around to watch the mobs still chasing him. As they grew closer, the sun grew higher. It caught each of them in its rays, setting them ablaze one at a time and leaving nothing but ashes behind.

Now that he got a good look at them, these creatures seemed different than the standard zombies that he'd encountered before. They seemed older, drier. Less like zombies and more like husks.

A warm, whispering wind blew in off the desert and swept the ashes away. Soon there was nothing left of the mobs at all.

Archie walked all day long, putting the lava far behind him. The moment darkness enveloped the land again, though, the low groans and rickety rattles of the undead filled the air behind Archie once more. He decided not to give them a chance to catch up with him this time, and kept marching as fast as his aching feet would carry him.

Rain started to fall then, pelting Archie with large, wet drops that soon had him soaked to the skin. It turned the sands of the desert dark, and the clouds that blanketed the sky made the night blacker than ever. Soon Archie could barely see beyond the ends of his arms.

He kept walking.

Just as the rain transformed from a shower into a downpour, Archie heard a particular kind of hissing that came not from creepers but from giant spiders.

He peered through the drenched darkness behind him and spotted a row of glowing red eyes that could only belong to those spiders. Unlike the undead mobs, the spiders were fast and could keep up with Archie's short-legged gait. He had to move faster if he was going to avoid them.

Though he feared he might fall into a pit, Archie tossed caution aside and picked up his pace. If he wanted to escape the giant spiders, he had no choice.

Something seemed to be drawing him forward. Something more than a simple sense of self-preservation. It felt less like he was fleeing something than closing in on it.

Lightning crashed, and Archie saw that he was approaching the side of a dark mountain, something that was almost invisible on that stormy night. He didn't see any crack in it, no pass or cave into which he could escape. It was like someone had planted a wall there, and the only choice he had now was to climb it, treacherous as that might be.

The ground sloped up sharply, but Archie kept toward it, moving away from the spiders as fast as he could. Soon he had to change from scrambling over the rock to clambering up it. While the rain made the rock slick, he still managed to find some decent handholds and footholds, and soon he was climbing straight up.

Archie looked behind him and saw that the steep slope did not deter the spiders in the slightest. They crawled right up it on all eight legs, moving nearly as fast as they would if they were walking on level ground. He couldn't match their speed, not vertically, and it was only a matter of time before they caught up with him.

Despite that, Archie kept climbing. As he went, he knocked a loose bit of rock off, and it went spinning off beneath him. At first the sight of it terrified him, as it reminded him that he could fall just like that at any moment. But then the rock smacked into one of the spiders and knocked it off the side of the mountain, sending it tumbling to its death below. If he'd had any breath to spare, Archie might have shouted in triumph. Instead, he kept climbing as steadily as he could manage, and any time he found a loose bit of rock, he sent it falling behind him.

Soon the last of the spiders following him had been knocked to its death. Archie stopped to rest for a moment, but another flash of lightning showed him that he wasn't that far from a ledge above his head. Happy to have found a place where he might be able to rest for a moment, he hauled himself up to it and collapsed on its rocky surface.

The thunder and lightning reminded him that he shouldn't stay outside if he could manage it. Now that he'd escaped the spiders, he needed to find shelter from the rain. It bothered him to settle down in one place during the darkness, for fear that mobs might catch up with him and trap him someplace, but exposed as he was on the side of this mountain, he didn't see any other option.

After taking a scant moment to catch his racing breath, Archie pushed himself back up to his feet and staggered forward. He moved slowly and carefully across the rocky, rain-slick shelf, making sure that he didn't accidentally stumble into an unseen pit. When he reached the far side of it, he discovered another wall, this one smooth and vertical, and he realized that climbing it would be impossible.

He wanted to collapse there into a dreamless sleep, but he couldn't bear the thought of a spider sidling up and sinking its fangs into his neck while he was unconscious and helpless. Instead, he forced himself to make his way along that cliff face in the hopes he might find some means of escape. He would have been satisfied with a reasonable slope to climb, although he wished he might stumble upon a protective cave as well.

To his amazement, he literally stumbled over an unlit torch. It was just lying there on the ledge, and he didn't see it until he tripped over it. At first, he thought he might have found a tree root, even up here, higher than the trees seemed able to reach, but when he closed his hand around it, he knew what it was.

Archie had nothing to light the torch with, and he feared it might be too wet to burn anyhow. But when he held it up, some sort of magic caused the tip of it to burst into flames. He didn't understand it, but he wasn't going to complain about it.

In the light of the torch, Archie could see a bit farther and noticed that the shelf he stood on seemed wide enough to house a small army. He wondered if there had been an easier way to reach it. The thought bothered him in two ways.

First, he felt a little stupid for having climbed up a sheer cliff face if he could have found a much easier trail up there instead. Second, if there *was* an easier trail, then mobs might use it to get to him. His momentary sense of safety vanished.

The new fear that gripped him at least spurred him awake, back from the brink of total exhaustion. He raised his new torch high, even though he worried that it might bring curious mobs toward him. It showed him a path carved off to the left, and he followed it.

The path wound into a pass that cut deeper into the mountain, around a few secondary peaks that stood much shorter than the one in the mountain's center. Once inside the pass, Archie could no longer see the land that sprawled below him, from which he had begun his climb. However, the rocky formations around him at least offered a little shelter from the whispering wind.

As Archie reached the end of the pass, he spied the flickering of torchlight ahead. He came around the final bend in the pass and gasped to see a massive doorway towering in front of him. Gigantic braziers mounted atop high shelves framed the double doors. When lightning flashed, he could see handles on the doors placed high above his reach.

Archie could only imagine who could have built such a place. If anyone had ever lived there, they seemed to have deserted it long ago.

The smart thing to do, he knew, would be to turn around and leave. To head back into the storm and face the horrible weather and wandering mobs that had plagued every step of his nights. But he couldn't bring himself to do that.

A horrible foreboding filled Archie's heart as he gazed up at the doors. It felt like whatever lay beyond them could only be swollen with the sort of horrors that swarmed through his worst nightmares.

Still, his curiosity prodded him forward. He couldn't stand the idea of leaving those doors alone. Of walking away from them and never knowing what might stand beyond them.

He steeled himself, held up his torch high, and pressed a hand on the massive doors.

They began to give.

CHAPTER TEN

To Archie's surprise the gigantic doors swung open as if they had been waiting for his touch. Inside, it seemed that nothing but darkness awaited him.

He crept through the doors and found himself standing on a large, flat expanse in a massive chamber that stretched so far he couldn't make out the ceiling or walls. All he knew was that the rain and wind that had howled around him outside could not reach him in here, and for the moment, that seemed like enough.

As he moved forward, his torchlight showed him that the shelf on which he walked ended abruptly. He found nothing but a bottomless pit on every edge but one. In that direction, a naked bridge of rock stabbed out into the darkness.

Something emitted a soft glow so far below the edges of the shelf that Archie couldn't make out what it might be coming from. A part of him wondered what he would find if he leaped over the edge, but the only thing he would be sure of then was a sudden and terrifying death.

Archie feared that the bridge might collapse under his weight if he ventured onto it, but he didn't see any other way to move deeper into the chamber. His throat suddenly dry with fear, he made his way forward as carefully as he could. He peered over the edges of the bridge as he went and saw nothing below him but that mysterious glow.

He reached the other side of the bridge without incident and discovered a steep slope waiting for him there. It seemed as if someone had hollowed out the mountain but left another peak inside of it for him to discover.

Archie shaded his eyes from his torch's light and spied a faint, golden glow coming from the top of the internal peak. Without an easy way down, the only way for him to go was up, so he set back to climbing.

The light grew stronger and brighter as Archie made his way higher and higher. The closer he got to it, the more he felt like a voice was whispering something in his head. In fact, he recognized it now and realized it had been whispering softly to him the entire day.

Closer, it said. *Closer.*

Archie froze as he finally understood the words. For hours he'd thought they had only been a part of the wind's whispers. To hear them now and know that they had always been words struck fear straight through his brain.

It's all right, the voice said, its tone growing in volume and strength. *Don't be afraid. Come closer.*

Archie glanced behind him. He could be down the slope, across the bridge, and out the door in a matter of seconds—

assuming he didn't fall to his death in his hurry. The glow from the top of the peak seemed far warmer and more welcoming than the one from below.

I am here for you. I offer you power.

Archie shook his head to try to knock the voice out of it, but it didn't do him any good. He tried to plug his ears instead, but that didn't work either.

Closer. The voice rang in his brain. *Closer.*

Archie found that he didn't want to argue with it. Not at all. The voice might be odd, but if it had drawn him in here, at least it was into a place that wasn't cold, windy, and wet.

He climbed higher, working his way up the slope one bit at a time until he finally reached the summit. As he clambered over the top, he saw the most amazing thing that had ever appeared before his eyes: a glowing orb that hovered over a wide and low pedestal.

Archie's eyes grew wide as he gazed upon the orb. It shifted colors while he watched it, moving from bright pinks to shining yellows to fiery oranges.

Welcome, the voice said to him. *I am the Orb of Dominance, and I am here to help you rule the world. It is your destiny.*

Archie didn't know how he felt about that. The idea that he could rule even his own destiny much less rule the entire world seemed so ridiculous he couldn't even laugh at it. He could only gawk in utter disbelief.

Even then, he felt himself being inexorably drawn to the Orb. He felt his feet moving him toward it of their own accord, and his arms reached out to grab for it.

The Orb pulsed in anticipation as Archie's hands moved to close around it. *Yes. Your time is finally here.*

The Orb seemed so eager that Archie pulled back for a moment. He knew that few things in life came to you without any strings attached, and because of that he inherently distrusted what the Orb seemed to be offering him. A little Illager like him didn't deserve such power.

But he was going to take it.

Yes. You are destined for greatness. Your miseries have come to an end. Your time to rule has come.

Heroes like Smacker and awful Illagers like Thord would never be able to hurt him again. With the power of the Orb, they would now answer to him!

Archie reached out and grasped the Orb in his hands. It began to tremble, and he felt unimaginable power course through him.

Sparkling lights began to swirl around him, encircling him in a glowing vortex. The Orb's might swelled through him, and he saw that nothing was impossible for him. Not any longer.

Yes. Now we are one. Now our fates are forever intertwined.

The mightiness of what Archie had just become overwhelmed him. He threw back his head and laughed. The gigantic cavern in which he stood echoed with his crazed cackles.

CHAPTER ELEVEN

The next morning, Archie awakened and wondered if it all had been a wild and ridiculous dream. As he opened his eyes, he saw that he was still clutching the Orb of Dominance.

Normally such an intense light would have made it hard for him to sleep, but this light seemed to calm him with its power.

Actually, *calm* wasn't the right word for something that emanated such incredible power. If it had been in the hands of someone else, Archie would probably have fallen to his knees and begged for mercy. Because it belonged to him, though, he found it infinitely comforting to have and to hold.

Good morning. Time to rise. We have a lot of work to do.

Archie's stomach rumbled in agreement. He stood and stretched as best he could while he kept the Orb tucked under his arm.

Daylight streamed into the cavern through the gigantic doors far below. Archie gazed down at it in relief. The undead were no longer a threat, at least for the remainder of the day.

They will never threaten you again. Not while you have me around.

Archie couldn't help but smile at that thought. He'd lived in fear for so long that it felt like the Orb had lifted a massive weight from his shoulders. He stood up straighter and taller than he could ever remember.

He gazed down and marveled at the Orb, still overwhelmed by everything about it. It looked glorious, and now it claimed to have the power to give him everything he wanted. To protect him. To keep him safe.

It still seemed like a dream, and he worried that he might awaken from it at any moment and discover that death had surrounded him. Perhaps he had suffered a blow to the head and become delusional.

This is real. Your worries are over.

Which was exactly what Archie figured his delusions would tell him. Still, doubting his good fortune would do nothing but make him miserable. He figured he should at least enjoy the comforts they brought him—until they proved to be fiction or reality, either way.

Let me show you what we can do. First, we must leave this place.

Apparently Archie's new best friend couldn't teleport him about the land. Or fly. Instead, Archie had to carry it down the treacherous slope.

He did just that, and he found it much easier than he would have guessed. He wasn't sure if it was the power of the Orb or not, but he felt confident with every step. Normally he'd have been half paralyzed with worry about slipping and tumbling into the apparently bottomless abyss that stretched on either side of him, but instead he moved down the slope like he was walking down a wide and pleasant street.

He crossed the bridge over to the platform in front of the door. As he did, he spotted a group of statues framing the door, three to each side of it. They resembled the iron golems that had protected Yumi's village, but instead of being fashioned from metal, they seemed to have been carved out of a living stone that glowed with a crimson light.

They have been standing watch over you, keeping you safe. Nothing could have harmed you in here.

"Are they alive?" As Archie peered at them, they separated from the walls they were leaning against and strode toward him. Their joints creaked as they moved, sounding like stones rubbing together. They hauled up short several feet away, like soldiers coming to attention before their general.

Nothing happened for a moment. Then the creature closest to Archie shuddered, which nearly sent him fleeing back into the darkness. The glow of the Orb comforted him, though, and he leaned closer to the thing instead.

As he watched, the golem shook the dust of years off itself. Its redstone limbs scraped against its body as it regarded him with eyes that glowed like the coals of a burning fire.

Archie didn't say a word to the redstone golem. It knew who he was and what he was to it. It took a step closer to him and then fell to one knee before him, acknowledging him as its master.

Archie laughed loud and long, right until his voice became hoarse and he started to choke. When he finally wiped the tears from his eyes and could see properly again, he discovered that all the redstone golems had fallen to their knees before him, and he started to laugh all over again.

They are yours to command.

Archie suppressed an urge to squeal with delight. The village had only a few iron golems to protect them, and now he had six of these redstone golems under his control. Already he couldn't imagine who could stand in his way. Even the heroes would tremble before his might.

Grinning widely, he moved forward and stared out the open doors. The sun was already getting lower in the sky. He'd slept most of the day away.

You were exhausted. You needed rest. I protected you. I healed you.

Archie felt a surge of gratitude, and the Orb glowed warmly under his arm. He looked down at it and decided that it deserved better than to be toted around like that. It was the most precious thing he'd ever seen, and it needed to be put on display in a way that everyone around could see it.

A wise notion, as befits one who is destined to rule. Your subjects will be fortunate to have you watching over them.

A beam of light arced out from the Orb and exposed a vein of metal running through the floor in front of Archie. Blocks of iron and gold rose up from the ground and hovered there before him. A moment later, they began to spin around and around like a top. The blocks whirled about, becoming taller and narrower, until they melded into a tall, straight pole with a small disk on its top.

Perfect.

The pole—which Archie now recognized as a staff—floated over and came to a rest right before him. He reached out and took it with one hand as it landed on the ground. It felt like it had been made for his grasp.

With his other hand, Archie took the Orb of Dominance and placed it on top of the staff. It stuck as if he had glued it there, but when he looked closer, he saw that it wasn't actually touching the staff at all. Instead, it hovered over the disk on top of the staff, just as it had atop the pedestal inside the hollow mountain.

That feels better.

Archie had to agree. He realized then that he was still starving.

A moment.

Just seconds later, a plate full of steaming-hot food appeared on top of a nearby boulder, at just about the height of a table. Another rock appeared next to it at the perfect level for Archie to sit on. He immediately did so and set to the food as if he hadn't eaten in weeks.

Every time Archie cleaned his plate, more food appeared on it. He kept eating until he was so stuffed he couldn't move. When he was finally done, he rolled off his stony chair and curled up on the ground once more.

A pillow grew out of the ground beneath his head, and a blanket appeared out of the air and settled down over him. As his need to sleep overtook him, he looked up to see the Orb of Dominance hovering above its spectacular staff, standing entirely on its own. The redstone golems had moved to encircle him, guarding him from anything that might disturb his rest. Full and safe, he quickly drifted off.

What seemed like moments later, the all-too-familiar sounds of groaning husks startled Archie awake. He threw off the blanket and scrambled to his feet, too terrified at the moment to even think of the Orb still shining over him or the redstone golems standing guard around him.

Do not fear. You are under my protection.

Archie glanced up at the glowing globe and wondered just how impressive that protection might be. It was one thing to carve a staff or conjure up a meal, but it was another thing entirely to fight off a horde of hungry husks. The redstone golem might be able to fight them off, but would they actually do it? Unsure of the limits of his newfound power, Archie grabbed the staff in both hands and held it before him like a weapon—one that he had no idea how to use.

He stared into the surrounding darkness, his eyes straining to see what was coming at him. Soon enough, a green-skinned, rotting humanoid came staggering toward him, its one good eye shining in the Orb's reddening light.

One of them would normally have been enough to send Archie scrambling back inside the hollow mountain and trying to slam the doors behind him. The groans rolling toward him indicated there were many more.

Hold here. You are in no danger.

Archie glanced over his shoulder at the open doorway behind him. It seemed like the safest route for sure. When he looked back to see how close the husks had gotten, he spotted another five or six of the creatures shambling behind the one in the lead. And who knew how many others might still be coming toward them in the darkness?

The redstone golems hadn't even bothered to turn toward the threat. They seemed like they'd be about as useful as statues. Maybe he could hide behind them?

Archie began to drop the staff, turn around, and flee, but he caught himself at the last moment. If he fled now—at the moment when he finally seemed to have come upon real power—he would never know what he could do. If he wanted to have such power, then he had to wield it.

Now.

Exactly. You could command the golems to do your work for you, but why bother? Use me. Destroy them all.

Archie raised the staff high over his head. The Orb of Dominance blazed atop it with the crimson color of the setting sun. It crackled with power as the husks approached.

As the closest one came within Archie's reach, he drew back the staff to clock the creature in the face. Instead, the Orb flared up with power.

Archie watched as the Orb's glow intensified. Beams lanced out from it, transfixing the nearest husks and igniting them. As the nearest ones incinerated, Archie began walking forward. The Orb's beams reached out to others, destroying them as well. Soon every husk in the entire area was gone, leaving behind several neat little piles of ash.

Archie gasped in delight. "Incredible!" he said out loud.

Are you pleased? The Orb sounded so eager.

"Definitely!" It seemed to Archie that the Orb could read his thoughts, but he preferred to speak to it out loud. The idea of having something else's thoughts ringing in his brain was strange enough. He didn't want to start communicating that way himself. At least not yet.

Of course, this meant anyone watching him would think he was speaking to himself. Given his location, he didn't believe the chances of that happening were very high. And with the power he now wielded, he didn't much care.

With the Orb of Dominance at his side, no undead mob would ever be able to threaten Archie again. He felt safe for the first time since he'd left Yumi's home. Maybe for the first time in his life.

I told you I would protect you. You need not worry again.

Gratitude surged through Archie. "Thank you." It seemed terribly inadequate, but he didn't know what else to say.

Allow me to show you the rest of your lands.

Archie shook for a moment. Lands? Like it wasn't enough that the Orb was there to protect him and make him feel powerful. It also came with lands?

Despite himself, he was eager to see what the Orb was talking about. "Where are we going?"

Wave my staff toward the rocks to the south.

Archie reoriented himself until he saw the rock formation the Orb had mentioned. He raised the staff high and shook it in that direction. As he did, a beam stabbed out from the Orb and grabbed a large block of rock, moving it aside. It was far heavier than Archie could ever have hoped to move on his own, but the Orb handled it like a bag of feathers.

Over and over again, the Orb moved one block after another, and soon Archie could see there was a path on the other side of the rocks.

To speed things up, you could order the redstone golems to help.

"A fine idea!" Archie turned back toward the redstone golems and discovered them right behind him. They had followed him over without him even noticing.

"Hey, you! I mean, um . . . My golems!" he said to them as he pointed at the rocks ahead. "Clear my way!"

The creatures lurched forward as one and set to work. With all six of them at it, the rocks were soon all cleared away, revealing a passageway toward a switchback path that led down the mountain. This, Archie knew instantly, was how the husks had made their way up here. They had squeezed through a narrow tunnel that had been nearly invisible, probably lured by the light of the Orb of Dominance. If they'd thought the light had come from the flickering torch of some poor wanderer who would make easy prey, they'd paid the ultimate price for their mistake.

That way lies your future. Let's find it.

Archie strolled down the cleared path as if he owned the entire mountain. Maybe he actually did.

As he made his way down the path, the first rays of the dawn broke over the horizon to the east. The storm that had soaked the region the previous night had broken, and the thunderclouds had fled to plague some other lands.

From the mountain path, Archie had a stunning view of the desert that stretched to the south. If he tried, he could even see past that to the mountains and forests that lay beyond it. Apparently he'd climbed up extremely high in the dark, trying to get away from those spiders. It still surprised him that he'd made it without somehow falling to his death.

Once he reached the foot of the mountain, the Orb started whispering instructions in his mind. For a moment, Archie considered ignoring them. He could have set off for the south instead and gone back to find the village. He wanted to find Yumi and let her know he was all right.

Most of all, he wanted to hunt down and take out Salah and Thord and all of the other people who'd made his life so miserable. That included those heroes who'd forced him out of the village. Included Smacker.

Especially Smacker.

All in good time. Even heroes such as those are no threat to you. Not individually.

But they do not work alone. When your foes band together, they can amass an overwhelming force. If we wish to defeat them—to remove them from the land once and for all—we need to find allies too.

We need to form an army of our own.

Archie liked the sound of that.

CHAPTER TWELVE

The Orb tugged at the top of the staff, leading Archie back toward the southern face of the mountain he'd just come down from. At the Orb's instruction, Archie began to use the staff and his team of redstone golems to alter the landscape.

All he had to do was point the staff in the right direction and think about how he wanted things to change, and the Orb and the golems took care of the rest. The golems actually did most of the work, while Archie and the Orb planned out the architecture of his new home.

It took days of planning and even more time to mine the necessary materials and craft them together into the wondrous new structure Archie's plans demanded. Still, the design was exhilarating, and the golems worked at their jobs tirelessly, even when exhaustion finally forced Archie to sleep.

"It needs to be humongous, with high walls and even taller towers. It needs to be something that intimidates people who even dare to look at it."

Yes. A castle fit for one who will rule all the lands. A place where you will be safe—and from which you can launch your armies.

"Exactly! It will be the most glorious building this world has ever seen!"

Such a proud structure needs an equally amazing name.

"Right! Something to tell people who hear the name that they would be fools to come near it." Archie racked his brain but couldn't think of anything appropriate. He'd lived his entire life in and out of Illager mansions, but all of them stacked on top of one another wouldn't measure up to the place they were building.

Highblock Keep.

At this point, Archie wasn't sure if he or the Orb had come up with the name. He only knew for sure that it fit perfectly, and he wasn't interested in exploring that question further.

Soon enough his plans came to fruition, and the structure itself was complete. It would take him time to furnish the place fully, but now he could finally move into it at least.

Welcome home.

Archie walked up the long, wide steps to Highblock Keep, which had been carved from the mountain's living stone. The scale of the place took his breath away. He'd never seen any structure so gigantic in all his days. And it was all his.

Although they had just built the place, in Archie's mind the keep didn't seem fresh and new. Instead, it felt like it had been there forever, waiting to be rediscovered, like a gorgeous statue hidden inside a flawless block of marble. Archie and the Orb hadn't built it but revealed it.

Enter and take possession.

As Archie topped the stairs, he found himself staring across a deep chasm at a gigantic gate, taller and wider even than the doors that had led him into the hollow mountain. He didn't see a way to get across the massive gap, which seemed wide enough that only a bird could ever cross it.

For a long moment, Archie didn't know what to do. Had he actually designed a home he couldn't get into? Then the voice of the Orb of Dominance echoed in his head once more.

I can help you with that.

Archie slapped himself on his wide forehead and chuckled. Of course. He had the power in his hand. He only needed to use it.

He held the staff up high once again and thought of a bridge. Large chunks of wood leaped up from the surrounding terrain and fastened themselves to the ledge on the far side of the gap, one at a time. As he watched, they continued to rise up and attach themselves to the edge of that wooden peninsula, growing closer and closer to him with every second.

Soon, the peninsula reached the near end of the gap and finished up. It had formed a wooden drawbridge across the wide-open air. Still, it didn't seem finished.

After a moment's pondering, Archie waved the staff again, and this time gigantic chains leaped from the corners of the bridge near him and stretched all the way to holes that formed in the highest corners of the gate on the far side of the gap. With these, the drawbridge could be hauled up, cutting off the remainder of Highblock Keep from the rest of the lands beyond, keeping whoever might be inside absolutely safe.

Archie didn't quite understand how a drawbridge worked, or how to design the mechanisms that would allow it to be raised, but the Orb took care of all that. It reassured him without any words at all, and he felt comforted that whatever he was doing there in Highblock Keep, it was perfectly right.

Thus fortified, Archie marched straight across the drawbridge with a confidence he had never felt before. When he reached the far end, the gate rose open before him, and he entered Highblock Keep proper.

Inside the keep's gargantuan walls, Archie began to explore. It was one thing to design a place and something entirely different to walk through it—especially a place as large and complex as this. Whenever he was unsure of which way to go, the Orb prodded him in one direction or another, and he learned to trust its instincts as if they were his own.

The place was massive, like it had been built for people much larger than the little Illager. Despite how imposing it was, he felt perfectly at home there. There was no need to measure up, as it all fit him perfectly.

At some point beyond the gate, a large, wide, stone bridge led from the front section of Highblock Keep over an open section of the sea. From there, it crossed to a mountainous island that seemed like it had been formed by a volcanic eruption that had frozen all of the lava in place while it blackened into the hardest stone.

The Obsidian Pinnacle, on which sits this section of the larger keep. This too is all yours. The start of your empire.

A wild grin formed on Archie's face, and he felt grateful no one else was around to see him. If they had been, they might have thought him insane.

As Archie strolled about, the redstone golems followed in his wake. The thrumming of their heavy footsteps comforted him, but he decided it was time to show them to their new chambers. He led them into a large, underground room that they had carved out back when they'd started the keep's construction. Like most of the place, it had ceilings so high that even they could move freely in the chamber without fear of scraping their heads.

Archie raised his staff high, and the Orb of Dominance illuminated the entire chamber. "Here you are, my redstone golems!" Archie shouted. "Welcome to your home!"

As the redstone golems settled into their places, Archie took a moment to marvel at them and the power they represented. Even just the six of them amounted to the most impressive fighting force he'd ever seen. His wildest ambitions had never stretched even this far, and now it seemed that they were only at the cusp of what he could manage to conquer with the Orb.

His rise was only beginning.

"What else?" Archie asked when he could finally catch his breath. "What else could the world possibly have for me?"

All of it. The entire world can be yours. You only have to take it.

That thought sobered Archie up. He hadn't thought of himself as a thief as much as a pillager. Among the Illagers, the penalty for stealing from fellow Illagers was stiff, and Walda meted out justice without mercy.

You are not stealing anything. You are claiming what is rightfully yours.

Archie didn't understand that at all. How could the rest of the world be his? To be honest, he didn't quite understand how the Orb of Dominance and Highblock Keep had come to be his, other than out of sheer luck that befell someone wandering in lonely parts of the world where he didn't belong.

You were not chosen by coincidence. This is your fate.

The Orb had said that before, but still, this confused Archie even more. Being picked by random chance at least made some sense to him. He'd been driven to the hollow mountain out of desperation, and he understood how few others would come this way without Undead mobs at their back.

Then Archie realized something that caused him to stop breathing for a minute. Perhaps the mobs hadn't been chasing him the way he'd thought. Maybe they'd been herding him instead.

That would explain why they never caught up with him. Why none of them had seriously harmed him throughout his terrible ordeal.

Again, Archie came up against something horrifying that he realized he didn't want answers for. The possible explanation scared him more than the mystery, so he was content to live with it remaining unsolved.

"Exactly how am I supposed to conquer the world?" he asked aloud instead. "I can't just wave my staff at it and make it happen." He hesitated. "Can I?"

No, but with my help and that of the army we will amass, such lofty goals are within your grasp.

Archie felt the staff tugging him upward. He returned to the stairs, leaving his redstone golems behind. They stood as he departed and watched him until he exited the room.

He followed the staff's pull up, up, up, moving higher and higher through the Obsidian Pinnacle until he reached the peak. There he discovered a chair carved out of the stone for him. He hadn't remembered including it in the place's designs—much of those busy days now seemed like a blur—but there it was, all the same.

As Archie neared the chair, he spotted a hole in the stone floor, right in front of the seat. It was the exact width of the staff.

Place me in there and sit down. I will show you what you need to see.

Archie slotted the end of the staff into the hole, and it sank down into the stone until the Orb of Dominance hovered just above the height of the chair's seat. He hesitated to let go of it for a moment, but forced himself to relinquish his grasp. To his relief, nothing horrible happened when he did. He sat down in the chair and found the Orb hanging there in the air before him, right at his eye level.

Peer into me. I shall provide you vision.

Archie didn't quite understand what the Orb meant by that, but he had learned to trust it. He opened his eyes as wide as he could and stared into the Orb's glowing surface until his pupils shrank into tiny dots.

Then he saw.

The Orb's glow faded away—at least to his eyes, which he had given over entirely to it—and a vision of the desert to the south of Highblock Keep appeared before him. This was a part of the desert he had avoided before, but he somehow knew exactly where it was located as he looked at it.

He seemed to be looking down on the land from a great height, as if he were a bird hovering above it. Night had covered the land in a blanket of darkness broken by the light of the moon overhead. A new dawn already colored the sky to the east, but it was far from alighting on the sands below.

Two forces met on the desert, engaged in a vicious battle. On one side, a horde of husks and skeletons streamed forth in an unending line from a massive temple carved out of sandstone. Archie had seen it from a distance when he'd skirted the edge of the desert, although not from this angle. Even so, he recognized it instantly.

On the other side fought an Illager raiding party. Archie gasped in shock as he recognized Thord in the thick of it. His old nemesis stood on the edge of the battle, conjuring vexes—small winged creatures armed with sharp swords—to enter the fight for him. Any time a husk came close to him, he threw up his arms and summoned a line of gigantic fangs from the ground to snap up and bite the hungry mobs.

Although Archie detested Thord, he had to admire the evoker's skill with his spells. He seemed untouchable as far as the husks were concerned. Sadly, the same could not be said of the others in the raiding party, who were struggling to survive the husk horde.

"Those fools!" Archie said. "They're losing!" As he said the words, he realized that this shouldn't have surprised him. The same thing had happened to the last raiding party he'd been in. Only he and Thord had survived, and that only by sheer luck.

At this point, though, Archie had begun to doubt there was such a thing as luck.

"Why are you showing me this?" Archie said, suddenly suspicious. Disgust at the raiding party's weakness swelled up in him. He wanted nothing more than to turn away from their impending failure, but the Orb seemed to ignore his wishes.

Because you need to see it.

CHAPTER THIRTEEN

As Archie watched from his seat at the top of the Obsidian Pinnacle, dawn finally reached the desert where the Illager raiding party still battled the Undead mobs. The flow had cut itself off, as the Undead knew their time to fight was running out, but those who remained continued to battle the Illagers with bites and bows.

The mobs continued to take down Illager after Illager until the sun brought their savagery to an end. They continued to fight even as they caught fire. The Illagers, for their part, turned and fled at that point, keeping the Undead from setting them ablaze as well.

Once the Undead had been reduced to ash, the fleeing Illagers ground to a halt and collapsed. A few of them tended to their wounds. Others simply needed to catch their breath. They would survive.

A good few of them, though, wouldn't. They hadn't even lasted long enough against the Undead to have the chance to flee.

With but a thought, Archie's viewpoint zoomed in farther. He could now see the faces of the people recovering on the sand, enjoying the moment of respite they had before the desert became unbearably hot. Among them, he spotted Thord.

The evoker began stomping around the others, ordering them to stand up and get ready to march. They seemed to be making a push toward somewhere, although Archie could only guess where or why.

It struck him that Thord had done the same sort of thing when Archie had been part of the raiding party, and he hadn't understood it then either. Why would the Illagers raid the Undead mobs? They didn't offer anything in the way of loot. There wasn't any profit in fighting them.

Archie had never been able to summon the guts to ask Thord the question. Most times when he had opened his mouth in the party leader's presence, his only reward had been a smack across the back of his head. But it had never seemed to him that Thord knew why they were fighting the Undead either. He just liked fighting, and anything that let him do that was all right by him.

Like all the rest of them, in the end, Thord had been following Walda's orders, Archie realized. She was the one who'd know what was going on, if anyone did.

Either way, the Illagers couldn't attack the Undead mobs forever. There seemed to be an endless supply of husks and skeletons, and Walda would eventually run out of Illagers.

"They need me," Archie said.

Yes, they do.

"Otherwise, the Undead mobs will eventually kill them all."

They are your people. They can form the troops for your army.

Army? The Orb had mentioned the idea before, but now it excited Archie more. He'd long detested fighting himself. It was dangerous, mean, and dirty, three things he hated. That was why he'd striven to avoid being part of the Illager raiding parties for so long.

But having someone to fight on his behalf? At his orders? That intrigued him.

Dead Illagers couldn't fight for him though. He had no way to control them. He needed them alive.

How could he save them? What could he do to intervene on behalf of the Illagers?

Should he take the Orb of Dominance and march into the desert? He could likely destroy the Undead the same way he had at the entrance to the hollow mountain, but that seemed risky. He'd only fought a handful of the creatures before, not an endless horde streaming from that temple.

You can send your redstone golems. They can fight on your behalf.

This made sense to Archie. Although if he had the redstone golems, what did he need the Illagers for? He could just let them die.

That thought appalled him. He'd been a part of that tribe for as long as he could remember. Even as badly as he'd been treated there, he didn't want them all dead.

But when it came to an army, wouldn't the redstone golems be enough? They looked so tough, Archie couldn't imagine what would be able to stand against them. Any one of them could step on him and squash him like a bug.

They aren't enough to protect Highblock Keep from a siege.

That thought brought Archie up short. He felt safe and protected here in his new home. Who would ever lay siege to such a place?

Had someone else once controlled the Orb? Whoever they were, they had probably controlled the redstone golems he'd found too. They might even have built the amazing creatures themselves.

What had happened to them? Why had they abandoned their power? Had they been run off or killed? And who would be powerful enough to have beaten them?

And would they be coming back?

No one could ever claim me from you.

Archie wondered how the Orb of Dominance could possibly know that for sure. Then he again decided that he didn't want to know the answer, which was probably wrapped up in how the Orb had fallen into his hands in the first place. Questioning his good fortune could only hurt, he thought.

There was no point in looking back, but he could move forward. He could save his people, and he could build his army at the same time. He just needed to bring them to him.

Archie leaped off his seat, snatched up his staff, and made his way down to the dungeons where he'd left the redstone golems. When he got there, he raised the staff high above him and said, "Arise! We have work to do!"

The redstone golems roused themselves and stood at attention before him. He inspected them carefully. Despite how hard he'd been working them, they all seemed to be in good shape. Not that he would know any different unless they were actually falling apart.

Archie gestured with his staff and climbed up out of the dungeon. The redstone golems followed right after him. They moved slower than he did, each of their heavy steps shaking the ground as they marched.

Archie grew impatient with the speed they were making. At this rate, it would take them forever to reach the Illager raiding party. Still, he felt sure the redstone golems were walking as fast as they could.

They moved up through the bowels of the Obsidian Pinnacle and made their way across the wide stone bridge to the front section of Highblock Keep. Once they crossed the drawbridge, Archie stopped and gazed back at the place. He'd only just gotten here, and he was leaving already. Would it be okay until he returned?

He hesitated for a moment. Should he do this at all? Would the Illagers want his help? They'd banished him, after all.

Just as important, would Highblock Keep be safe without him? It wouldn't be much help to gather an army, he thought, if it cost him his stronghold.

As he pondered these mysteries, the Orb of Dominance surged in brightness. A moment later, the drawbridge began to rise.

The last of the redstone golems was still standing on the wooden bridge. The instant it began to move, though, it hustled forward and leaped off the end, landing on the rocky shelf next to Archie.

The Orb had done that without Archie ordering it to happen. He wondered, had the Orb simply read his mind—as it seemed capable of doing—or had it anticipated his request and taken care of the matter for him? And since it could manage that, did it mean that the Orb of Dominance didn't really need him in the end?

More questions that Archie didn't think he wanted answered.

"Thank you," Archie said aloud. "I wasn't sure if I should leave some of the redstone golems behind to protect the place or not."

Highblock Keep will be safe without you. And you will need all the help you can get against the Undead who plague both your people and the desert.

Archie started for the stairs, which would take him straight to the desert's edge. The redstone golems lumbered after him, taking care not to damage anything. He was glad they had made the steps to Highblock Keep so deep and wide. Otherwise, creatures like these wouldn't have been able to navigate them at all.

Once they reached the ground, Archie felt vulnerable again. Even with the redstone golems marching behind him, he missed the comfort of the walls of Highblock Keep.

"Could I not have sent the redstone golems out to help the Illagers on their own?" he asked. That way he could have remained safe inside his new home and not risked himself at all.

The redstone golems are not very smart. They need guidance from someone who can understand the situations they might find themselves in.

Archie nodded at that. As much as he didn't like the answer, it made sense. The iron golems that protected villages worked something like that. They were strong and tenacious but relatively easy to fool. But with someone like him guiding them with a strong hand, they would be truly dangerous.

"An army needs a leader." Archie thought he could hear the Orb chuckling softly in agreement.

With that, Archie led his current army—small in number, but large in size—into the desert. The redstone golems followed him without question or complaint as they rumbled along beneath the scorching sun. Archie thought about commanding one of them to walk close enough to him to provide him with some shade, but the fear of being squashed by a wayward foot made him put that notion aside.

As they traveled, Archie realized that he had only a rough idea of where he could find the Illager raiding party. He knew where they had been at dawn when he'd been watching them survive the battle with the Undead mobs, but he didn't know where they might have gone since then. He considered trying to use the Orb to look for them again, but it seemed like perhaps that wouldn't work properly if he wasn't sitting in his chair at the top of the Obsidian Pinnacle.

We will find them.

Archie didn't even want to ask how. He'd put all his faith in the Orb of Dominance up until now. This would be a rotten time to start arguing with it.

As they moved deeper into the desert, Archie spotted the temple out of which the Undead had been streaming. It stood silent at the moment. Not a living thing moved on or around it, not even a bird. It seemed like it had been built and abandoned untold centuries ago.

Give the Desert Temple a wide berth for now.

"I thought the redstone golems would be enough to protect me."

They should be sufficient for most purposes, but they are a force, not an army.

"Can they at least take on the Undead attacking the Illagers?" For an instant Archie wondered if the Orb had brought him out here to die.

You need not worry about my loyalty. I serve you, and only you. We are bound together.

"You didn't answer my question."

The golems should be able to take on a force of Undead similar to that which you witnessed this morning. Especially if the Illagers will help us.

Archie's stomach twisted into a knot. He didn't know if the Illagers would be happy to see him. He hoped that they would welcome the opportunity that he and his redstone golems would be able to offer them, but Thord wasn't his biggest fan.

There was a chance the Illager evoker would sneer at Archie and refuse his help. There was even a possibility that he'd order the raiding party to attack Archie and his redstone golem band. If that happened, Archie would be forced to defend himself—and that would be terrible all around.

They will not attack us.

"You don't know them like I do."

If they attack us, we will exterminate them.

The idea of finally having the upper hand over Thord appealed to Archie. In the past, he'd preferred to avoid fights in general, mostly because he knew that he would lose them. The fact that he might win a fight now didn't make him any more eager to start it—especially if it meant that he might wind up ending some of his fellow Illagers in the process.

But if he could humiliate Thord in front of the others? He wouldn't mind that a bit.

"What if they hurt the redstone golems?" Archie had only a handful of them to rely on. If he had to fight the Undead with them, he didn't want to waste any of his mighty subjects on fighting people who should have been his allies rather than his enemies.

We can always make more.

Archie gasped. If they could manufacture more redstone golems, then why were they wasting their time looking for the Illagers? Other than to save them, of course.

It just seemed like it would have been simpler to make more subjects than to bring Illagers into the fold. The redstone golems followed his orders without question, and they never mocked him or talked back. He didn't feel like he'd get nearly the same kind of respect out of his fellow Illagers.

Plus, he wouldn't have had to leave behind the safety of Highblock Keep!

Making new redstone golems is not a simple process. It requires more heat than can be found in Highblock Keep.

Heat? Archie knew where he could find plenty of heat.

CHAPTER FOURTEEN

By the time the sun set, Archie and his redstone golems still hadn't found the Illager raiding party. They had made it all the way around to the southern side of the Desert Temple, but no matter where Archie looked, he couldn't find any members of his former tribe.

The Undead, though, began to appear the instant the sun's rays no longer fell on the gates of the Desert Temple. One by one they came shuffling or clattering out of it, forming a well-spaced line that stretched toward the darkest parts of the desert. They didn't seem to have any destination in mind, but they clearly hungered for fresh prey.

Despite the size of the redstone golems, Archie did his best to keep them out of the way of the Undead mobs. To his amazement, they managed it. The mobs ignored them, barely even looking in their direction.

With the fall of dusk, Archie was ready to give up on finding the Illager raiding party until the morning. He looked around for a tall dune on which he could set up camp, and he wondered if he could manage to climb up on one of the redstone golems' shoulders and fall asleep there. He didn't think it could be any worse than snoozing in the branches of a tree.

The Illagers are not far off.

"How do you know that?"

Archie suppressed a moment's irritation at the Orb. Did it know where the Illager raiding party was? Had it known the entire time they'd been wandering around lost?

Listen.

Archie opened his mouth to snap an angry retort at the Orb, telling *it* to listen to *him*, but before he could manage it, he realized what the Orb meant. He shut his mouth carefully and held his breath. He closed his eyes, cocked his head to the side, and reached out with his raised ear.

Off in the distance, over the groaning of husks, he heard the twanging of bowstrings, the clash of steel, and the cries of the injured and the dying.

He opened his eyes and swung his head about as if it were on a swivel. He took the measure of the sounds as he did, until he managed to determine the direction from which they echoed across the dunes.

Then he finally remembered to breathe.

"That way." He marched off in that direction, using the staff as a walking stick. The redstone golems fell in line behind him.

Eager to get a good look at what he'd been hearing, Archie hustled ahead. The sounds became louder as he approached their source, but the desert played tricks on him. Every time he topped a dune, he fully expected to see the battle playing out before him, but he was disappointed several times before he finally came upon it.

When he finally reached the fight, Archie skidded to a halt in the sand at the peak of the final dune and took it all in. Below him, a horde of Undead mobs fought in pitched battle with the Illager raiding party.

There were more husks and skeletons this time than before, and tonight they were being ordered around by a skeletal figure wearing a bejeweled circlet on its head and long, priestly robes. It wielded a staff, much like the one Archie held, but without a glowing Orb floating atop it. The figure hovered just above the ground, its feet never touching the sands below it.

A *necromancer. An ancient wizard that uses death magic to control the Undead.*

That sounded like the worst thing Archie had ever heard of, even in his cruelest nightmares. He'd run into Undead before, but he'd never thought too much about where they might come from. They just showed up every night—kind of like bats in the darkened sky—and disappeared in the daylight. The idea that they might be directed by something—or someone—chilled him to the bone.

That explained, he supposed, why the husks and skeletons had managed to surround the Illager raiding party tonight. Generally the Illagers were faster than the Undead and managed to keep away from them until they were ready to bring the fight to them. Somehow, though, the creatures had penned the Illagers in on all sides, and they were closing the trap around them in the deadliest ways.

Archie didn't know what came over him. He hated fighting

and wanted to stay as far away from it as possible. In the past, he would have frozen up and simply watched the battle devolve into carnage until there were no Illagers left to scream to him for help.

Now, though, he stood tall in front of his redstone golems, pointed toward the Undead with his Orb-topped staff, and shouted, "Charge!"

The redstone golems obeyed without hesitation. They lumbered straight into the battle with no concern for their own safety. They wanted only to please their master.

The Undead didn't pay much attention to the assault. They had their hands, bows, and teeth full dealing with the Illagers they were attacking. The fact that the desert sands were suddenly thrumming under their feet didn't bother them in the slightest.

The necromancer spotted the redstone golems, but not before they were only a dozen strides away. It spun about and waved its staff, ordering some of the Undead to break off and face the incoming threat, but it was too late for them to do much about it.

The redstone golems slammed into the Undead like a roaring tide smashing into a beach. They swept aside husks like they were tiny children, and they stomped the skeletons to pieces and ground their bones beneath their feet.

A shout of surprise went up among the beleaguered Illagers, and then a raw-voiced cheer. They had started to flag with exhaustion and had prepared themselves to face their final moments with their inevitable defeat. Newly heartened, they raised their weapons once again to aid in the destruction of the Undead.

Archie felt like cheering himself as he watched the battle play out from a relatively safe distance, just beyond bowshot, should an enterprising skeleton get any heroic notions into its skull. The redstone golems were doing better against the Undead than he could have hoped.

Then the necromancer waved its staff again. Every one of the husks still standing turned and focused their silent hunger on a single one of the redstone golems. They surrounded it on all sides and pulled at it with their rotting fingers and bit at it with their broken teeth while the Illagers and the other redstone golems busied themselves with beating the skeletons to pieces instead.

Archie watched in horror as the husks overwhelmed the victimized redstone golem. The creature swung recklessly at anything within reach, knocking husk after husk away from its rocky self, but every creature it slammed aside was replaced instantly.

The relentless onslaught wore the creature down. Its leg gave out, and it fell to one knee. In an instant, the husks clambered over it like it was a small hill and tore at it until it fell onto the sand in a glowing heap.

Archie knew right away that the redstone golem was done.

Despair filled his heart. He only had so many of these creatures, and the Undead appeared to be limitless. Even if he carried the battle that night, would the losses leave him with enough redstone golems to protect Highblock Keep? Was he going to be a hero one night only to lose everything he'd gained the next?

You need an army. If you fail here, the most you can hope for is to spend the rest of your days sealed in Highblock Keep with the drawbridge raised.

Archie wasn't convinced that would be so bad. It would be lonely, sure, but he was used to being lonely. And it would be much better than how he'd lived when he'd been wandering the land on his own. At least he'd be safe and warm.

You don't really want to waste such power by hiding it away. Power is meant to be used.

Someone had hidden the Orb of Dominance away, Archie knew, but not for what purpose. The fact that Archie had never heard of that person or the power of the Orb perhaps proved that point. Did Archie really want to live quiet and forgotten when he could become a legend?

He'd never dreamed of such a destiny before. He'd had a hard enough time keeping himself from being beaten up. But now, with all this power at his disposal, how could he bear to waste it?

With renewed determination, Archie took his staff and pointed it straight at the Undead leader. "Take down the necromancer!" he shouted.

The remaining redstone golems turned as one to execute Archie's order. Ignoring the skeletons still firing arrows at them, they lumbered directly toward the necromancer.

When the necromancer realized the redstone golems were coming after him, he thrust his free hand in the air and recalled the husks to his side. They abandoned the downed redstone golem, which was now nothing more than a heap of glowing rubble, and hurried to their master's aid.

Meanwhile, the skeletons broke off from the redstone golems and the heartened Illagers and made straight for Archie. This turn of events surprised him, as up until that point he'd felt like he'd been untouchable. The first arrows fired at him fell well short of hitting him—but not short enough for his liking.

He thought of turning and fleeing into the desert. Surely the redstone golems and the Illager raiding party would be fine on their own. Once the redstone golems killed the necromancer, the other mobs would be easy for them to deal with.

You are a leader. Leaders do not flee.

Archie groaned out loud. He knew the Orb of Dominance was right, but he felt like he would personally be much better off as a living coward than a dead leader.

You can defeat any Undead who dare come near you. Do it.

Archie looked up at the glowing Orb and realized it was right. He was panicking over nothing. He only needed to use the power it had granted him.

He held his staff high and willed the Orb to destroy the incoming Undead.

Archie had worried that the Orb wouldn't be able to reach the skeletons until they were too close for comfort. It had been one thing to destroy those husks atop the hollow mountain. The Orb could destroy long before they managed to put Archie in any real danger. But could it defeat the skeletons before they drew close enough to fire their arrows into him?

He shouldn't have worried. The Orb had not once steered him wrong so far, and it didn't do so now. It fired out powerful bolt after bolt so fast that it incinerated the skeletons closest to him just as they were about to loose their bowstrings. Their weapons clattered to the ground where they had once stood, their arrows rolling away behind them.

Archie let out a little cheer of his own. Perhaps that wasn't the thing a strong and confident leader would do, but he didn't care. He was too thrilled to keep his excitement to himself.

Fortunately, the necromancer didn't have a similar means of responding to the redstone golems. Its husks had rallied to its side, but the much-larger golems were busily stomping them into paste. As Archie watched, one of the golems broke through the husks and smashed a redstone fist right into the necromancer's face. The necromancer reeled back, staggered by the blow.

Meanwhile, more of the skeletons approached Archie, following the necromancer's last orders to them, which must have been something like, "Kill the person with the glowing Orb on a staff."

They didn't seem to have any sense of self-preservation. They just kept marching toward him, and the Orb kept lancing fresh bolts of power through them.

The Illager raiding party had stopped fighting at this point. The ones who were still on their feet were checking on their injured friends, seeing what they could do to help them. Without the Undead mobs attacking them, they could haul the ones who could be saved away from the battle and then get ready to leap back into the fracas should their savior not prove up to the task.

Another of the redstone golems went down under a pile of husks. The loss caused Archie to groan in dismay, but the resultant movement of the husks toward the downed golem opened up a gap in the line they'd formed in front of the necromancer. Two of the remaining redstone golems dashed forward and began knocking the necromancer back and forth between them like a bony punching bag.

In a matter of moments, the necromancer crumbled to the ground in a heap of broken bones.

When that happened, the other Undead mobs lost their unity. The husks were content to keep attacking the golems, but the skeletons decided that perhaps it was best to keep their distance from Archie and his stunningly effective Orb.

Secure with the Orb hovering at the top of his staff, Archie marched over to the redstone golems and let the Orb eradicate any of the husks too stubborn to leave once their friends began turning to ash. In the end, three of the golems stood next to Archie, tall and mostly unharmed. The others remained crumbled in the sand, unmoving.

Some of the Undead mobs moved in the direction of the Illager raiding party, but they did so as individuals rather than as a group. The Illagers picked them off one at a time as they came closer. Between that and Archie lancing away any Undead that came near him, the area was soon emptied of such mobs.

It was then that the leader of the raiding party came over to introduce himself to their savior. Archie let the glow of the Orb of Dominance return to its standard intensity so the Illager could stop shading his eyes. When the leader lowered his hand, Archie immediately recognized him as Thord, who gawked up at him as if he had returned from the dead.

"Archie?" Thord said in awe. "Is that you?"

CHAPTER FIFTEEN

If Archie thought the Illagers in the raiding party had been happy to see him before, they were flat-out thrilled to discover that he was one of their own. They smiled from ear to ear and clapped him on the back and congratulated him on having done so well for himself. They were too astonished at being alive to summon much jealousy of him, at least for the moment.

None of them mentioned the fact that he had been banished from the Illager camp for having supposedly ruined the last raiding party. Archie wasn't foolish enough to think that was due to them realizing Thord had lied about that. They were just too craven to dare to disappoint their new Illager hero.

He had to admit, he enjoyed every bit of their praise and attention. He'd known many of them for years, but before this, few of them had been willing to do more than sneer at him as they walked by. To have them give him unreserved adulation warmed every bit of him.

Thord, for his part, remained silent. At first he simply seemed to be in shock—perhaps from having nearly been killed in battle once again—but later Archie caught the evoker looking at him and shaking his head in disbelief. He just couldn't wrap his head around the idea that Archie had gone from such a weakling to becoming the most powerful Illager ever.

Archie decided not to lord this over Thord—yet. It was more satisfying to pretend he didn't notice the Illager's evident dismay rather than rub his nose in it.

He is jealous of you. He believes he should have control of me instead.

Archie gripped his staff tightly, with both hands. He would never let anyone take the Orb of Dominance from him. Never.

Do not worry. My destiny is intertwined with yours, not his.

That allayed Archie's reflexive fears, at least for the moment.

When the hubbub all died down, Archie beckoned Thord over to speak with him. The evoker hesitated for a moment, unsure of how it would look for him to be showing Archie such respect, but he complied.

"Thank you for saving us," Thord said reluctantly. It clearly hurt him to say out loud that he had needed Archie's help. "Walda will be happy to hear of our triumph."

"It's been a while since you've had one," Archie said. He discovered he was unable to resist needling Thord. The Illager had bullied him for so long that he certainly deserved it. "I seem to recall your last raiding party was a total disaster."

Thord coughed in surprise and then immediately changed the subject. "We need to get back to the camp to report to Walda."

We can't just let them walk away. We need them on our side. Invite her to meet with you.

Archie nodded to Thord, as if he'd been considering what the Illager was saying rather than listening to the Orb of Dominance. "Please tell her that I would like to speak with her in my fortress."

Thord nearly choked. "Fortress? You have a fortress?"

Archie pointed off to the north. "It's called Highblock Keep. It's on the northeast coast. Head north from here but keep well away from the Desert Temple. You can't miss it."

Thord frowned. "Didn't your monsters kill the necromancer already?"

Archie stopped to ponder that. If the necromancer was dead, maybe Thord had a point.

The Desert Temple is the home of many necromancers. Killing one of them is hardly enough to put an end to their reign of terror.

"Don't be foolish," Archie told Thord. "That was just one necromancer. The desert is lousy with them."

Thord grunted. He might have sensed that Archie wasn't being entirely straight with him, but he wasn't about to call him a liar—not in front of all the other Illagers he'd just saved.

"All right. I'll let Walda know."

"I expect to see her—and the rest of the tribe—soon," Archie said. With that, he turned on his heel and marched back into the night. He made a point of not looking back as he went.

Archie led his three remaining redstone golems back toward Highblock Keep. He surveyed them as they trundled after him, and he felt dismay that he'd already lost so many of them in the battle with that necromancer.

If the Desert Temple was the home to several necromancers, Archie was in trouble. It wouldn't take too many more fights like that before he ran out of his redstone golems.

"You said we could make more of the golems," he said aloud, once they were long out of earshot of the remnants of the Illager raiding party. Even so, he kept his voice low. He didn't want anyone to know he was speaking with his Orb.

We just need a source of redstone—and incredible heat. Then we can build the Fiery Forge, where crafting such golems is done.

Archie thought once again of the river of lava that he'd raced past while trying to avoid the Undead on his way north. That seemed like maybe it would fit the bill. If lava wasn't hot enough to feed this special forge the Orb was talking about, what else could be?

Yes. The lava fields to the west should work nicely. Well done.

Archie felt a little glow at the fact that he'd brought something to their partnership that the Orb of Dominance hadn't expected. Perhaps there was a good reason the Orb had wound up in his hands after all. It was easy for him to doubt his good fortune, and bits like that made it feel more like he actually deserved it.

He was eager to head straight for the lava fields and get to work, but he worried that Walda and the Illagers might show up while they were there. If that happened, he didn't want them to turn around and leave. After all, he needed them for his army, right?

We will prepare Highblock Keep for their arrival. They can help us build the Fiery Forge.

Archie liked that plan.

The sun was high in the sky before they made it back to Highblock Keep. Once they were over the drawbridge and back on the island of the Obsidian Pinnacle, Archie finally felt safe. He returned the remaining redstone golems to their dungeon and then went looking for a place to rest.

The Orb led him to a fantastic set of chambers in the highest tower of Highblock Keep. It featured windows that looked out over the lands to the south so that Archie could always see anyone coming his way. To his relief, no one was heading in his direction, so he felt like he could finally relax.

The Orb showed him to a bed that seemed so fresh and new that the Orb must have crafted it for Archie on the spot. He wanted to discuss the plans for furnishing the remainder of Highblock Keep in appropriately grand fashion, hopefully before Walda and the rest of the Illager tribe arrived. He wanted to stun them with his wealth and power, after all.

The moment his head hit the pillow on his massive new bed, though, Archie instantly fell asleep.

When he awakened, he saw the rays of a new dawn breaking. He had slept throughout the entire night and into the next day. While the good rest left him feeling ready and refreshed, he worried that the Illagers would be knocking on his door at any moment.

He spent the rest of the morning working with the Orb of Dominance to get as much of Highblock Keep in order as he could. While the Orb was immensely powerful, there was so much to do that it felt like an impossible task. For the first time, he understood what the Orb meant when it said that Archie needed an army. Even when it came to furnishing Highblock Keep, he couldn't do it alone.

The moment his ambitions went beyond that, he'd run into disaster, at least as far as his redstone golems were concerned. Sure, he'd beaten the necromancer, but it had cost him dearly. If he couldn't replace the golems—or, better yet, increase their numbers—he wouldn't be the ruler of Highblock Keep for very long.

Archie labored all day long to get the keep in shape. With waves of his staff, he summoned rich, thick carpets to cover the floors of the largest rooms. He put beds in the rooms and barracks, waiting for Illager heads to rest upon their pillows. He conjured up countless blue banners to hang on the walls, lending a badly needed splash of color to the place. To that end, he also designed stained-glass windows in many rooms, which filled the place with dazzling patterns when the sunlight hit them just right. He even spent time crafting statues of himself in strategic areas—all of them a bit larger than life, to make him seem even more impressive—if only to remind his guests who owned the place.

It was hard work and seemingly endless, but Archie wanted to make a good impression on the other Illagers. If they showed up to a dump that felt like little more than a pile of rubble stacked up against the sea, many of them would start to wonder what they'd gotten themselves into—and how soon they could leave. When they arrived, he wanted to stun them with the luxury of his home and inspire in their hearts both jealousy and awe.

After all, his Illager clan wasn't the only one in the land. Once his tribe settled in, he would send some of them back out into the world to spread the news. To tell every Illager they could find that there was a new place they could gather. A new banner under which they could rally. A new Illager ruler who was sure to lead them all to untold glories.

At the end of the day, the Illagers still hadn't arrived at Highblock Keep. In retrospect, Archie should have realized that would be the case. Thord and his raiding party would have to limp all the way back to the Illager mansion and then convince Walda they weren't lying or at least hallucinating about Archie having become so powerful since his banishment began.

Then Walda would want to pack up all of the Illagers and their things and bring them along with her. She never went anywhere without her people. Sure, she would send the raiding party out to attack things, but she never departed from the mansion. Her place was there, she always said.

And moving that many people at once always took longer than it should. They'd get there, but it would take time.

We can be patient. We will need them all.

Archie agreed with that. However, he didn't want to sit around the keep for days, even if there was plenty for him to do. He wanted to ignite the Fiery Forge.

So we shall.

Archie was so excited about it, he decided to start out that night. He no longer feared the Undead or any other mobs that might be wandering around in the dark. Not while he had the Orb of Dominance at his side.

The Orb insisted that they bring along one of the remaining redstone golems on their trip, and Archie wasn't inclined to argue. A part of him wanted to leave them all behind to protect his new home, but if he was killed while strolling about, what good would control of the keep do him then?

This time, he—rather than the Orb—led the way. He strode out of Highblock Keep and turned west. After skirting around the hollow mountain, he followed his old path back toward the lava rivers he'd spotted on his way there.

It seemed like perhaps the sun had decided to rise in the west, but he knew that the glow came from the heat of the molten rock flowing through that land. Soon after that, the lava flows heaved into sight, and Archie came to a halt to take in the view in all its awe-inspiring glory.

The last time Archie had been in the area, he'd been too busy fleeing the mobs hounding his steps to take any time to appreciate the stark beauty of the area, especially at night. The glowing lava lit up the region, casting a reddish glow over everything around. It flowed from the tops of the mountains that ranged before him all the way down to the level on which Archie stood.

The light, the heat, and the stench of ash and sulfur in the air gave the place an otherworldly feel. It seemed so far removed from the plains the Illager tribe generally wandered, and Archie had to wonder what—if anything—could actually live there.

Creatures made of redstone can live here. They can be crafted here. They can thrive here. But they require your protection from heat like that.

At first, Archie wasn't sure what the Orb meant, but when it pulsed with power, he realized its intent. "Ah," he said as he waved his staff at the redstone golem he'd brought with him. A bit of the Orb's glow seemed to separate from it and drift out to the creature. There it settled upon it, coated it from one end to the other, and then seemed to be absorbed into its rocky skin.

Immediately thereafter, the redstone golem strode forward, right past Archie. The fact that it had begun moving on its own surprised him, and he scrambled to catch up with it. The massive creature walked straight down to the nearest lava flow and stood by its edge as if it was contemplating walking straight in.

Then it did just that.

Archie gasped, afraid that the redstone golem would be destroyed. Rather than melting into the lava, though, it stood there, knee-deep in the glowing rock, as if it had just waded into a delightful hot spring. After a moment, it turned around to regard Archie again.

It knows where you need to go. Let it take you.

Archie didn't understand what that meant until the redstone golem reached out over the edge of the river of lava with its massive hands. When the hands came down to Archie's level, he carefully climbed up on top of them. As the redstone golem straightened back up, he scrambled onto its shoulders without any concern for how undignified he might look.

Without prompting, the redstone golem turned and waded farther into the river of lava. As the lava rose over the creature's waist, Archie began to question the wisdom of letting the golem haul him deeper into the withering heat. He glanced back at the shore with a longing look.

Over his better judgment, he let the golem forge ahead. At no point did the lava rise higher than the redstone golem's armpits, which was plenty close enough for Archie. He began sweating profusely and wondered how far into the region they would have to go before they found what the golem was after.

After the redstone golem made it across the river of lava, it turned and headed toward the deepest crevasse in the region. Once they reached the edge of it, the golem carried Archie down a series of switchback trails that led deep below the surface. Eventually, as dawn broke in the sky high above them, the golem found the entrance to a cave, and it stopped for Archie to climb down from its shoulders and stand on his own feet.

That is where we need to go.

Archie wasn't fond of the idea of exploring whatever lay beyond the cave's entrance, but with the Orb at his side and the golem right behind him, he felt as safe as he could possibly be. He passed through the mouth of the cave and found himself in a massive cavern that extended as far as the Orb's glow could reach.

Redstone and diamond lined the walls, and he realized he'd discovered a place filled with more riches than he could ever have conceived.

This is exactly what we need.

Archie strode into the cavern, straight down its sloping floor, where he discovered a gigantic pool of lava formed by a cataract that tumbled down from the chamber's distant ceiling.

Here is where we can start to build the Fiery Forge.

Archie was relieved to hear that. Now that they'd found the location, though, he wasn't sure how to start.

First you need to build a mold. Then we can mine redstone to fill it.

That made sense to Archie. He just needed to find something strong enough to craft the mold out of. It needed to be tough enough to withstand the heat and the power he would have to bring to bear on it. Only one substance would do.

He raised his staff and waved it at the nearest wall. Raw diamond cleaved away from the rock there and floated over to him. He worked like this until he had enough of it, and then he began to form it into the large shape of a golem.

Perfect. Now procure some redstone to place into the mold.

Archie pointed his staff at another part of the wall. The stone there cracked and gave way, and a large chunk of redstone emerged from it. At Archie's direction, it floated over to the diamond mold that he'd made, and he brought it down to rest on top of that. He repeated this a number of times, until the mold was full.

As he watched, the tremendous heat from the lava cataract—or the lavafall, as he thought of it—went to work on the redstone. Archie realized that while the heat wouldn't normally be enough to melt the redstone, the diamond must have helped intensify the heat to the point at which it could. The redstone grew even redder than before, and it soon lost its form and melted into a large pool of the substance within the mold.

"Amazing," Archie said in awe. A sense of triumph overcame him, stronger than even the one he'd felt when he'd singlehandedly defeated the Undead attacking the Illagers. It was one thing to destroy and something else entirely to create!

Allow me to help you.

The material inside the mold looked like a statue of a redstone golem, a facsimile of it that lay there entirely bereft of life. Archie held the staff up high before him, and the Orb pulsed with power. After a moment, there was a sharp flash that seemed to move from the Orb directly into the inert redstone, setting the entire creature aglow. For a moment, it flared so brightly that Archie could barely see.

As the glow faded, Archie blinked away the spots before his eyes, and the statue inside the mold began to move. At first it struggled there like it was trapped, shaking from side to side. Then with a loud *crack* it broke free. A moment later, it sat up in the mold and gazed at Archie, recognizing its new master.

CHAPTER SIXTEEN

Archie left the new redstone golem at the Fiery Forge with orders to start preparing the raw materials for more of its own kind. To that end, it would need to carve out as much redstone as it could find and place it into the mold. As it found more, it would stack up the extra next to the mold for later use.

Archie would have to return to imbue the new redstone golems with life. That was something only the Orb could manage.

Perhaps you should stay here and oversee the operation.

Archie knew all that was true, but it couldn't be helped. He had to return to Highblock Keep before the Illagers arrived there. He didn't trust them alone near the place—especially Thord. The last thing he needed was to get there and discover that someone else had stolen his seat at the top of the Obsidian Pinnacle.

You mean your throne.

Archie honestly hadn't thought of the chair like that before. To him, it had only been a place to sit while he stared into the Orb of Dominance. Thrones were meant for rulers.

You are a ruler.

That felt wrong. Didn't rulers have subjects? People they ruled over? Without those, how could anyone be a ruler? Just ruling over the redstone golems in Highblock Keep didn't seem to qualify.

Your subjects will arrive at your keep soon.

Archie frowned at that. He wasn't sure Walda would agree to make him the leader of the Illagers so easily. She hadn't seen him since she'd banished him from the tribe.

Once the story of how he saved the raiding party reached her, perhaps she would change her mind. It was a long way from admitting you were wrong about someone to handing over your entire tribe to him though.

You don't need her endorsement. The Illagers will follow you.

Archie hoped the Orb of Dominance was right.

He climbed back on top of the redstone golem that had brought them there and set off back toward home. When they returned to Highblock Keep, no one was waiting for them. However, Archie could see a large group of people marching toward them through the desert to the south. That had to be the Illagers, and from the look of them, they must have brought the entire tribe, exactly as he'd hoped.

Archie lowered the drawbridge and entered the keep. He went down to the dungeons and retrieved the rest of the redstone golems. They joined him back at the drawbridge in plenty of time.

Archie wanted to show the Illagers his strength—or some of it, at least—without actually hurting anyone. The redstone golems seemed like the best way to manage that. He was used to hanging around with them now, and they still impressed him. He knew how the Illagers would see them.

It was late in the day when the Illagers finally arrived. Archie was bored of waiting for them by then, and he sat leaning up against one of the redstone golems until the tribe was in shouting distance. Then he pushed himself to his feet and held his staff—topped with the Orb of Dominance—before him.

Walda walked at the fore, the entire tribe trailing in her wake. They carried everything they had with them, ready to put down stakes wherever they liked—or had to—for the night. They looked weary, but they generally did when they were traveling. They had probably crossed the entire desert to get there, after all.

"Welcome to Highblock Keep!" Archie called out as they neared.

A low cheer went up from the approaching Illagers. Archie noticed that neither Walda—nor Thord, who appeared from behind her—joined in that particular bit of fun. They seemed less relieved to have made it here than they were concerned. They both wore extremely serious looks, and Walda cut off the celebration with a harsh glance backward at the others.

The Illagers remained silent until they reached the end of the drawbridge. At that point, most of them spread out in a semicircle around the entrance while Walda and Thord stepped forward to speak with Archie. They did not smile at him or embrace him.

This was not a family reunion or the greeting of a prodigal son. This was business, and they did not seem happy about it at all.

"Hello, Archie," Walda said in a grim and proper tone. She met his eyes as if she meant for him to kneel to her. "I understand we have you to thank for the survival of our raiding party."

Archie tried to be magnanimous about this inarguable fact as he met her gaze. He stood up as straight and tall as he could manage. "They would have been wiped out for sure. I was happy to help."

"How fortunate that you happened to be in the area." She said this in a way that implied it could not possibly have been a coincidence. The glare that Thord shot Archie from over her shoulder convinced him that Thord might have spent the last couple days pouring such poison in her ear.

"I only wish I could have gotten there sooner. I spotted the trouble from my, ah, observation post on the top of the Obsidian Pinnacle." He gestured behind himself to the very peak of the rear section of Highblock Keep. "It took me a while to reach the raiding party from there."

"So, this is supposed to be your home?" Thord said in sneering disbelief as he gazed up at the structure. He couldn't help but marvel at it, but that only added to his belief that no one so far beneath him as Archie could possibly own such a place. As little as he wanted to be impressed by Archie, he still didn't emerge from behind Walda, keeping her between himself and Archie at all times.

"It is." Archie wasn't about to argue the point or dignify Thord's doubts. If the Illager wanted to take Highblock Keep from Archie, he was welcome to try. Even if he could somehow manage to rally all of the Illagers behind him, he would fare no better.

Now you're getting it.

Archie chuckled to himself as he surveyed the other Illagers. They seemed overawed at the very sight of Highblock Keep, the redstone golem guards, the Orb-headed staff, and even—maybe especially—Archie himself. None of them would question his authority.

If there was one thing that Illagers respected, it was strength, and Archie had plenty of it on display. The regular Illagers instinctively gravitated toward that. If they had come here on their own, they would already be pledging their loyalty to Archie.

The only things stopping them were Walda and Thord. They wore their defiance in their posture. They were proud Illagers, unwilling to bend for anyone.

Well, at least Thord was, but he'd always been a bully and a fool. No one had ever successfully stood up to him, and because of his magic and the reputation he cultivated, few had even tried. They were just happy to watch him pick on someone like Archie rather than them.

Thord had climbed up the ranks of the tribe's hierarchy by carefully choosing his battles. He hit the people above him when they were at their weakest.

It would only be a matter of time before he came for Walda. Everyone knew it, including her. But now Archie had leapfrogged ahead of them all.

Even if Thord was an idiot, Walda was smart enough to know when she was beat. She favored Archie with the edge of a smile. "I would like to thank you for your good deeds and—as I understand it—your offer of hospitality."

"It was no trouble at all." Archie didn't mention how dismayed he'd been at losing some of his redstone golems in the battle. With the Fiery Forge up and running, he hoped to recover from that setback soon enough.

He decided to press ahead. "I'd like to invite you and the rest of my fellow Illagers to join me in Highblock Keep. Those who do, I promise to keep housed and fed and as safe as these walls can make them."

That, he realized as the words left his mouth, wasn't enough. The Illagers were a proud people, and they didn't care nearly as much for comfort as they did for power. If he was to lead them, he would have to show them not that he could care for them but that he could bring them to the greatest glories they had ever seen.

He would have to promise them the world.

"Together, we can destroy any who would oppose us. We can grind the Villagers down and put them in their places. We can gather all of this land's riches for ourselves. Together, we can conquer the whole of the land."

Archie repressed a gasp of surprise as he made this pronouncement. The idea that the Illagers would be able to take over the Overworld from sea to sea was radical enough, but that he would be the one to lead them?

They cannot do it without you.

Archie allowed himself a knowing smile, and he let Walda and Thord bathe in it.

"If you follow me, I can promise you the greatness for which our people have always been destined, but that has escaped us so far. The days of our losses at the hands of even the most powerful of heroes are over. We will crush our foes and drive them before us. We will claim their riches as our own."

He paused for a moment to let his words sink in. "Under my leadership, no one will stand before us ever again."

The assembled Illagers raised their voices and pumped their fists in a resounding cheer. This was exactly the sort of thing they wanted to hear, and they didn't care whose mouth the words fell from.

Walda pursed her lips as she considered this, impressed. She had to have known that something like this offer had been coming, but perhaps she wasn't quite convinced she should take it yet. In any case, she wanted to let her reactions play out for the other Illagers to see.

Thord, on the other hand, wasn't quite cunning enough to see there was even the remotest chance of Archie's triumph. He assumed that—like himself—Walda would never give up power unless it was taken from her. He snickered at Archie in anticipation of Walda laughing in the smaller Illager's face.

"The changing of the leadership of our tribe is not some trifle to be handled lightly," Walda said carefully. "The fate of all our people is bound to that of our leader, and it has been my honor to carry the tribe's compass as we've navigated our way through this world on our own terms."

Thord glanced about, ready to crow in delight at the smackdown he saw coming Archie's way. Walda heard him fidgeting over her shoulder and silenced him with an ice-cold glance. He stared at her in abject horror as he realized that he had make a terrible mistake in his judgment.

"You have clearly risen fast in this world and come to possess an amazing power all your own," Walda said to Archie. "I do not wish to question your good fortune, especially when you have been kind enough to offer to let your people share in it. That's especially generous of you given your banishment."

The smiles grew on the rest of the Illagers' faces as they realized that Walda had judged the direction of the tribe's temper properly. Several of them began shouting in savage delight.

"We accept your offer," Walda said with as little resentment as she could manage. "Where you go, we shall follow."

Thord actually fell to his knees in despair and seemed about to start wailing and complaining about the unfairness of it all. The rest of the Illagers, though, saw him and thought he was bending the knee to their new ruler. Taking their cue from his apparent display of humility, they fell on their knees next to him.

This all happened in back of Walda, who stood at the front of the Illager tribe. She had ignored Thord when he collapsed, not wanting to reward his theatrics by giving him any attention, but when she heard the rest of the tribe fall to their knees, she let out a little gasp of surprise.

Walda glanced behind her on both sides and saw that she remained the only Illager still standing before Archie. In spite of that, she stayed standing, spreading her arms wide as if she were presenting the other Illagers to Archie.

You cannot allow such defiance.

Archie's eyes flashed with anger. He understood that Walda was a proud Illager—one who'd led the tribe for as long as he could remember—but if she wanted to remain in his good graces, she would eventually have to bend the knee.

Maybe he should have struck her down then to make his point, but Archie was too stunned at the obeisance of the others to let his temper overtake him. A huge grin threatened to spread itself across his face, but he bit his cheek to prevent it from taking over. This was a solemn moment, not a time for gloating, and he needed to take this transfer of power seriously if he wanted the other Illagers to do so as well.

No matter. She will come around. Give the rest of them some time on their knees to absorb the import of this day.

Archie took a full minute to relish the moment. In his wildest fantasies, he'd never imagined anything as incredible as this. To become the leader of the entire tribe? To have that power handed over to him willingly? It blew his mind.

It had been wild enough to come across the Orb of Dominance and the redstone golems inside the hollow mountain—and then from there to construct Highblock Keep—but that had been a lonely triumph with no one to witness it. To have the bulk of his tribe on their knees, acknowledging his ascendancy? That was priceless.

You still think this was all an accident? Random chance played no part in it.

Archie wasn't sure what he thought of that. It was easier to believe that he'd just gotten lucky. That way meant there were no real expectations of him—from himself or anyone else. If it all fell apart the next day, he could say that he had an amazing ride and was only sorry that it inevitably had to end.

But if he was truly destined for greatness, he had a responsibility to rise to that challenge. It wouldn't be enough to simply move his tribe into Highblock Keep just so they could live like peasants in his palace. He had to develop goals—lofty, ambitious goals—and drive them all to it.

Yes. That's perfect.

Archie allowed himself a self-satisfied smirk—only for a fleeting moment—and then raised his staff before himself so that his people could bear witness to it as the symbol (at least) of his power. "Rise!" he told them. "With you at my back, there is nothing I cannot do. There is no prize we cannot have. This entire land—and everything in it—will be ours!"

The Illagers shot to their feet, roars of approval erupting from their lips. Only Thord and Walda were less than full-throated in their approval, but even they managed to join in.

Walda stood there, unmoving, until the last echoes of the roar had died down. Then she walked toward him to offer him her hands. As he took them, she towered over Archie, but she suddenly seemed much smaller than he.

"As you say, so shall it be," she uttered to him in the most formal tone he'd ever heard from her lips. "You need only point us in the right direction, and we shall fight whatever stands in our way."

You know where you need to lead them.

It took Archie only a moment to ponder the Orb's words, and the answer to that mystery popped straight into his head.

"Enter Highblock Keep," he said as he stepped aside and swept his arms toward the far end of the drawbridge and what stretched beyond it. "Rest and heal! Drink and dine! And prepare yourselves for our greatest battle yet!"

He allowed a vicious smile of triumph to play over his face for all to see. "For soon we will conquer the village, and all the people in it!"

CHAPTER SEVENTEEN

Archie wanted to let the Illagers get comfortable in their new surroundings, but the Orb of Dominance counseled him against that. In its opinion, allowing people to get too used to the idea of having him in charge and taking care of them—rather than demanding things of them—would only guarantee that Thord or even Walda would make a move against him. To maintain his power over them and the rest of the tribe, he needed to keep his potential rivals off balance, and he needed to deliver to the rest of the Illagers what they wanted.

Archie wasn't a typical Illager. Most of his life, all he'd wanted was to survive. If the bullying would have ended on its own, that would have been all he really needed—or so he told himself.

Illagers in general, though, were raiders. They made their living by stealing from others. Mostly this involved robbing the few

Villagers who were foolish enough to travel the land on their own. Sometimes it meant taking down a foolish hero who let down their guard at the wrong moment. Either way, it was about fighting and taking, and even though they were now safe and sound in Highblock Keep with plenty of food, drink, and shelter, that's what the Illagers still wanted. What they ached for.

And Archie had to give it to them.

There was only one target that would satisfy them, and he'd already announced his intention to take it: the village. The best part was that he would finally get his revenge on Salah and the rest of the people who'd run him out of the place in the middle of the night with torches and pitchforks.

The only trouble with his plan to raze the village to the ground was Yumi. He didn't want to hurt her at all. He only hoped that she would show enough sense to get out of the way once he and his forces arrived.

Despite his misgivings, he headed out for the Fiery Forge the next morning, and he took a vanguard of the best Illager warriors with him. He left Walda behind and put her in charge of Highblock Keep while he was gone, but he insisted that Thord come with him. He didn't want the two of them plotting against him together. Besides which, he wanted to impress upon Thord how absolutely futile it would be to try to resist his rule.

This time, Archie brought all of the remaining redstone golems with him as well. He required them to help with completing the construction of the Fiery Forge far more than he needed them back at the keep. He hoped Walda would see it both as a sign of the trust he had in her—and as a sign that he was so strong and confident that she had no chance to turn his people against him.

When they reached the Fiery Forge, Archie had the redstone golems help him construct a bridge across the lake of lava. If he was going to have Illagers working in the forge, they needed a way in and out of the place, and the redstone golems could handle the heat to construct it.

Once the barest length of the bridge was complete, Archie led the other Illagers across it and down into the Fiery Forge. There they found the redstone golem Archie had left, standing over a diamond mold filled with copious amounts of redstone. The whole group gasped in astonishment at the amazing wealth on display, and Thord's eyes began to water at the sight of the golem-mold itself.

"Hold back!" Archie warned the others as he raised the Orb of Dominance high and used it to bring the newest redstone golem to life.

When it cracked its way free of the mold, the Illagers raised a mighty cheer. Archie turned to enjoy the look of utter amazement plastered on Thord's face. "This just seems impossible," the evoker said breathlessly.

Archie just laughed. Then he assigned a group of the Illagers to remain behind with the new redstone golem and get to work on helping it mine and craft a new one. It struck him then that if he stationed Illagers there permanently—especially some of his best warriors—he was asking for trouble. They would eventually turn on one another out of boredom, and the ones who survived that would be sure to come after him next.

We will have a ready supply of workers—once we capture the Villagers.

Archie had been thinking more in terms of raiding the village and razing it to the ground, but what the Orb said instantly made sense. With the Villagers under his control, he could force them to work in the mines of the Fiery Forge instead, with a smaller force of Illagers set to oversee them. It would work wonderfully.

"We'll set the Villagers to work in here once we conquer them!" he announced just before he led the rest of them back out toward the bridge. All of the Illagers cheered the choice to enslave the Villagers, although the ones who were left behind griped about not being there to see it happen.

When Archie and his retinue arrived back at Highblock Keep, the Illagers there welcomed the new redstone golem with glee. Even Walda clapped with excitement over how another such creature would add to the tribe's might. The fact that Archie's army would only get stronger over time heartened him. Still, part of him wanted to wait until he had an overwhelming army of redstone golems to work with before he set out on his campaign to conquer the entire land.

It is not necessary. You can take the village with the forces you have. One victory at a time.

Archie wasn't so convinced about that, but it was Thord who changed his mind.

With the quick help of the Orb of Dominance, Archie had converted one of the largest rooms in Highblock Keep into his throne room, a place where he could meet his fellow Illagers and confer with his advisors. In fact, he had only one living—well, one breathing—advisor to whom he would listen at that moment: Walda. She stood by the side of his throne and whispered things into his ear as he met with other Illagers, giving him the context he needed to make his decisions.

In that respect, she was much like the Orb of Dominance, but with her only power being her extensive familiarity with the members of the tribe. However, if Archie had been forced to choose between the two creatures, he would have tossed Walda into the sea without a moment's hesitation.

He suspected she was aware of that. She didn't, of course, know that the Orb spoke to him and provided him with counsel, but she had to realize that he considered her dispensable, despite her unique set of knowledge. She was more valuable to him than any of the other individual Illagers, but that wouldn't be enough to keep her prestigious position safe if she failed him.

Perhaps that was why she suggested that he needed a title.

At first, Archie didn't understand why she wanted to make such a fuss. The leaders of the Illager tribe had always been just that: leaders. They weren't kings or emperors or anything else. They didn't have fancy names or special clothes or anything that marked them as exceptional—just the respect of their people.

"This is different," Walda told him. "*You* are different. We never had a home like this before either."

She gestured to the high-vaulted ceilings of the throne room and, by extension, all of Highblock Keep. "You're building something entirely new. Something that ambitious requires new words to show off the new way of thinking. You need a title that declares that to the world."

Archie mulled this over, but he didn't get the chance to make a decision about it before Thord derailed him. The bully called him out in front of Walda and all of the other Illagers in the room—the few that Archie hadn't assigned to various details around Highblock Keep—and he made a point of not being quiet about it.

"You're weak," Thord said as he jabbed a finger up at Archie, who looked down at the bully from his newly fashioned throne.

"You might have everyone else here fooled, but just because you lucked your way into this place doesn't change anything. It doesn't change you. Don't forget: I know who you are."

He is a threat to you and your power. Make an example of him. Defeat him now.

Archie recoiled at the idea of taking out Thord on the spot. With the power he had at his command, the bully was no longer a real threat to him—at least not physically. And Archie didn't want to be the kind of ruler he knew Thord would be, one who crushed any who dared to speak up to him.

Who lorded it over everyone else.

Who ruled by fear.

Better to rule by fear than to be conquered.

Archie realized that the Orb had a point. If he wanted to maintain his power, he needed to crush any dissent from Thord at once. The bully was testing him now, perhaps because the visit to the Fiery Forge had illustrated how little Archie had to fear from him. The only hope Thord had was that Archie would somehow still let himself be bullied, perhaps out of habit more than anything else.

Archie knew, though, that if he showed any actual weakness in front of the other Illagers bearing witness to their conversation, he would lose much of the popular support he'd earned. If he was honest, a part of him still felt like cringing in front of the bully, but after the kind of power he'd now tasted, he wasn't about to give in to it.

Instead, he let loose a little snarl and then opened his mouth to speak. Walda interrupted him before he could form a single word.

"How dare you question the bravery of our ruler?" she said to

Thord in a scathing tone. "After all he's already done for us? You should be crawling around here on your hands and knees to show your gratitude."

Thord laughed. "Oh, I'm grateful enough for all that." He gazed around at the throne room as if he would soon own it. Eventually his eyes settled back on Archie. "Don't think I don't appreciate everything you've done for us Illagers. But also don't think you can hide up here inside your keep and not have someone call you out on it."

"I'm not afraid of anything." Archie saw exactly what Thord was doing. If the bully could paint him as a coward, his rule over the Illagers would be as short as he was and as brutal as Thord.

Remove him.

Archie opened his mouth to do just that, but at the last instant, a concerned look from Walda stopped him. Then he realized that he'd been about to make a mistake. If he removed Thord, it might end any troubles with the bully, but it would make him seem like maybe Thord was right—and that he had struck too close to home.

Don't worry about that!

Archie ignored the Orb. It didn't have to deal with being in charge. That was his job.

"I was only letting you heal up after the second disaster that happened to a raiding party under your watch," Archie told Thord. "If you are already eager to enter battle again, we will leave for the village in the morning."

Thord froze. He'd been prepared to taunt Archie for being a cowardly wimp. This change in tactics had thrown him. "Tomorrow?" he said in a frail voice.

Archie slid down from his throne. "Is that not soon enough?

We can leave tonight if you like. I am ready for the fight of our lives. Are you?"

Thord scowled, frustrated that his gambit had been thwarted. "Me? Of course! But it would be safer to start our journey during daylight, don't you think?"

Archie thumped the bottom of his staff on the ground for emphasis. "Night and day make no difference to me. The creatures who roam the dark can't be more dangerous than the battle we'll face at the end of our journey. And we're sure to win that as well!"

Thord gave Archie a little bow, out of surprise and sheer reflex rather than intent. The fact that he recognized Archie's power—even in such a small, involuntary way—gave Archie heart. He told himself he'd been right to ignore the Orb of Dominance's advice about the bully.

For now.

Word went out from the throne room, and the other Illagers immediately set to their preparations. For his own part, Archie wasn't sure what to do with himself. He settled for doing his best to look busy yet inspirational, which included brooding on the keep's ramparts as he considered the battles to come.

After mulling it over, he decided to leave behind one redstone golem to protect Highblock Keep in his absence—plus the one at the Fiery Forge. That meant he could bring three of the massive creatures with him. Once he got back, he would go and imbue life into even more of them.

He wished he could have waited until he had forged more redstone golems, but Thord's taunts had forced him to move up his timetable. He was just going to have to make do with the army he had.

The next morning, as dawn slid over the eastern horizon, Archie led his people and his ready contingent of redstone golems out of Highblock Keep's front gate. He raised the drawbridge behind him with the help of the Orb of Dominance and then set off into the desert.

The caravan gave the Desert Temple a wide berth. Archie wasn't sure exactly what was inside it, but he knew he didn't want to bother with it at the moment. He was sure to have his hands full with destroying the village and didn't need to waste any of his resources on adventuring through a complex of unknown size and depth.

Archie worried that Thord might try to draw him into heading into the Desert Temple then and there. When he glanced back at the evoker, though, he saw Thord staring at the distant place and shuddering, likely at the memories of the Undead that had streamed out of it and nearly killed the Illager raiding party—twice.

It took them a few days to make it all the way back to the Squid Coast. Despite Archie's eagerness to reach the village, he ordered them to stop each evening to set up camp. This included posting guards and placing a line of torches around the area to keep any curious mobs away.

They had remarkably few interruptions, for which Archie was grateful. The last thing he needed was for the Illagers to get spooked by random mobs before they even reached the village. Of course, he needn't have worried. As he recalled as he looked over the scattered tents one night, the tribe's raiding parties were used to camping out in the open and dealing with such things.

They neared the village late one day, and Archie stood atop the shoulders of one of the redstone golems to address his Illagers. He'd already started to think of them as "his," and he reflected that in his speech.

"My fellow Illagers!" he said. "This village, which stands ripe for the pillaging! This village, which hoards the land's food! Which keeps the land's animals! This village will soon be ours!"

The Illagers cheered for him, even Thord and Walda. Then, at his direction, they all set to preparing themselves for battle.

After night had fallen over the village like a glittering blanket of blackness, Archie led his people to the ridge that overlooked the place. From there they could see the torches of the village burning below, keeping the people there safe—or so they hoped.

"We attack all at once," Archie said. "We charge them from out of the darkness and take them by surprise."

"What about heroes, if they show up?" Thord asked in a defiant tone. "What are we going to do against them?" He wore a defiant yet amused smile, like a child who'd just caught a parent making a mistake.

"Most nights there aren't any heroes in the village. And if there are?" He pointed to his redstone golems. "We'll take care of them."

Thord's taunt had raised another question in Archie's mind though. *What about Yumi?*

He couldn't exactly order the others to leave one of the Villagers alone. They would become suspicious of his motives, and Thord and maybe even Walda would accuse him of sympathizing with their foes.

Don't worry about her. She isn't worth the trouble.

Archie stifled the urge to shout at the Orb. He understood how the Orb felt—part of him felt that way too—but he couldn't bring himself to just abandon Yumi to the mercies of his fellow Illagers. She'd shown him so much kindness.

And what good did that do you?

For a moment, Archie actually considered tossing the Orb

aside, but he realized that would be the most foolish thing he'd ever done. Without the Orb's power, he was nothing. But he wasn't going to give up on saving Yumi.

The only thing he could do, then, was race straight toward her home and hope she was there and that he could talk her into surrendering to him straight away. He had to admit to himself that it wasn't much of a plan, but it was all he had.

CHAPTER EIGHTEEN

At Archie's order, the Illagers charged into the village and began destroying the place. Most of them set to banging down doors. Others took the torches set up around the town and tried to set fire to the houses there. A few even decided to attack the village's cows and pigs, figuring any damage they could do was a good start.

Archie ordered two of his redstone golems to find the village's iron golems and attack them. The golems were, put bluntly, dumb as rocks, but they would follow Archie's orders to the letter. Better yet, they wouldn't take orders from anyone else — or at least anyone who didn't have control over the Orb of Dominance. Archie expected Thord to betray him at some point, but at least he wouldn't be able to convince the redstone golems to turn against him.

You can count on me as well.

Archie still didn't know what he'd done to deserve the loyalty of the Orb, but he treasured it. When he'd brought the other Illagers into Highblock Keep, his worst fear had been that the Orb would decide that one of them—most likely Walda or, worse yet, Thord—was worthier of the Orb's power than he was. He'd taken that risk anyhow, and he was relieved to have had it pay off.

Otherwise, he would never have been able to mount this attack.

The Villagers sounded an alarm straight away. It would only be moments before the entire place was up in arms. Archie knew he didn't have much time, so he headed for Yumi's home.

When he got there, she was already standing in her open doorway, an iron golem at her side, her eyes wild and ready. She spotted him instantly.

It would have been hard to miss him on a good day—an Illager storming into a village—but with the redstone golem lumbering behind him in the night, he might as well have had a spotlight on him. She couldn't see his face in the light coming from behind him, and she snarled at him. "Get out of here, you awful Illager!" she shouted. "Or I'll hand you your head!"

Archie threw up his hand as he raced toward her. "Yumi! It's me!"

She had been about to order the iron golem to attack, but she raised her hand to stop it and squinted at the oncoming figure instead, which seemed much shorter than she had expected. "Archie?" she said in shock. "Is that you?"

He skidded to a halt just in front of her, and the redstone golem did the same a few feet behind. She took a step closer to the iron golem, out of instinct more than anything else. Then she reached out and wrapped him in her arms for a hug.

"What happened to you?" she asked. "Where have you been?"

"It's a long story." He enjoyed her embrace so much he never wanted it to end. If only he hadn't brought an army of Illagers along with him—but if he hadn't, he'd never have been able to return to the village again.

She released him and held him at arm's length to get a good look at him. She seemed overjoyed just to see him alive. Then she glanced up at the redstone golem towering over them, and her breath caught in her throat. "Who's your friend?"

"That's part of the story." He took her by the hand. "I'll tell you everything later. Right now, we need to get you out of here."

Yumi rattled her head, confused. "Wait. What's going on? It sounds like the village is under attack."

"It is," he said. "That's why you need to leave."

Suddenly suspicious, she yanked her hand out of his. "But why is it under attack?"

She gazed out past him and the redstone golem and saw some of the buildings on the edge of the village starting to go up in flames. Horrified, she covered her mouth with her free hand. "Oh no, Archie. What have you done?"

Archie frowned. He had to get her out of there now, or everything would go wrong. "Just take my word for it, Yumi. You don't want to be here."

She scowled down at him. "Are you trying to rescue me from this, or are you part of this?"

He sighed, defeated. "Can't I be both?"

She gaped at him in shock. The redstone golem adjusted its posture behind him, and she stared up at it too, then back down at him as she realized the truth. "You're not just part of this. You're behind this!"

Somewhere behind Archie, the sounds of battle clashed and rose as the fight was truly met. The Villagers' other iron golems weren't about to just let the Illagers raze the place to the ground. They were ready to fight.

Archie looked up at Yumi, his eyes pleading with her, begging her not to be one of the Villagers they dragged away to work in the Fiery Forge. "Please," he said. "Come with me."

She blinked away tears of confusion and rage and shook her head. "I just can't believe this. I can't believe you would do this!"

"I had to," Archie said. "The situation demands it. You should be able to see that."

He reached for her again, but she pulled away. That's when Archie heard a familiar voice holler something at him. He couldn't understand the words, but the tone clearly meant, "Hey you!"

He spun about and spotted the hero there—Smacker—storming at him with his iron sword raised and ready.

Archie's heart sank. If one hero was here, that meant there could be others, and if that was the case, the Illager raid was doomed.

Still, he had to try. He patted the redstone golem on the leg to get its attention and then pointed straight at Smacker. "Get him!"

The gigantic golem brought up its massive fists and began swinging them at Smacker. The hero, for his part, seemed absolutely delighted to be attacked. He grinned widely and crowed loudly and swung his sword about with reckless and amazing abandon.

Yumi grabbed Archie by the shoulder. "You need to stop this!"

"I'm not going without you. This town is doomed—the people will soon be mine—and I don't want you doomed with it."

She goggled at him in dismay. "You're an idiot! After all I did for you? I brought you into my home! I treated you like a friend!"

A large thump cut her off, and Archie spun around to see that Smacker had lopped an arm off of the redstone golem. The creature kept on fighting as best it could, but it was clearly losing the battle. It just wasn't fast enough to keep up with someone as strong and agile as the hero.

"Stop it!" Archie shouted at Smacker. "Leave it alone!"

Yumi knelt down next to Archie and spoke straight into his face. "You led an attack on this town? And you expect us to just let you destroy the place?"

"He ruined my life!" Archie said. "He needs to stop! I'm going to make him stop!"

You need to bring the others to fight him.

Archie knew what the Orb meant. If he could get the other redstone golems here, they might have a chance against the hero. They were probably still busy fighting the iron golems that watched over the town, but even so, he needed them here. If they could beat Smacker, they could still win.

Archie wished he'd done what he'd wanted and stayed at Highblock Keep until the Fiery Forge had created a full-on army of redstone golems for him. Then no hero could have stopped him. It was too late for that now though.

Far too late.

Archie pulled away from Yumi's grasp and stumbled toward the center of town, moving wide around the battle between Smacker and the redstone golem as he did. "You traitor!" Yumi shouted after him. "You'd better run!"

With a clap on the back of her iron golem, she sent it lumbering after Archie. As it chased after him, she wiped the tears from her face.

Archie thought if he ran as fast as he could, he might be able to find at least one of the other redstone golems and get it to team up against Smacker. He didn't get far, though, before he realized something was terribly wrong. The central part of the village wasn't filled with Illagers stampeding through the place, like he'd expected.

Well, it did have that, but not *just* that.

In some places, the Illagers were busy attacking the Villagers as hard as they could, but in others, they'd stopped and turned to battle a new and unexpected force of skeletons and husks.

Archie stared at the scene for a moment, too stunned to understand how his planned victory had come to this. What could have possibly caused it to fall so terribly apart? He raised his staff to defend himself against any incoming Undead, but they all seemed too busy to notice him.

He realized that the Undead mobs hadn't come from nowhere. They couldn't just have stumbled upon the battle by accident. They must have followed the Illagers all the way from the Desert Temple to the village.

That meant that someone was controlling the Undead mobs—maybe even purposefully keeping them out of the Orb's reach. Otherwise they wouldn't have been able to restrain themselves for the entire journey. They would have attacked the Illagers at some point along the way.

Instead, they had remained hidden from the sun during the day, and they had tracked the Illagers all the way here, moving only by night. They had been patient and cunning, and they had waited until the Illagers began their attack on the village before they made their move. They had held off until the worst possible moment—and now they were here, trying to destroy everything in sight.

We need to leave.

Archie hated to admit it, but the Orb was right.

"Stop fighting!" Archie shouted at his Illagers—and the red-stone golems if they could hear him. "The battle here is over!"

He could tell right away that there was no way for the Illagers to defeat the iron golems, the hero, *and* the Undead mobs. Plus the necromancer that had to be hiding somewhere on the edge of town. They'd lost the element of surprise now, and the Undead had taken that edge instead. They were doomed if they remained.

The only option—much as he hated to admit it—was to retreat.

Thord was sure to use this against him. He'd paint Archie as a coward, someone who turned and ran the first moment things went against him. No matter what, though, Archie couldn't stand to watch his people get destroyed. They needed to try again another day.

Otherwise, they were sure to lose everything today.

"Listen to him!" Yumi shouted out to her own people. She'd appeared behind Archie with her iron golem at her side. They might have chased the little Illager here to attack him, but the shocking sight of the Undead raging through the place had stopped her cold, just like it had him. "Don't bother with the Illagers anymore! Focus on the mobs!"

Everyone but the Undead stared at both Archie and Yumi for an instant, entirely confused.

"Leave them alone!" Archie said to the Illagers. "Let their iron golems fight the Undead!"

"You have to be kidding!" Thord shouted in disbelief as he emerged from the fray. He cut down a husk lurching after him as he stalked toward Archie. "We can't leave now! We're winning!"

"There are too many of them!" Archie said as fiercely as he could manage. "We'll all die!"

His commanding tone wasn't enough. Thord had never wanted to listen to him in the first place, and now that he had an excuse he was going to ignore Archie entirely. "Fine!" he shouted at Archie in defiance. "You run! I'll stay here and fight beside my Illagers!"

Archie opened his mouth to protest, but before he could speak, an arrow caught him in the back.

You are hurt!

Surprised at the pain that shot through his body, he turned to Yumi to say something, but nothing came out. He just wanted to ask for her help. Together they could take out the Undead, he knew.

But then another arrow caught him in the chest, and he discovered he couldn't breathe. No matter how hard he tried to suck in enough air, he felt like he was leaking the entire time.

Hold on. I will preserve you.

Archie did the best he could. He clawed at Yumi, who grabbed him by the arms and tried to keep him on his feet.

He felt his knees buckle beneath him as darkness began to curl around the edges of his vision. It pressed in harder by the second until all he could see was a long tunnel that seemed to go on forever, ending in the Orb of Dominance, which still hovered on the end of his staff.

"I hate to say it, but you deserved that," Yumi said as she laid Archie's lifeless body on the ground.

Those were the last words he heard before everything faded away.

INTERLUDE

Karl had been sleeping in some Villager's house—he didn't really know which one—when he heard the alarm bells start to ring. He'd just taken the closest home when he barged into the village that evening, and when he got to the door of the place, he wasn't at all sure where he was. He only knew that there was some kind of emergency, which he figured would be all kinds of fun.

What he found when he burst out of the home, his sword already spearing from his fist, did not disappoint him. A band of Illagers had invaded the village in the middle of the night, raiding and pillaging. That was just the kind of thing a hero like him needed to break up the boredom.

To top it off, the Illagers had brought a trio of redstone golems with them. Even better!

Karl hadn't seen redstone golems before. He'd fought an iron golem once, though, in a village where he'd apparently overstayed his welcome. He still didn't understand how the people there could have been so ungrateful for his help that they'd finally sent their metal-bodied guard after him to kick him out.

He would have left that village without a scuffle if they'd just been straight with him and asked him to. The fact that they only spoke their silly pidgin language that he didn't understand a word of may have gotten in the way of their ability to even attempt that, but he didn't care. It was just rude.

That's why he'd taken that iron golem apart with his sword, danced on the leftover pieces, and then never looked back.

The people here seemed to tolerate him a lot better. At least they'd never sent one of their iron golems out to deal with him. And now they'd somehow even managed to deliver him some prime entertainment for the evening!

Karl charged straight toward the first of the redstone golems he spotted. He cut down an Illager or two along the way, but they didn't really concern him. The Villagers could likely avoid them for the moment, and he could mop them up after he'd personally dealt with the massive mobs instead.

Karl pointed at the redstone golem and bellowed, "You are mine!" With that, he cranked his sword high up over his head, sprinted toward the creature, and brought his blade down with all his might. The two-handed blow lopped off the mob's right arm, and it thumped on the ground as heavy as a felled husk.

Karl hooted with delight and set to dismantling the rest of the redstone golem, limb by limb. While he went at it, he noticed a squirrelly little Illager watching him at work.

The tiny guy looked familiar, like Karl had seen him before. That didn't seem too likely though. Most Illagers Karl ran across wound up never bothering anyone else again.

Plus, this one was holding a staff with a bright Orb hovering over the top of it like it was held there by a giant magnet. Karl was pretty sure he'd remember something like that if he'd seen it before. Still, he couldn't shake the sense of familiarity.

He ignored all that, though, when he saw that the battle had just gotten a lot more complicated. As if it wasn't bad enough that Illagers had raided the village, they'd somehow attracted a crowd of Undead mobs too.

To tell the truth, that kind of excited Karl. He liked a challenge. Just not too much of one.

He wasn't sure if he should be afraid yet or not. If things got too tough, he could always head for the hills. It wasn't like he was all that attached to anyone in the village, after all. At least not enough to brave certain death for them.

As it turned out, he shouldn't have worried for a moment. The Undead hadn't come there with the Illagers—which would have been weird. Karl had never seen Undead and Illagers working together before.

Instead, the husks and skeletons seemed just as eager to attack Illagers as Villagers, which made everything a whole lot easier. At least for Karl and maybe for the Villagers too. All they had to do was lock themselves in their homes again and wait for the Illagers and the Undead to knock themselves to pieces.

Before Karl could hustle the Villagers back inside, though, he saw that tough woman Villager—the one who took care of the iron golems—talking to the squirrelly Illager with the glow-topped staff. While they spoke, the little guy took a couple cheap shots from some sneaky skeletons right through his rib cage. He went down like he'd never bother the Villagers again.

That seemed to upset the Villager for some reason, but Karl didn't concern himself about that. Instead, he finished taking apart the now-armless redstone golem lumbering around in front of him—a couple sharp slashes to the knees put an end to its walking days—and then he started shouting for a retreat.

Not everyone listened to him, including that tough lady Villager. She seemed to be trying to keep the Illager alive, which didn't make a lick of sense to Karl. If she stayed out there, she was sure to get herself killed, so he did the heroic thing and grabbed her.

She fought him at first, but only until she realized who he was and what he was doing. She came to her senses after that and let him shut her into a nearby house.

It was for her own good, after all.

With the useless Villagers out of danger and the Illagers and their other redstone golems on the run, Karl had free rein to take the battle to the Undead mobs roaming through the streets. He started hunting the husks and the skeletons one by one, and then began taking them down in groups. They weren't any match for his speed and skills, especially since most of them were busy banging on the doors and windows of the Villagers' homes. That meant Karl could come up behind them and get a good whack or two in on them before they figured out what was going on and turned around to defend themselves.

Karl had a ball smacking the Undead mobs into pieces. He knocked one skeleton into a pile of bones with a single blow. The rest of them just hung around and waited for him to get to them—at least for a while.

Karl was in the middle of taking down a particularly hungry husk when he realized that he didn't have any others lining up behind that one to get the same kind of special treatment. Once he finished up with that creature, he glanced around to find himself utterly alone. The village streets stood empty.

The Villagers, of course, were huddled in their homes. The Undead seemed to have disappeared too, but Karl didn't understand where or how. Most of the time such creatures kept at it until Karl defeated them all or the sun came up. He was pretty sure, though, that he hadn't torn apart every one of the mobs he'd seen rampaging through town.

Sure, it was possible that Karl had lost track of the numbers of his defeated enemies in the excitement. It wasn't like that hadn't happened before—maybe more than once. But when he surveyed the village streets, they were just way too quiet.

Unsure if this was cause for celebration or caution, Karl kept his sword in his fist as he stalked around the vacant village, hunting for any stray mobs that needed ending. Not one creature presented itself to be cut down by his blade.

At that moment, he wished the other heroes had been staying in the village that night. For some reason they'd decided that commandeering homes from Villagers was the wrong thing to do, and they'd built their own places to live in. He'd never seen the point of wasting so much time on building a personal fortress when he could just borrow a perfectly fine one in the village whenever he wanted.

Despite what the others might think, that had worked out to the mutual benefit of the Villagers. If he hadn't been sleeping in one of their beds when the Illagers attacked, the entire place might have been burned to the ground. Especially when you tossed in the attack of the Undead mobs at the same time.

For a night that had raced from a dead sleep to a raucous brawl to an epic battle, it had gone dead silent awfully quick. Even after looking down every one of the village's streets, Karl still didn't trust it. He contemplated going back to bed, but he didn't want to fall asleep and then have to come back out and save everyone once again.

Besides, he was still wide awake from the adrenaline of the fight. It was going to take him forever to nod off this time.

He was just about to give up and try that anyhow when the other heroes showed up. They strolled into the village like it was the middle of the day, fearless of anything the night might be hiding from them.

"What are you all doing here?" Karl asked, instantly suspicious. He'd had a wild night and wasn't about to put up with any more lectures from them about respecting the Villagers' rights and property.

Pinky gave him a grim nod. "We heard the sounds of a battle and came to help."

Karl waved his sword all around, gesticulating at the empty streets. "You're a little late. I took care of it."

"Nice work," Stache said with grudging approval. "You took out all these enemies yourself?"

"What do you think?" Karl sheathed his sword and put his hands on his hips, arms akimbo. "After all, who protects this place while you folks all sleep in your own comfy beds?"

Scarface knelt down next to the base of a building. "This place took a lot of skeleton arrows." They pointed to the wooden stand for the alarm bell nearby. "That got marked up by an axe."

Karl felt the others all looking pointedly at his sword and his clear lack of a bow or an axe, but he was too shameless to blush at the attention. "Fine. Of course I didn't take out *all* of the bad guys," he explained. "I mean, they'd already started in on each other by the time I got out here. If I hadn't saved the day, though, we'd have a lot more Villagers missing tonight."

"Sure," Red said in a tone that almost sounded convincing. "They must be happy to have you here."

"They ought to be," Karl said, just a hair indignant but not wanting to show it. "I mean, who wouldn't be grateful to not have their homes burned to the ground."

"What happened to the Illagers?" Pinky asked as they glanced about, confused. "Did they all get beaten, or did some of them get away?"

Karl glanced around, unsure what he should say. He wanted to claim he'd beaten every last one of them, but he didn't want to get caught in another blatant lie. The others would only put up with so many of those in a row before they called him out on it.

"I don't know," he said with a carefree shrug, as if the question itself was beneath him. "Do you see any of them walking around here anymore? That's all that matters to me. I mean, it's not like I'm keeping score, right?"

The other heroes chuckled at that. They knew that Karl often did keep score, and that fact had become a running joke among them.

"We spotted a line of Undead mobs marching away from here as we entered the village," Stache said. "But not any Illagers."

"I think some of them left earlier, after the husks and skeletons showed up. They must have just run off in a different direction."

"Kind of odd to see Undead moving in a line like that," Scarface said. "They had a floating skeleton of some sort leading them away. They were all following it."

That news sent a shiver down Karl's spine. He might not have been the smartest hero around, but the idea that someone was controlling Undead mobs couldn't be good news. Sure, that meant they'd retreated after he'd emerged to thrash them, but it also meant they could be much smarter about attacking him if they ever met up again.

"I must have had them running scared!" Karl said with as much bravado as he could muster—which was plenty for anyone, really.

"They seemed like they were carrying someone with them," Red said. "Is anyone missing from the village?"

Karl shrugged. "Seriously? You think I know every last person here in the village? Any dozen of them could go missing, and I would never know the difference."

Pinky sighed. "Whoever that was, I hope they're going to be okay."

CHAPTER NINETEEN

Archie woke up and found himself bound hand and foot to a skeleton. The creature seemed to no longer be Undead but entirely unliving and unaffected by any motivating enchantment, as it didn't move to object when Archie began to struggle against his bonds.

Frustrated by his failure to be able to sit up, Archie glanced all around and saw that he was moving, even as he was strapped down. Someone had taken the skeleton and tied it to a couple of long sticks to make a battlefield litter out of it, and then they'd thrown Archie's unconscious form on top of that and carried him off.

He had no idea how long he'd been unconscious. He could only tell that it was night—either still or once again. The stars swirled overhead until Archie realized they were doing that because his head was still swimming from his injuries. He gave up his struggles and froze, and with a great deal of effort he finally managed to make the sky stop moving around too.

He tried to assess the situation he was in, but it beggared belief. The last thing he remembered was being shot in the back by a bunch of skeletons that had ambushed him—along with the rest of the people in the village. He'd thought he was dead for sure, but apparently someone had taken the time to at least bind his wounds. He actually felt pretty decent, all things considered.

I told you I would preserve you.

The Orb of Dominance! Archie felt around for his staff but it wasn't in his grasp. It must have been taken from him while he was unconscious, but if he could still hear it in his head, then it couldn't be too far away.

Or could it? He wasn't sure how its magic worked. Maybe it could communicate with him from across an entire land. He had no idea.

I am here with you.

The Orb pulsed, glowing brighter for a moment, and Archie realized it was floating somewhere above his head, just out of his eyeline. If he'd been able to sit up and turn around, he would probably have been able to see it.

They laid me down next to you on the stretcher.

Archie breathed a sigh of relief at that. If the Orb was still around, then maybe he still had a chance to get out of this situation alive.

The Orb's pulse seemed to have drawn the attention of the Undead, and Archie could understand why. If he could get control of it, he might be able to use it to turn them all to ash. He struggled against his bonds once again, but he couldn't muster the strength to break free.

The necromancer swam into Archie's view then and floated

closer as Archie wrestled with the straps that kept him tightly in place. The creature gazed down at him with the empty eye sockets in its bare skull, and Archie wondered if it would speak to him. If so, how?

Magic, he supposed. Magic always explained everything strange in his life.

Before Archie could say anything to the necromancer, though, it smacked him across the head with its own staff, and darkness took him once again.

Archie awakened an untold amount of time later. This time, he was lying on a cold stone floor, but he was free. Or at least nothing was tying him down.

At least he was alive.

He looked around and found himself in a windowless room. The Orb of Dominance stood on its staff, leaning in a corner. Its glow provided the place's only illumination, and by that, Archie could see that the place was bare but for himself and the staff.

Once again, he was surprised to not be dead. He would have bet anything that the only way he'd have avoided being immobile forever was by being transformed into a husk or a skeleton himself. He was amazed to have escaped that fate—so far.

We are in the Desert Temple.

Archie almost died of fright from that simple statement. If the necromancer had brought him all the way from the village to the mysterious structure that rose out of the middle of the desert, he might have been better off dead. What kind of fate could the creatures who lived in this place have in mind for him that they would have dragged him here?

We are about to find out.

The door to the room opened, and a necromancer floated in,

its feet hanging above the rough stone floor. It didn't say a word to Archie. It simply nodded at him and then gestured for the little Illager to follow as it turned around and left.

Archie wasn't sure what he should do, but getting out of the cell seemed like a much better idea than remaining inside it. He snatched up his staff—with the Orb of Dominance still securely hovering atop it—and pattered after the necromancer.

As he emerged from the room, he found himself in a long hallway that trailed off into darkness in both directions. Other rooms lined the way, their doors all closed. No lights shined through the bars fixed into each of the small windows cut high into each of those doors, and no sounds emerged from them either. As far as Archie could tell, he was utterly alone, with the exception of the necromancer, who steadily floated farther away on his left.

Not wanting to delve deeper into the dungeons beneath the Desert Temple without any sort of guide, Archie followed the necromancer. He figured if he saw a path to freedom along the way—as unlikely as that might be—he could make a break for it. Until then, he could only keep his eyes open and be ready if the chance presented itself.

For a moment he considered using the Orb to destroy the necromancer, and finding the way out of the temple entirely on his own. He wondered if this necromancer was the same one from the village. The same one that had knocked him out when he'd been stretched out across that skeleton.

He decided it didn't matter. If whoever was in charge here wanted him alive and had gone to all the trouble to bring him here that way, he wanted to meet them. Even if his head hurt from the treatment he'd gotten, it was still on his shoulders.

They'd piqued his curiosity enough that he at least wanted to hear them out.

You are getting wiser.

Archie took some heart at that compliment as he followed the necromancer in a winding path through the Desert Temple. They passed all sorts of coffins, catacombs, and sarcophagi.

Many of them stood open and empty, their occupants having either been dragged away or wandered off on their own. Others sat closed, and Archie realized his curiosity didn't extend to figuring out if they were empty too or still remained occupied.

They eventually emerged into a long, high-ceilinged chamber lined with tall statues on either side. At the far end hovered a gray-skinned figure dressed in a blue-and-green outfit that covered its shoulders and legs but left its chest bare. It wore a large, ornate crown with an enormous emerald set in the middle of it, and it bore a staff that resembled Archie's, except that it had a black shaft with an emerald orb hovering atop it.

"Welcome, stranger," the creature said as it moved forward, off a large dais on which sat a throne just as ornate as its crown. "I am known as the Nameless One."

Archie declined to give his name. It didn't seem nearly as dramatic and important as *the Nameless One*, and in the end he didn't suppose it mattered.

"Why did you bring me here?" Archie asked. He wasn't in the mood to trade pleasantries with someone who had kidnapped him to drag him into a conversation. As he spoke, the Orb pulsed just a bit brighter, which Archie hoped would be taken as the implied threat he meant it to be.

The Nameless One's emerald pulsed in reply, and Archie wondered just what powers it might have. What would happen if the two of them faced off against each other? Would one of them prevail? Or would they wind up killing each other instead?

Archie wasn't eager to find out.

"I have waited for your rise, as was long foretold," the Nameless One said in its deep and hollow voice. "I have been patient for countless lifetimes, but it has paid off. You are finally here."

Your destiny precedes you.

Archie thought he detected a note of pride in the Orb's voice. As if it had been right in choosing him and the Nameless One's interest in him had proven that.

"I haven't heard a thing about you," Archie said, wondering if the Nameless One would take that as an insult.

"I had no reason to reveal myself until everything was ready. That moment has come." The Nameless One floated closer to Archie. It took an act of will on his part to stand his ground and keep his staff from trembling.

"You still haven't answered my question," Archie said in as steady a voice as he could manage. "Why did you bring me here?"

"I would think that would be obvious to one with your ambition." The Nameless One stopped several feet from Archie and gazed at him with its vacant eye sockets. "People with power like ours are fated to rule the land, and by forging an alliance with each other, we can guarantee our destinies."

Archie narrowed his eyes at that, concerned. He didn't want to upset the Nameless One, so he chose his next words with care. "If we're both supposed to rule the land, wouldn't that make us rivals rather than allies?"

The Nameless One laughed at that, a dark and horrifying noise that seemed to echo from countless coffins at once. "There is enough of the land for us to share it, each according to our natures." It gestured at Archie's staff and then at its own. "You will rule the day. I will rule the night."

Archie glanced around the gigantic room. He spotted husks and skeletons waiting in the wings, stuffed between the statues that lined the length of the place. Given the size of the entire complex, the Nameless One could have had hundreds if not thousands more creatures stashed inside the place, ready to do his bidding at a moment's notice.

An important question sprang into Archie's head. He hesitated to ask it because it seemed like doing so might weaken his position, but he felt sure the Nameless One had already considered it. He licked his lips and then said, "If you're so powerful, what do you need me for?"

The Nameless One shook a bony finger at Archie. "You are just as sharp as I suspected you would be. That's an excellent question."

It pointed at the Orb of Dominance. "Are you aware of the full potential of the artifact you carry with you?"

Archie suppressed a shudder. He'd foolishly hoped the Nameless One didn't understand the power of the Orb, which was why it had let him keep hold of it. If the Undead leader knew all about the Orb, then the fact that Archie still had it under his control was an even bigger mystery.

"I take it by your silence you are still coming to terms with it. In many ways, your staff is a twin to my own." The Nameless One waved his emerald-topped staff gently about. "The power of mine stems from the night of this world. Your Orb's power, however, comes from somewhere far beyond."

Archie didn't understand what that meant, but an important realization dawned on him. "So you need my power to help with your plans."

"Precisely. You are a quick study."

Archie held his staff out before him and looked up at the Orb hovering above it. He wondered what would happen to the Nameless One if he unleashed the Orb's power here inside the Desert Temple. Would the creature be destroyed? Or would its emerald orb make it immune?

Archie suspected the Nameless One hadn't gotten to be so ancient by exposing itself to needless danger. He also guessed that if he fired up the Orb to attack the ancient Undead, he would be made to regret it.

He might have been able to fight his way out of the place. He might even have made it back to Highblock Keep alive. But he would have been making a powerful enemy if he left like that.

"What do you need from me?" he asked.

The Nameless One floated forward until it was just out of reach of Archie's staff. "The Orb of Dominance has the power to make my minions—all of them—immune to the ravages of sunlight."

Now Archie really understood. "With that, your forces won't have to hide when the sun is out. You can travel throughout the land at any time of day and let your mobs range as far as you want."

"Precisely."

It's too much. You can't let the Nameless One have everything.

Archie considered that assessment. The Orb was right. "And what do I get in exchange for this?"

"Other than an escort to bring you home safe and sound to Highblock Keep?"

Archie gave the Nameless One a grim nod. "By itself, that would hardly seem enough. You need me."

The Nameless One hovered a little higher and gazed down at

Archie from above. The emerald atop his staff glowed *darker*, if that was possible. "I believe you treasure life far more than I do."

Archie knew that the Nameless One meant to intimidate him, but all it made him do was laugh. "If you could have taken the power for yourself, you would have done it by now, and I'd be lying dead in the village."

The Nameless One lowered itself closer to the ground. "Or perhaps you'd be the latest husk recruit in my Undead army."

"Too true." Archie swallowed an urge to vomit at the idea of being one of this creature's eternal slaves. "So, what is it worth to you?"

The Nameless One focused its empty eye sockets on Archie, and he could feel it trying to size him up. "What do you require?"

Archie allowed himself a wry smile. "Well, I do need a proper army . . ."

CHAPTER TWENTY

When Archie strode back to the entrance of Highblock Keep, Walda stood there waiting to greet him. He peered past her and checked out his fortress. It seemed to be in particularly good shape. Maybe better than ever.

"You got the drawbridge down, and you've been fixing things up," he said to her. "I'm impressed."

Walda motioned nervously toward the army of husks and skeletons that had followed Archie home. He glanced behind himself to see them fidgeting about in the broad daylight, unsure of how to handle themselves in a world in which everyone could always see them coming. "You brought an Undead army with you. I'm the one who's impressed."

Archie shrugged as if he'd forgotten the mobs had been behind him. He'd had plenty of time to get used to the idea of leading an Undead fighting force, he supposed, although he didn't think he'd ever become jaded about hanging out with creatures that would try to eat him given even half a chance.

"We thought you were dead," Walda said, not taking her eyes off the Undead. "We held a wake in your honor."

"That was kind of you, but premature."

"Clearly."

Archie craned his neck and tried to take in the whole of the Obsidian Pinnacle from where he stood. "And you took charge in my absence?"

Walda shrugged as if that would clearly have been how he wanted it. Despite her casual air, she glanced at him to size up his reaction, just in case. "It seemed like the wisest course of action. We've had a number of other tribes join us to rally here under your banner. If I hadn't taken over, one of their leaders certainly would have—and don't think they didn't try."

Archie snickered at that. "I assume Thord tried to contest your authority too."

"Of course."

"And where is he now?" A part of Archie hoped that Walda had thrown the bully into the sea from the keep's highest tower.

"Looking after the redstone golems in the dungeons."

"That doesn't sound like a terrible enough job for someone who directly challenged the leader's authority."

Walda grunted, understanding Archie's disappointment in her. "Despite what he thinks—and perhaps you do too—leadership doesn't work particularly well if you simply punish everyone who challenges you."

Anger welled up inside of Archie. "Then why did you banish *me*?"

Walda wobbled back and forth a bit on the end of the wide-open drawbridge, clearly unsure how she should answer. Eventually she seemed to come to a decision and let out a nervous sigh before she spoke. "Honestly, I didn't want to. Given a choice, getting rid of Thord would have been far wiser. If we were Villagers, that's what I would have done."

"So why didn't you?" Archie could feel the Undead massing behind him now, and he relished the way they made Walda squirm with unease.

"Because we're Illagers. We don't have that sort of luxury. Thord was a better Illager than you by almost every means of measure. So when it came down to having to choose between the two of you, I went with Thord."

She braced herself as she waited for Archie's reaction.

She made a mistake. You should make her pay.

He found himself steaming with anger over the way Walda had treated him—and over the fact that she'd taken over Highblock Keep the instant it seemed like he might be dead. He stared hard at her and wondered what he should do with her.

"I'm sorry," she added in a surprisingly meek voice.

Archie accepted her apology with a sharp nod. "I'll forgive your transgressions—for now," he told her. "But don't get any ideas about replacing me. As you can see, I'm a lot harder to defeat than you might have guessed. You serve here in Highblock Keep at my pleasure. Never forget that."

Excellent.

Walda's shoulders tensed in fear, and Archie relished the look on her face. She was learning to fear him the way he'd once feared her.

"As for Thord . . ."

Walda tensed up once more. The two of them had a long history together as the leaders of their Illagers. While she was in charge of the full tribe, no one had contested Thord being in charge of the raiding parties for as long as Archie could remember.

"He's a good leader too," she said. "If you need people on the field of battle, you can't do better."

"The last two times he ran a raiding party didn't go so well," Archie pointed out. He knew he wasn't being fair. The first time, no one could have predicted that Smacker would ruin everything, and the second time, well, Archie had actually been in charge. If anyone was to blame for that disastrous assault on the village, it was him.

Of course, Smacker had ruined that too.

Archie thought he was starting to see the real problem. Smacker had been a thorn in the Illagers' collective side for far too long.

Walda waffled. "Well, you can't do better among Illagers, at least."

Archie gave Walda a condescending pat on the arm. "We need to do better. And we will."

With that, he turned and raised his staff. The Undead mobs all stared at it as if they were aware he could kill any of them with it in an instant. "Remain here!" he ordered them. "Protect the entrance to the keep."

He had no idea if any of them really understood anything he was saying. The Orb demanded their attention, though, and got it. Uncertain if they would obey him without its direct threat still pointed at them, he turned and led Walda across the drawbridge and back into Highblock Keep.

Halfway across the bridge, he turned around to see the husks and skeletons milling about there. They might not have been following his orders enthusiastically, but he'd never really been able to understand what motivated them in the first place.

"I cannot wait to see the look on the others' faces," Walda said as they walked into the keep. "They're going to be even more shocked than I was."

"I take it they haven't been behaving themselves?" Archie said. "Our Illagers require a strong hand."

Walda tried to ignore the jab at her leadership. Instead, she glanced over her shoulder at the Undead mobs and asked Archie a nervous question. "Are you sure they're not just going to invite themselves in?"

Archie hefted his staff. "I have complete control over them. They won't hurt us. Not as long as I'm in charge."

Walda grunted with grudging respect. "Yet another reason to leave your leadership unchallenged then."

Archie glared at her. Perhaps he'd been too lenient with her after all. "Did you have designs on that?"

"Me? Of course not."

He didn't believe her for a second. The fact that she pointedly didn't speak for the rest of the Illagers—and not for Thord particularly—did not escape Archie.

The army you have assembled is still not enough.

Archie had worried about that the entire way back to Highblock Keep. The Illagers hadn't been enough to help him take the village, or to protect him from the Undead army—which, now that he thought about it, had clearly followed them to the village and waited until the worst moment to attack just so the Nameless One could get Archie alone.

Now that he had the Nameless One as an ally, he shouldn't have to worry about trouble from that quarter in the future—barring a terrible betrayal. Sure, a roaming cluster of Undead mobs might randomly attack, but they wouldn't have enough force behind them to be a real threat.

The Undead were never the real threat. It's the heroes you need to worry about the most.

That made sense. The Undead had certainly disrupted the attack on the village, but once again, it had been Smacker who'd started turning everything wrong.

There are others too.

Archie groaned inwardly. Smacker had been the only hero in the village the night they'd attacked, but now that the Illagers had failed in their first attempt, they might not find the place so poorly defended in the future. At the very least, Archie and his army might have to contend with beefed-up defenses, but there was also a good chance that the Villagers would beg every hero in the land—and maybe even beyond—to come to their aid.

That was the last thing Archie needed.

He'd thought that his redstone golems might be enough to handle his hero problem, but that hadn't been the case. Smacker had dismantled the first redstone golem he ran into like it was little more than a pile of rocks. Bringing the Undead along to attack the village would help, but the heroes would make quick work of them if Archie couldn't stop them directly.

Would having more redstone golems help? It would be a good start, for sure. None of the Villagers or even their iron golems could stand up against the creatures. If Smacker's success against that first one was any indication, though, Archie would need dozens of them to be sure they could prevail against even a handful of heroes.

You cannot wait forever to build your army. If you do, the heroes will find their way here to take care of you before you can muster enough strength to attack them.

Archie had no idea what he could do to prevent that from happening. Their loss at the village had set certain wheels in motion, and he didn't know how to stop them. Perhaps there was a way to get them pointed in a different direction at least.

You need more muscle. Something that can equal the heroes in might.

Archie stared at the Orb of Dominance. Wasn't this powerful artifact supposed to be the thing that gave him the edge he needed? Maybe it wasn't as omnipotent as he'd hoped.

He supposed he couldn't feel bad about that though. The Orb had hauled him up from the most miserable point of his life and given him more power than he'd ever dreamed of wielding. He couldn't be disappointed because it didn't hand him the entire land on a platter. He would just have to take the tools it had given him and work for it.

There is more you might be able to do with the power of the Fiery Forge.

That idea intrigued Archie. The forge had already given him the redstone golems. What other powerful aid might it be able to supply?

Besides which, Archie needed to visit the Fiery Forge again to make even more redstone golems to supplement his forces. After all, they weren't going to spring to life and wander off to Highblock Keep on their own. Before he headed out, though, he had a few other things to do. He decided to head to the Obsidian Pinnacle and at least check up on the place.

Archie dismissed Walda and then started the climb toward the top of the Obsidian Pinnacle. He met a few other Illagers along the way, each of them working on different tasks to which Walda, presumably, had set them. To a person, they greeted him with shocked delight.

Apparently, to them at least, he was immortal. As he climbed, his legend grew.

Archie's thoughts wandered toward what he might do to improve his forces, and one idea kept coming back to him over and over again. If the redstone golems weren't powerful enough, perhaps the answer wasn't to make more of them. Instead, what if he made something bigger.

That's it. Exactly.

An image of a gigantic creature sprang into his mind, something like a redstone golem but much larger. It would require a bigger mold and much more diamond and redstone, but if he could pull it off—if the Orb could animate it—he thought it would be worth it.

I like the way you think.

Archie smiled at that, pleased with himself. If he wondered whether the idea had come from him or had been planted in his mind by the Orb, he didn't let it bother him for more than an instant.

By the time Archie reached the chair at the top of the pinnacle, he was feeling pretty good about himself and his Illagers. He'd gone from being banished to becoming their champion, and that was a position that he vowed he would never surrender. To his mind, the only one he had to worry about in that respect was Thord, but even thoughts of that bully couldn't bring him down at the moment.

As he had done before, Archie set the Orb of Dominance's staff into the hole drilled in front of the chair. Then he sat down and peered into the shifting colors of the Orb's glowing surface.

The outside of the Orb slowly shimmered away, and an image of the Fiery Forge—or at least the lava-drenched volcanoes that spilled into it—appeared before Archie. As before, he seemed to be watching from a bird's altitude, and it took him a moment to manage to maneuver his viewpoint down into the underground complex of caverns where he could spot the Fiery Forge itself.

He zoomed down into it and saw the golem mold there was filled with cooling redstone. The creature there was ready to be imbued with life. All it needed was some help from the Orb.

Archie realized then that he didn't see the redstone golem that he'd set to watch over the Fiery Forge. It should have been standing right next to its sibling-to-be, but it seemed to have wandered off.

The little Illager pulled his viewpoint back out again and scanned the cavern for the missing redstone golem. The other Illagers he'd stationed there still remained, working away at their jobs as he'd ordered them. They were mining the walls, building tracks and carts to carry the precious ore about, and generally doing a fine job.

He wondered if any of them had even heard that he was supposed to be dead. Probably they were unaware or they might have abandoned their posts. Had the redstone golem somehow figured that out and gone rogue?

After many panicked moments of panning around and maneuvering his viewpoint throughout the cavern complex, Archie finally spotted what he was hunting for. The redstone golem had moved farther into the cavern that housed the Fiery Forge, much deeper than Archie had ever ventured. And it had someone riding on its shoulders.

Even as Archie zoomed in, he knew whom he would see there, and he was right. Thord stood perched on the shoulders of the golem, which had apparently carried him to their current location. The golem seemed to be dragging a makeshift sled filled with diamond and redstone, a fortune in raw materials, and it was heading toward another exit from the place, one that Archie had never seen before.

Thord was robbing the Fiery Forge.

You need to defeat him. Now.

Archie had figured that out already. Thord was simply too much of a threat to his authority to be allowed to continue. The only question was whether Archie needed to march out to the Fiery Forge to take care of that task or whether he could wait for Thord to return to Highblock Keep instead. After all, Thord didn't know he was alive, so it was possible that he would walk right back into Archie's grasp.

But Archie was no longer in the mood to wait for that.

CHAPTER TWENTY-ONE

Archie set off for the Fiery Forge right away, bringing one of the redstone golems with him. He didn't bother to check in with Walda or anyone else before he left. He wondered if she knew about what Thord was up to, but he figured that if she did know she'd just lie to him about it. And if she didn't, then he didn't want her to have that knowledge.

It was bad enough that Thord was trying to rob him. Archie didn't want to let the other Illagers think the evoker actually had a chance of succeeding. If they did, they might start choosing sides, and Archie worried that would go poorly for him. He didn't want to have to crush a full-on rebellion within his ranks.

On top of that, Archie was just as furious with Walda as he was with Thord. She'd been in charge of Highblock Keep when he'd been missing. That meant she had to know—at the very least—

that Thord wasn't there. She could have told him about that, but she hadn't.

Which probably meant she knew what Thord was up to and supported it.

You cannot trust anyone but yourself.

That had become abundantly clear to Archie. He'd already known that, of course, from long before Walda had banished him from the tribe, but he realized that he'd harbored hopes that the situation might change with his rise to power. For most of his life, he'd felt terribly alone, but he'd thought that becoming the leader of the Illagers would mean he might finally have some real friends—or at least Illagers he could count on.

Instead, he found himself more isolated than ever. At least before, no one had tried to take anything from him, mostly because he hadn't had anything to take. Once he had power, though, other people wanted it, and they were apparently willing to go to great lengths to get it.

Looking back at the attack on the village, Archie wondered if Thord had somehow been working with the heroes. Or perhaps with the Nameless One, hoping that the Undead ruler would kill him rather than strike a bargain with him.

He just couldn't tell what might be true anymore.

The only person who'd shown him any real kindness and friendship was Yumi, and in his attempt to solidify his power, Archie had ruined that too. The look on her face when she realized that he'd led the attack on the village haunted him. He'd tried to save her, of course, but she hadn't seen that—just that he and his army were trying to destroy everything she'd ever held dear.

She would never forgive him. He decided he could never forgive himself either. But that didn't change what he had to do.

As Archie and his redstone golem tromped out of Highblock

Keep, he saw his new army of Undead mobs clustered around the end of the drawbridge. He wondered if they might turn on the Illagers while he was gone. If so, maybe they deserved it.

Archie felt a pang of jealousy for the Nameless One. To know that the creatures under your command were always on your side, no matter what. How amazing would that be?

They are only tools.

Archie wasn't sure what the Orb meant by that. He supposed the Nameless One would have to be lonely too—and had been for far longer than Archie had been alive. Sure, the Undead mobs did as they were told, but then they were only animated corpses, not real, living people.

That didn't seem like a fair trade. But then, constantly worrying about traitors wasn't much better.

Archie stopped at the end of the drawbridge and held up his staff. The husks and skeletons all turned to stare at him, ready for his orders.

For the barest instant, Archie considered sending them into Highblock Keep to destroy the other Illagers there. He could put the problems of having to deal with the living behind him. He could become another sort of Nameless One, commanding the Undead—perhaps even the remains of his fellow Illagers—to do his bidding.

He shuddered and shook that idea off.

"Stay here," he told them. "Protect Highblock Keep until I return."

He knew that left a lot of room for interpretation, but he didn't have the time or inclination to give each of them individual orders. He needed to get to the Fiery Forge and confront Thord before he got away.

The way there was easier than Archie remembered. It was a

cloudy day, but none of the worst mobs were wandering about in the muted sunshine. Those creatures he spotted scattered immediately, not at the sight of him but at the redstone golem dogging his heels.

It was well past dark when Archie spotted the telltale glow of the lava flows rising red in the west. When he reached the lava river, he stormed across the bridge and then let the redstone golem carry him down the trail to the cavern wherein lay the Fiery Forge.

The Illagers working in the cavern glanced up when Archie and the redstone golem entered, but they just as quickly turned away. He suspected they knew what Thord was up to, but either way, he was glad to see them cower at his presence. If he could not be loved, he would settle for being feared.

The golem-to-be that Archie had spotted in the diamond mold still lay cooling there, ready to be called to service. The darker parts of the redstone still glowed a bit, but they were finally beginning to turn to the gray color through which the crimson part of the redstone shone. He considered stopping to use the Orb to get the new redstone golem moving, but he was too angry to think about that then.

Working from memory of his last viewing through the Orb from the Obsidian Pinnacle, Archie headed toward where he hoped to discover the traitor.

Even with guidance from the Orb of Dominance, it took him a few tries. He wasn't sure if it was due to a faulty memory, the difficulty of the terrain, or the fact that Thord was moving about, perhaps in an effort to evade detection. Or possibly some combination of those things.

Archie located the exit he'd seen Thord using, and he followed a series of passages that led up, up, up until he finally reached the surface again. Once there, he found himself emerging from the side of a mountain, right near a cataract of lava that cascaded down from high above and splashed into a wide lake of lava that lit up the night. The land seemed peaceful enough—abandoned, really—but for the metallic rhythm of someone using a pick.

Off in the distance, Thord was methodically whaling on a large vein of diamond that he'd unearthed near the edge of the lava lake. As he worked, the traitor glanced over his shoulder in a nervous way and spotted Archie and his redstone golem coming toward him.

Shocked, Thord cursed in horror and then sprinted over to where Archie's missing golem stood watching over him. Clearly not in the mood to talk, he produced a bow and arrow from somewhere behind the creature's legs, nocked an arrow to his bow, and dipped the tip of it into a nearby pool of lava. The arrow burst into flames, and Thord turned, aimed at Archie, and let the missile fly.

The arrow fell well short of Archie and his golem as they approached. It skittered toward them but snuffed itself out long before it came anywhere near them. Before Archie could even laugh at the futile shot, Thord had already nocked another arrow and was setting it ablaze as well.

"Stand down!" Archie shouted at the evoker.

"I knew it!" Thord said as he let his next arrow fly. "I knew you weren't dead! I knew it couldn't be that easy!"

This arrow landed closer to Archie but still fell well shy of him. He sneered at the pathetic attempt.

"You turned against me the moment I fell!" Archie said.

"*Against* you?" Thord barked out a bitter laugh. "I was never *for* you! Just because a loser like you lucks into finding something as powerful as that Orb doesn't make you a leader!"

"Being a bully didn't make you one either!"

Archie held his staff out in front of him like it was a shield. Thord's next arrow sailed into the night sky, carving a flaming arc of fury, but a ray from the Orb struck out and disintegrated it. Only its ashes reached Archie, splashing across his chest.

Thord threw down his bow with a frustrated snarl. Archie thought he might go for his sword, but Thord reached out and grabbed the redstone golem next to him by the leg instead. "Get him!" he growled at the golem. "Kill him!"

The redstone golem turned and regarded Archie as if seeing him there for the first time—which Archie supposed was true. Golems weren't particularly observant, after all. Would it follow Thord's orders without question? Or could the Orb change its mind?

Thord's redstone golem strode straight toward Archie like it was going to trample him. Archie kept his staff before him and walked out to meet the creature. His own golem followed right behind him.

"You think you can stand up against me?" Thord shouted as he drew his sword. "Let the golems beat each other up. While they're busy, I'll take you down!"

Do not fear.

Archie allowed a confident smile to creep across his face. Out of everyone and everything in the world, he trusted the Orb of Dominance most. If it told him not to fear, then he wouldn't. It would either save him from the oncoming golem, or he would die.

"Yes!" Thord shouted, as he started marching toward Archie, swinging his blade around to get the balance of it once again. "Take down that little runt! Grind him into paste!"

The way Archie figured it, if the Orb was going to kill him, it had a dozen other ways to pull that off. If it was going to betray him, it could have done that countless times already—including taking up with the Nameless One over him. And if it suddenly changed its mind and went with Thord right now? Then Archie was better off with a quick death.

When Thord's redstone golem reached him, rather than attacking Archie it veered to its right and walked past him. Then it spun about and fell into step behind him. The other golem made room for the new one, and the two settled in next to each other.

Thord gaped in astonishment at his golem's betrayal. He'd bet everything on the creature following his orders, and to see it turn against him with not even a word from Archie crushed his hopes as if they'd fallen from the top of the Obsidian Pinnacle and smashed into the ground. He turned on his heel and fled in the other direction.

Unfortunately, the diamond vein Thord had been working sat at the end of a peninsula that stabbed out into a lake of lava. If Thord had gone in another direction he might have had a chance to get away. It would have been a slim one, perhaps only delaying the inevitable, but a tiny chance would have been better than none.

Archie really hoped that Thord wouldn't rob him of his vengeance. Not like that.

He got his wish.

Thord ran all the way to the end of the peninsula and saw that there was no escape from there. He spun to the left and then to the right, seeing much the same thing: a wide expanse of molten rock that would surely incinerate him with a touch. He turned back around then and saw Archie and the two redstone golems marching right for him.

Thord paled at the sight, but he wasn't ready to give up yet. He threw up his arms, ready to start casting spells, and shouted, "Come on, Archie! You're not going to hide behind those things forever. Prove to me you're a *real* Illager! Step on out from behind them and take me on yourself!"

Archie laughed at Thord's transparent attempt to trick him into risking his life in an open battle with the evoker. He would have loved to personally return all of the beatings he'd taken at Thord's hands over the years, but it wasn't worth it to get within reach of the fangs or the vexes the evoker could summon.

That sort of wisdom is why I chose you in the first place.

Archie stopped where he was and motioned for the redstone golems to come around and stand in front of him. They did so to either side, forming the equivalent of a redstone wall between him and the stricken Thord.

The bully stared up at the creatures and tried to put on a brave face. He failed, though, and the facade quickly cracked. "Hey!" he tried to shout around the massive creatures. "You don't need to do this. We can come to some sort of arrangement, right? We can make a deal!"

Archie pointed his staff at the bully, and the pair of redstone golems took their cue from that. They surged forward, pressing Thord between themselves and the molten lava.

CHAPTER TWENTY-TWO

After the business with Thord was over, Archie returned to the cavern to see about executing his latest idea. To his delight, he discovered that the Illagers he'd left there had kept busy in his absence. They'd amassed a tremendous amount of diamond and redstone, even more than he actually needed.

Originally, Archie had thought to use the diamond to create more molds for redstone golems so that he could make many of them at once. While that had been a fine notion, he realized now that he'd been thinking too small. Using the Orb, Archie took the pile of diamond and arranged it into a massive mold near another section of lava. If the mold for the redstone golem had been large, this one was gigantic.

While Archie had modeled the redstone golems on the iron golems found in the village, he took some liberties with his new design. He wanted it not only larger but stronger, meaner, and uglier than ever. He wanted the very sight of it to be able to strike terror in the heart of anyone who witnessed it.

When he was done, he realized he had drawn a crowd of Illagers who were curious about what he was up to. He immediately put them to work filling the mold with redstone while he watched. It took them a long while, but Archie discovered he needed the rest. It turned out he didn't mind watching Illagers work for him, and as he relaxed, he dreamed about forcing Villagers — especially the ones who had chased him off with torches and pitchforks — to handle such chores instead.

Once it was all ready, Archie used the Orb to cut a channel into the ground and guide the lava from the lake to the edge of the new mold. The heat from the lava lake melted the redstone into one large glowing pool that filled the entirety of the massive mold he'd built from top to bottom. It took forever to cool, but when it was ready, Archie held the Orb high once again and willed it to bring his new creation to some semblance of life.

The mold had been so large and complicated that Archie wondered if he'd ever be able to build something like it again. He could only hope that all of his efforts would pay off.

As he waited, something inside the mold shuddered, and a crack appeared in its diamond shell. A moment later, the shell began to crack. It calved away from its center, one large chunk at a time, each diamond piece shattering as it smashed into the ground.

Soon Archie's latest and most incredible creation towered before him, a redstone creature that dwarfed even the two golems at Archie's side. The other Illagers trembled before it in blood-freezing fear, and Archie couldn't help but throw back his head and laugh.

Archie dubbed it the Redstone Monstrosity. One look at it was all anyone would need to see why.

The monstrosity stood half again as tall as a golem and half again as wide. That would have been enough for it to strike terror into anything facing it, but the vicious horns that topped its skull transformed its already horrifying visage into something far worse. Nothing Archie had ever seen could hope to stand before it.

It was perfect.

Without delay, Archie headed back toward home. This time he had the Redstone Monstrosity carry him atop its massive head. He was exhausted enough to want to sleep the entire way, but too excited to close his eyes for an instant.

When he reached Highblock Keep, the Undead mobs stood milling about the front gate, but the drawbridge had been pulled up, keeping them from moving inside. The sea of creatures parted for him as he had the monstrosity lower him to the ground. He strode through them, the golems and the monstrosity trundling in his wake. When he reached the drawbridge, he raised his staff, and the chains that held up the giant slab of wood rolled out, lowering the bridge into place.

The Undead wanted to surge forward into the keep, but Archie turned around and raised his staff before them, holding them at bay. They recoiled to a safe distance and watched—the husks groaning with hunger—as Archie strolled into the keep.

He brought the golems with him, but he left the monstrosity behind to stand guard at the end of the drawbridge. It was less that he didn't trust the Undead to stay out of the keep than that he wasn't sure the bridge could hold the massive monstrosity's weight.

Walda met him at the other side of the bridge. She was so busy gaping at the Redstone Monstrosity that he had to snap his fingers at her to get her attention.

"What happened?" Archie demanded. "Why was the drawbridge up?"

Walda winced as she answered. "You were gone for so long the Undead became restless. They started to attack some of our people."

Archie nodded, understanding. "And you thought it would be better to separate them rather than fall into an all-out battle with our supposed allies."

Walda tensed, thinking that Archie might be trying to lead her into a verbal trap here. She hesitated for a moment before she owned up to what she'd done with a stiff nod.

"Smart move," he said. "This is why I have decided to not execute you yet."

Walda relaxed with his first words and then went straight back into a panic as he ended his sentence. "Yet? But why would you want to do that?"

Archie fixed her with a withering glare. "You knew where Thord went. You knew what he was doing, and why. And you never breathed a word of that to me."

Walda opened her mouth to respond, but Archie cut her off. "You thought he might kill me. And you hoped that if he failed you could just deny everything. Well, he did, but you can't."

He raised his staff before her and let the glow of the Orb of Dominance wash over her. "I know it all."

She flinched in fear and threw her hands up before her to protect herself from his fury. Archie had rarely had the pleasure of having someone grovel before him, but he discovered that he enjoyed it.

This is as it should be.

Archie wasn't entirely sure he agreed, but it was hard to argue with the Orb's results. People who were afraid of him seemed much less likely to betray him. Thord hadn't feared him in the slightest—much as he clearly should have—and that was what had made him so brazen about his treachery.

Archie had known that the Illagers respected his power—the power the Orb granted him—but that had ramped up when he'd returned to Highblock Keep after everyone had presumed him dead. The fact that he had gone into the wilderness and taken care of Thord—and returned with the Redstone Monstrosity in tow—certainly would burnish his reputation even further.

The way Walda cowered before him, he knew. No one would dare to betray him now.

"You—you don't understand," Walda finally said once she realized that Archie wasn't going to turn her to ash on the spot. "Your people adore you. We know that you—and only you—are the one who can bring us all to the greatness that we've so long deserved."

Archie didn't bother to hide his disbelief. The other Illagers would never love him, but he would be satisfied if they feared him at least. He wondered if he should reconsider sparing Walda. A very public execution of her on the front steps of Highblock Keep would do a lot to let everyone else know exactly who was in charge around there.

You are supreme.

Archie smiled at that, and Walda mistakenly took that as him granting her permission to speak. "To that end, we've—ah—been planning a celebration for you. A ceremony!" The desperate words tumbled from her lips in spontaneous bursts.

That caught Archie's attention. "A what?"

She straightened up, hope flickering in her eyes. "A ceremony to officially crown you as the greatest Illager leader ever to live."

Archie blinked. He knew she was appealing to his vanity. He wasn't foolish enough to ignore that. But the idea that others might recognize him as a great leader stunned him.

He had to admit, she had a point about how amazing he was, mostly because the bar for great Illager leader had been set staggeringly low. To be fair, Walda was the only Illager leader Archie had ever met, but he'd heard of others too. Walda was reported to be the best of the lot.

But Walda's wildest ambitions had only involved keeping her people together and fed. They'd not tried to bring others into their fold. They'd not attempted to take any territory. At best, they'd only harassed any village they came across. At worst, they'd spent days if not weeks fleeing from heroes who'd decided to try to rid the land of them.

She'd never considered trying to conquer the entire land, but Archie—who'd only come into his true power a short time ago—already had his people on the precipice of actually managing just that. He could see why his people would want to lionize him. He had no doubt they'd be singing his praises for generations. Long after those who knew him in life had passed away, he would be a subject of myth and legend.

Why not enjoy a bit of that attention in the here and now?

"A crown, you say?"

Walda brightened. "Yes! To go along with your title! The perfect thing to symbolize the heights to which you have climbed. A tall crown, fashioned from gold and adorned with precious jewels."

Archie pursed his lips, confused about this. None of the Illagers had the skills necessary to craft such a phenomenal piece of regal headwear. "Where did you find such a thing?"

It comes from the keep's vault. I fashioned it for you myself.

Walda froze, unsure of how to reveal the answer to Archie. When she saw the angry look on his face, though, she instantly confessed. "While you were gone—when we thought you were dead—we took the opportunity to explore every bit of Highblock Keep. In the dungeons, we discovered a vault filled with the most amazing riches."

It lies behind the room in which sits the throne.

Archie realized that he should have been mad about the fact that Walda explored the depths of Highblock Keep while he was gone. He didn't recall making that room himself, but the construction of the place had been a blur. Still, he was too intrigued by the appearance of a proper, glorious crown to be too worried about it at the moment.

How had the Orb come up with a crown for him? And a vault filled with treasure to go with it?

I peered into your heart and saw how best to fulfill your deepest desires.

The idea that the Orb could read into even his subconscious thoughts disturbed Archie, but not so much that he was going to fail to enjoy the results. He wondered what else the mysterious thing had seen and what it might do with that information . . .

"We were going to show it to you when you returned from the dead, but you took off so quickly to deal with Thord that we never had the chance," Walda tried to explain.

Archie wasn't at all sure he bought it, but he motioned for her to go on.

"While you were gone, we took the opportunity to plan your, ah, coronation. Now that you're back, we can get it started right away."

"When?"

Walda looked at him, unsure of what he meant and afraid to express that to him.

"When will the coronation take place?" he clarified.

"Oh!" she said. "Tonight, if that works for you. If you need to rest, we certainly understand and can postpone to another date—whenever you like, of course—but the people are excited about having an amazing ruler like you in place. They would do it right now if you were ready for it."

Archie waved her off. He was tired from his journey back from the Fiery Forge and needed to clean up and change into clothes that would be fitting for a ruler of his stature. Looking down at himself, he realized he didn't have any.

"I've already had your best people working on your wardrobe," Walda said, correctly anticipating his concern. "You'll find the perfect set of clothes waiting for you in your royal chambers."

Royal chambers? The Illagers had been busy in his absence. Archie had no doubt that Thord and even Walda had once had their own plans for those chambers. With them both put in their proper places, though, Archie felt no compunction about assuming those chambers for himself.

Not that he would have in any case. Highblock Keep was his. Everyone else inside it was his guest, and they should accord him the respect of the rightful and undisputed owner.

"This works for me," Archie told Walda.

Her relief was palpable. She started to breathe regularly again and even fanned herself with her hand. "Excellent," she said.

"The one thing we haven't worked out for you is your title. We have some suggestions, but we thought your input would be the most vital."

"Right. My title." Archie had been too busy to put much thought into the issue till now. She had a point though. If he was to rule over the land, people would need to call him something other than Archie the Illager.

He'd been called all sorts of unkind things over the years, including several painful zingers coined by Thord. He wasn't sure he could counter all those with a new title, but he was willing to entertain the possibility. "What did you have in mind?" he asked Walda.

"*King?*" she said uncertainly.

Archie frowned and shook his head. "I need a kingdom to be a king, don't I? And this has never been about the land as much as it's about our people."

She grimaced. "I suppose you're not going to like *emperor* then?"

Archie shrugged. "Building an empire seems even less likely than coming up with a kingdom."

For now.

The Orb of Dominance, at least, had plenty of ambition for them both. After everything it had done for him, Archie wasn't about to stand in its way. If he might someday rule an empire with the Orb's help, then so be it. But he still thought that declaring himself an emperor would be premature.

"You never had a title for yourself, Walda," Archie told her. "Why would you insist on one for me?"

She raised her eyes and glanced about to indicate everything that surrounded them. "Well, I never had a keep or an Undead army or an Orb of incalculable power to call my own either. I think those are the things that separate us."

He chuckled at her discomfort, and that spurred her to speak again. She looked down at Archie with power-hungry eyes.

"You're going to be able to do things I could never have dreamed of, and you're going to bring the Illagers to greater glories than we could ever have imagined on our own. A conqueror like you deserves a crown and title to go with it."

Archie pondered that for a moment, savoring her flattery, and then nodded. "All right. What else do you have?"

Walda put up her hand and counted off the various titles as she ran through them. "Monarch. Majesty. Overlord. Prince—never mind, that's less than a king. Sovereign. Commander. Governor. Sultan. Potentate?"

She was clearly running low on ideas. She sighed at him as her shoulders sank. "None of those are working for you? At all?"

Archie shook his head. "It should be something unique. Something powerful. Something to strike awe in all who hear it."

Walda sucked at her teeth, acknowledging how tall that order was for her. She was a ruler, not a writer. "I'll see what we can come up with."

"We have until tonight."

A wide, relieved smile broke out on Walda's face. "So you're up for holding the coronation then?"

"The sooner the better," Archie said. "After all, we don't have any time to waste."

"Why is that?" Walda said, uncertain once more.

Archie chuckled at her lack of vision. "We have a land to conquer. It will only wait for us for so long."

CHAPTER TWENTY-THREE

"**W**e have a problem," Walda said when Archie emerged from his chambers that evening. He noticed she didn't have the crown with her.

"Are we going to have to push off the coronation?" The idea made him angry. Despite how silly he'd found it before, the more he thought about such symbols of power, the more he wanted them.

She shook her head, not at his question but at the entire notion that the coronation was something to worry about at that exact moment. "The Undead attacked and killed some of our people."

"What?" Archie couldn't believe it. "Who lowered the drawbridge?"

"We're hunters and gatherers," Walda said. "Some of the people wanted to go out and get some more food for the feast. The only way to do that was to lower the drawbridge. They figured the Undead wouldn't bother them during the day, at least."

Archie closed his eyes and pinched the bridge of his nose. "No one realized that these Undead haven't just disappeared in the sunshine every day?"

"The mobs have been pretty sedate up until now. We hoped that the daylight—while it didn't harm them—was at least keeping them calm."

Archie opened his eyes again. "But that didn't turn out to be true."

Walda shook her head, her eyes wide and horrified. "Not one bit."

"Tell me you raised the drawbridge."

"We tried—we really did—but the Undead had already gotten onto it before we realized what had happened." She held up her hands to stave off any interruptions until she was finished. "We did manage to lower the gates on this side of the drawbridge, but the Undead are still trying to claw their way in."

"Which they will continue to do until I order them otherwise," Archie said.

"The sun really doesn't affect them?" Walda seemed not to believe that. "Not at all?"

Archie hefted his staff before him. "I granted them immunity to limitations like that. They are on our side, after all."

"They don't seem to be acting like it." Walda started to raise her voice, but she remembered to whom she was talking and managed to tamp it down.

Archie strode past her and made his way downstairs to the gate. She trailed in his wake, as did everyone else they passed on the way. Word about the disaster had spread through the keep, and every one of the Illagers wanted to know if they had to fear for their lives from the Undead army that seemed to have turned against them.

You need to stop this.

That was something Archie didn't need to be told. Not by anyone.

When he reached the gate, the Illagers who'd been stationed to keep watch at it were standing well back from it. They all had their weapons out and ready, but they weren't attacking the Undead mobs through the gate. In fact, many of them had taken up positions around the corner from the gate, to keep themselves safe from the skeletons who'd taken to climbing on top of one another so they could fire arrows through the thick cluster of husks pressed up against the gate's bars.

Archie peered around the corner and had a volley of arrows fired at him for his trouble. He ducked back to recover from the surprise and noticed that everyone was staring at him in abject fear. It was up to him to solve this problem.

That was something he could do.

He held his staff out before him, the Orb of Dominance glowing brightly, and he stepped around the corner once again. "Hold it!" he shouted as he emerged.

Thankfully, the skeletons did just that. They had stretched back the strings of their bows, but they kept them clutched tightly between their bony fingers, unloosed. Similarly, the husks—who'd been groaning in a disturbing chorus of hunger—all fell silent.

Archie strode toward the gate with unfazed confidence. As he grew closer, the Undead mobs stared at the Orb with unblinking eyes or sockets, focusing exclusively on it.

"You are not to set foot in this building!" Archie declared, raising his voice so the creatures in the back could hear him as well. "Remove yourselves and wait for me in the field beyond the front steps! Highblock Keep is for the living, not the dead!"

The Undead mobs actually fell over themselves trying to comply with Archie's orders as fast as they could. Perhaps some of their speed sprang from the fact that he could have obliterated each and every one of them with lancing rays from the Orb, but it seemed that they were actually eager to please him. After all, he was their recognized master now.

The Undead have short memories.

That explained why they'd decided to ignore Archie's previous orders. They'd literally forgotten what they were supposed to be doing. That didn't seem like it would be much of a problem as long as he was around to keep them in line, but it meant that he couldn't trust them with long-term plans.

These were limitations he could work around. In fact, they gave him an idea.

He spun around to discover the entire hallway behind him packed wall to wall with curious Illagers. Each and every one of them was gawking at him and the power he'd just displayed. Slowly their slack jaws formed relieved grins, and a cheer went up from the back of the hall.

As the echoes of the first cheer were dying, another went up. Then another, and another. Soon the walls of the keep reverberated with Illager chants. They kept shouting, "Archie! Archie! Archie!"

Right then, Archie knew what his title had to be.

He waved for them to be silent, and they cut themselves off almost immediately. He cleared his throat and then spoke loudly again, this time for the Illagers in the keep rather than the things on the bridge.

"Thank you!" he said. "As long as I am in charge of Highblock Keep, you will be safe inside it! Remember that!"

A cheer went up once more, but he cut it short before it rolled into something larger. "Tonight, you are all invited to my coronation! We will meet in the throne room when the sky is fully dark! I look forward to becoming your official ruler!"

The cheers went wild, and this time Archie didn't try to stop them. Instead, he strode into the keep, and the howling Illagers parted before him, giving him a wide berth.

He went directly to the throne room, and Walda rushed in after him. She slammed the door behind herself, cutting off the still-roaring exultations.

Archie paid no attention to her. He simply strolled over to his throne and sat down on it.

"Thank you," Walda said to him. "That was very well done."

Archie tilted his staff to one side as the Orb atop it shifted colors the way it often did. "It's easy when you know how."

"It's one thing to wield power," Walda said with respect. "It's another entirely to know how to lead. You've taken to leadership quickly."

"Apparently I'm a natural at it." Archie thought about that night in the village when he'd been shot and kidnapped, despite all his power. That had not been one of his better moments, but he wasn't going to dwell on that now—or ever.

"I've had a lot more practice at it, and even if I had the power you control, I'm not sure I would have done quite so well."

Archie favored her with a knowing smile. She was flattering him again—lying to him, really—and they both knew it. Given the chance, she'd wrest the Orb from him and become the supreme ruler of the Illagers instead.

She just didn't know how to do it. Perhaps it was that she was too frightened to try. After all, look how Archie had handled Thord for his betrayal. She couldn't expect he would treat her any better.

She cannot take me from you.

Archie gave Walda an easy smile that she couldn't possibly understand. It was based on the confidence he felt that neither she nor any of the other Illagers could come between him and the source of his power. In that sense, he was untouchable, and that comforted him far beyond words.

"Let the others in," he told her.

She obeyed instantly and left his side to open the doors. As soon as she did, the rest of the Illagers in the keep filed into the throne room, moving in silence and respect. Few of them had ever been in a throne room before, much less witnessed something like a coronation, and they were one and all cowed by the prospect. Except, perhaps, for Walda.

The sun outside had fallen beyond the horizon, and full darkness would be upon them soon. Even from up as high as they were, Archie could hear the husks groaning outside and the skeletons clattering about. At his gesture, Walda set people scurrying to light torches in the sconces all around the edges of the hall, as well as in tall candelabras sitting on either side of the dais on which the throne stood.

A proper coronation requires proper lighting.

The Orb flared for a moment, and a brilliant light appeared in the ceiling directly above Archie. It shone down on him like a spotlight, declaring him the most important person in the massive room. If all eyes hadn't been on him before, they certainly were now.

He basked in the light for a moment before realizing that doing so maybe didn't make him look as serious and regal as he wanted. He pasted a mild frown on his face and narrowed his eyebrows instead. The people around him seemed to respond in kind, taking the moment as seriously as he required.

Once everyone was in the room and ready, Archie stamped the end of his staff on the ground three times, and the murmuring in the room went silent, as if he'd cut the noise with a diamond-edged knife. Walda strode up to the dais with the crown cradled in her hands. It sparkled in the torchlight, and Archie had to suppress a gasp at the sight of it. He'd never seen anything so gorgeous in his entire life.

It is exactly as you dreamed.

It was tall and fashioned from gold. It bore a gigantic ruby on the front, toward its ornate crest, with a sapphire of similar size just below that. Altogether, it was probably worth more than an Illager raiding party could gather in a year or more.

Walda stood next to him, on his left-hand side, and hefted the crown in front of him. He nodded at her where he sat, and she carefully placed the crown on his head.

Despite how tall and narrow it was, it fit perfectly. It felt heavy for an instant, but when he stood up on the seat of his throne to bring himself to even higher than his full height, the weight of the crown seemed to vanish.

He stamped his staff down once again, and everyone in the hall bowed their heads and bent their knees before him. The sight filled him with a sense of incredible power, even more than when he'd first grasped the Orb. His people would honor him here at his home and follow him into the heart of battle without question, he knew, and nothing could be better than that.

He looked to his left and saw Walda staring down at him. Perhaps she was too astonished to move, but she hadn't bowed her head or bent her knee.

Archie could not withstand that sort of disrespect at that most important moment. The Orb of Dominance's glow intensified with his emotions, and it flashed from golden to crimson as he swung it around and smacked Walda upside her head with it.

Without complaint or protest, she realized her mistake and bowed deeply. This brought her head lower than Archie's, which satisfied him — for now.

He turned and stared out at the Illagers filling the hall. The sight of his subservient subjects filled him with incredible satisfaction. He wanted to hold on to that for as long as he could. And he knew there was only one way to do that.

Armies that don't fight turn against themselves, as you saw earlier today. Give them a target, and they will serve you — just as you serve me.

The idea that Archie might be the one serving the Orb of Dominance rather than the other way around shocked him, but he wasn't about to start an argument with it in the middle of his coronation. Besides, if they both got what they wanted, why split hairs about who was controlling whom?

But was this really what he wanted? To control a vast army capable of taking over the land? To cut down any and all who would stand in the way of his ultimate triumph?

When this started, all Archie had wanted was to find a place where he belonged. Where the people would accept him for who he was and treat him like a valued member of their community.

Somewhere along the way, it had gotten far more complicated than he had anticipated.

And now he was about to be crowned . . . what?

He gazed out over the people assembled in the room. They'd come to abase themselves before him and to pledge their loyalty to him. They wanted to bear witness to a coronation, and he refused to disappoint them.

"Rise, my people!" he said to them. "Rise and meet the one who will lead you to greatness! Rise and greet me, your Arch-Illager!"

CHAPTER TWENTY-FOUR

"Arch-Illager?" Walda said the next morning as she greeted him in the throne room. "What a stroke of inspiration."

The feast last night had been fantastic, and the people were now roused and ready to do anything for him, Archie knew. He only needed to point them in the proper direction and give them their orders. Now.

He gave Walda a suspicious side-eye. "You don't like it?"

She composed her response carefully. "I'm not sure I understand it."

"It's a play on words, based on my name and who I am. *Arch* means *leader* or *chief*. And well, *Illager*, that's who I am. Who we all are."

Walda nodded in understanding. Archie still wasn't quite sure she approved, but then again, he didn't require her blessing at all.

"We move today," Archie told her, changing the subject. "Our Illager army is strong and ready and itching for a fight, as are our Undead allies."

"Most of your army is sleeping in after the feast last night," Walda pointed out. "Could we perhaps push the launch of our campaign against the Villagers off until tomorrow?"

That should be fine, but no longer.

Archie made a sound of disgust. "Fine, but we can't wait any longer than that. Our destiny awaits us, and I—for one—am eager to claim it!"

"As you say, Archie."

He arched an irritated eyebrow at her. "What did you call me?"

Walda sucked in her breath. "My apologies, *Arch-Illager.*"

Archie permitted himself a perfectly self-satisfied smile at the sound of his chosen title rolling off his former leader's lips. He almost wished he could bring Thord back from the dead so he could hear it from him too.

It occurred to Archie that although the Illagers needed a day to recover from the celebration of his coronation, the same didn't apply to the army of Undead clustered outside the gates of High-block Keep. Besides which, he was worried about the Illagers traveling alongside the Undead. It would only require a small problem with those mobs for the entire affair to devolve into chaos. He needed his fighting forces focused on their enemies, not worried about each other, and he had the perfect plan to make that happen.

First, though, he needed to do some research. He excused himself from the throne room and headed to the top of the Obsidian Pinnacle again. Once there, he placed his staff in its regular slot, sat down on the chair there, and peered into the Orb of Dominance.

What do you want to see?

"The heroes that stand between me and the village," he said. "I need to know where they are and what they're doing."

The surface of the Orb dissolved in front of Archie's eyes, and he found himself looking down at the village from an incredible height. The Villagers there had built more fortifications around the place in an effort to protect themselves better, but they clearly had no idea of the forces Archie had at his command now. The defenses might be enough to protect the place against the Illagers, but the redstone golems and—better yet—the Redstone Monstrosity would make quick work of them.

The only thing that would put a kink in Archie's plans was the presence of a hero. Any one of them alone would be able to take on a redstone golem, and together they might even present a reasonable threat to the Redstone Monstrosity. But if they weren't there . . .

Archie zoomed the viewpoint in and searched around the village for any sign of a hero. To his irritation, he spotted five of them chatting with one another in the center of town. They had apparently been helping with the fortification of the village, and they didn't seem to be done with their task.

The longer you give them, the tougher the village will become.

Archie knew that the Orb was correct. The sooner he moved on the village, the better. Otherwise, the heroes might throw up a castle's worth of defenses around it, and he'd find himself thwarted.

But with the heroes there, it wouldn't matter. Even without the defenses, they might be able to destroy his army, no matter how augmented with redstone mobs it was. He needed to get rid of the heroes.

Fortunately, he had an idea about how to do that.

"Show me their homes," Archie said. "The places they care most about."

The viewpoint in the Orb shifted wildly. It spun high up into the sky, whirling about until Archie had to clutch at the sides of the chair. He was so dizzy he thought he might throw up. Fortunately, just before that happened, the viewpoint stabilized, and he found himself gazing upon a serene scene far below.

As Archie peered into the Orb, he spied four different buildings scattered about the landscape. Even the closest of them stood at least a half day's walk away from the village, maybe more.

The buildings sat in different parts of the land. One stood atop a mountain. Another overlooked the sea. A third had been built inside an amazing tower. The last sat mostly underground but for a glassy staggered pyramid that emerged from the earth to allow in all the sunlight possible.

Each one of them seemed large enough to house a tremendous family, and they were tricked out with the most amazing architecture. Archie spent some time zooming in with the Orb and examining the places, and he'd never seen such incredible marvels. To think that each of them housed only a single person seemed like a tremendous waste.

They can be yours.

Archie liked that idea. One day, he would rule the entirety of the land, from sea to sea. Today, though, he was only interested in the village. Taking that would be a huge victory for him and would supplement the force of workers he needed to build more redstone golems. From there, he could roll on to take out the heroes one by one.

All he needed to do was get them out of the village so he could attack it.

He studied each of the places and their locations, both relative to each other and to Highblock Keep. Then, when he was finally ready, he went to find Walda.

She was in the throne room, making decisions for him in his absence. Fortunately—for her—she was sitting in a simple chair off to the side of the central dais. If she'd been on his throne, he would have been tempted to execute her on the spot.

All eyes swung toward Archie as he entered the room. He ignored them and strode straight for his throne. He relished approaching it with his fantastic crown sparkling on his head—almost as much as he enjoyed the respectful attention.

It seemed like everyone in the place held their breath until he was seated. Just as they began to breathe again, he crooked a finger toward Walda to summon her to his side. "A word," he told her.

She immediately excused herself from the conversation she'd been having and stood up. "Clear the room!" she called out clear and loud.

The others in the throne room vacated it immediately and without objection. The last of them closed the double doors that led into the room behind them with a resounding boom.

"Yes, Arch-Illager?" Walda said as she stood before him. She was so tall that even when standing lower on the steps of the dais, as she was, she could still look him in the eye. The height of Archie's crown still made his head officially taller, though, so he decided he could tolerate that.

"I have orders for you," he said. "I have chosen you for a most important mission."

Walda's face fell. "Will this take me from your side during the invasion of the village?"

"I'm afraid so," he said, "but it will ensure the invasion's success."

She let the frown on her face transform into a look of sheer determination. "Then I am yours to command." A dissatisfied look from Archie prompted her to hastily add, "As always."

Archie ordered her to produce a pen and paper. She complied immediately, taking some from the supply she'd set up next to her desk. He then drew her a rough map of the land. He would have made her do it, but she had no concept of the shape of the place.

In her younger years, she had led nomadic Illagers throughout much of the land—before she had settled down in their tribe's woodland mansion—but that only gave her an Illager's view of the place. With the help of the Orb of Dominance, Archie had access to the view of a bird.

The view of a god.

That statement disturbed a part of Archie for reasons he couldn't put into words. Another part of him was absolutely delighted.

Once he was done with the outline of the map, Archie marked off the different regions he was sending Walda through. He also included the locations of Highblock Keep, the village, and even the Desert Temple—which he instructed her to keep well away from, just in case, although he didn't say exactly why.

Then he marked the locations of the homes of the four heroes.

"I need you to take the Undead mobs and attack these places," Archie said to her.

Walda grew pale. "You're putting me in charge of the Undead?"

"It's a position of great power," he said in an effort to keep her from breaking into a full-blown panic. "You'll lead fully half of our forces, and on a mission of the utmost importance. Without your help, the attack on the village will fail for sure."

She swallowed hard and nodded firmly, as if she was trying to convince herself that an apparent suicide mission couldn't possibly be that bad. "And when do I leave on this mission?"

"Immediately," Archie said. "Now. As soon as you can pack your things, go."

Walda blew out a long breath as she tried to acclimate herself to the idea of marching off alone, the only living being at the head of an army of Undead mobs. A trip that would have those husks and skeletons following her through the night.

"If you move quickly, the mobs should recall their orders long enough that they won't turn on you. If you fail, well, you'll suffer the inevitable consequences."

"All right," Walda said after only a moment's hesitation. Archie could tell she wanted to refuse such a terrifying task, but she feared even more what he would do to her if she defied him.

He smiled at her. "I appreciate your loyalty."

She nodded, still trying to absorb the horrors that lay ahead of her. "What is the mission?" she asked, distracted by those stray thoughts.

"I need you to find the homes of the four heroes that like to hang around the village, and destroy them."

If Walda had turned pale before, now she blanched white. She hadn't led a raiding party in years, preferring to leave that duty to Thord, but with him gone, she seemed like the natural choice. Even she could see that.

The idea of destroying a hero's home, though, gave her pause. Archie would have been shocked if it hadn't, maybe enough to pull her away from the mission. Anyone who would promise to take care of something like that without any trepidation was clearly either insane or a liar—or both.

"You don't need to dismantle them to their foundations," Archie said. "Actually, I would prefer if you didn't. I want you to hit each one hard, set it on fire, and then go on to the next."

Realization dawned on Walda's face. "You don't want to hurt them. You just want to distract them."

Archie grinned at her. "They're all in the village right now. We just need to draw them out to give ourselves a chance."

She cocked her head at him. "You don't think your redstone creatures can tip that scale for us?"

"Possibly," Archie said. "But there's too much that can go wrong in a battle. I want to guarantee our success. To do that, I need to at least reduce the number of heroes in the village, if not get rid of them entirely. Every one of them you can draw away will be a huge boon to us."

Walda gave him a firm nod. "All right," she said as bravely as she could manage. "I will not fail."

CHAPTER TWENTY-FIVE

*Y*ou *have done well.*

Archie didn't *need* the approval of the Orb of Dominance, but he appreciated it. Regardless of its encouragement, though, he'd begun to have his doubts about the upcoming attack on the village.

That hadn't stopped him from launching his army out of the doors of Highblock Keep the morning after he'd sent Walda off with the Undead mobs. The Illagers who came with him had been relieved to not have to forge through all the husks and skeletons to find their way south, and he couldn't say he blamed them. Any day you didn't have to deal with Undead mobs was a good one.

The march toward the village was mostly uneventful. Despite his arrangement with the Nameless One, Archie steered his army well to the east of the Desert Temple. He didn't want to tempt the Undead leader into anything that could spoil his plans now.

Because many of them were nomads—or at least hailed from a tribe that had once been—the Illagers were used to such long marches on foot. They hadn't resided in Highblock Keep long enough to become soft yet. If Archie had his way, they never would. They were a warrior people, always looking for a fight, and to shut them all up inside Highblock Keep forever would destroy the core of who they were.

Once the village and all the heroes were destroyed, Archie knew of no one else who could challenge his supremacy. He could gather even more Illager tribes under his banner, and he could solidify his power from coast to coast.

After that, Archie planned to send his Illagers far and wide. With the Villagers as their unwilling workforce, building more and more golems for them, they could sail across the seas and conquer even distant lands. They could take whatever they wanted without fear of reprisal.

No one would be able to stop him. The wealth of the entire world would be his. Perhaps he would have his empire after all.

At that point, he'd have to figure out if he could really bear to share the land with the Nameless One or not. He had little doubt that the Undead ruler was already plotting against him. It was in the creature's nature.

The question was: What was the best way to stop that? Should Archie simply try to contain the Nameless One in the desert? Did circumstances demand that he limit its reign to the Desert Temple alone? Or did he really have to crack the entire fortress open and root the Nameless One and its Undead minions out?

Those were problems for another day. First Archie needed to

destroy the village. Until he managed that, everything else was just fodder for daydreams.

As his army grew closer to the village, though, his doubts grew too. If he wanted to destroy the heroes—who were the real threat to him and his power—did he really have to raze the village?

Do you remember what the Villagers did to you?

Archie recalled it all vividly. They'd distrusted him at first—especially Salah—but they'd eventually taken him into their village and treated him fairly well. All of that had been due to Yumi's kindness. If she hadn't been willing to stick up for him and let him stay in her place, perhaps no one would have.

The day before Archie had left, though, even Salah had been treating him better. Grudgingly, maybe, but better.

If it hadn't been for Smacker picking on him, Archie might still be living there. A large part of him still wished for that.

Sure, he had incredible power at his disposal. He had control of Highblock Keep and over every Illager in his army. But he still missed the camaraderie he'd found in the village.

He still missed Yumi, his friend.

And now he was going to her home to destroy it and to make her people work in his mines.

If you want to destroy Smacker and the rest of the heroes, you need to destroy the village too. The heroes know the place and the Villagers who live in it. They barter with them. They care about them. Obliterating it will hurt them in a way that even burning their homes to the ground cannot.

Archie understood that—or at least thought he did. Having the Orb whisper things into his head for so long and at any moment of the day had made it hard, sometimes, to keep his own thoughts separate. He wondered if he should put it away for a moment, just so he could walk for a ways on his own, without it reinforcing certain ways of thinking for him.

A great fear that someone might steal his staff from him—along with the Orb of Dominance—seized him then. He knew intellectually that no one would dare try such a thing, but emotionally he couldn't shake the bone-deep conviction that without the Orb he would be nothing. He needed to cling to it with all his might.

He actually clutched his staff tighter. He didn't want his people to think he was faltering, so he turned toward the Redstone Monstrosity and ordered it to pick him up. It did so and set him down upon the top of its head.

From up there, Archie could see his entire force of Illagers and redstone golems assembled around him. Together with the Redstone Monstrosity, they formed the most powerful army he had ever seen.

He wondered what Yumi would think when she saw it? More important, what would she do? Would she be wise enough to flee? Or would she be too brave and decide to make a doomed stand with her fellow Villagers?

And how could Archie keep that from happening?

You need not worry about her. She is beneath your notice.

That was the last thing Archie wanted to hear. He didn't want to attack the village if it would mean Yumi's defeat. At the very least, he wanted to protect her from his own people.

Ideally, he'd get her out of there before the attack came, but he didn't see how he could manage that. He'd tried that the last time he'd led an attack on the village, and that had only ended with him being shot—nearly killed—and kidnapped to the Desert Temple. The way she'd dug her heels in the last time told Archie that he probably wasn't going to have better luck with her this time.

Maybe if he went into the village alone ahead of time he could warn her. He could disguise himself as a Villager, and with luck, no one would recognize him. Of course, the moment someone did, everything would go sideways. The last thing he needed to do was get captured.

Plus, his great plan depended on him attacking the village before the people there could call for help. If the Villagers managed to alert the heroes and call them back before the full-blown attack, all of Archie's preparations would be for nothing.

We need those workers. We are on the edge of realizing our goals.

The Orb clearly didn't want Archie messing around with their plans, and he understood why. Going to save Yumi ahead of time was ridiculously risky—especially when it did nothing to improve their chances of winning the upcoming battle. But Archie just couldn't find it within himself to leave Yumi's fate to chance.

You cannot protect her always. You were not so worried about her when you were at Highblock Keep.

That was all true. Archie supposed he could have checked in on Yumi regularly via the Orb to see how she was faring, but he honestly *hadn't* worried all that much about her. Life in the village was fairly tranquil almost all of the time—with the exception of the occasional Illager raid. Since Archie was in charge of the Illagers now, no such raid would happen without his orders, which meant—in theory—Yumi was safer than ever.

Now that he was about to lead an attack on her hometown, though, he was going to upend that safety. He knew he couldn't keep her safe constantly, but he could at least make sure that he—or his people—didn't threaten her life.

Couldn't he?

You are overstepping your bounds.

Wait. What?

Archie looked up at the Orb hovering atop his staff. When he'd first laid hands on it, he'd assumed he was in charge of the artifact. At this point, he wasn't quite so sure it wasn't the other way around.

The Orb had often talked about his destiny with him. His fate. That was something he'd never thought of as being in control of before that.

But was the Orb of Dominance controlling *him*?

It struck Archie that manipulating him wouldn't be that hard. After all, what did Archie have to lose? His life had been absolutely awful until he'd come across the artifact. Why would he want to argue with the Orb?

Why indeed?

That didn't make Archie feel any better about it.

He decided to set his doubts aside for now. Or at least he thought he did.

As they drew closer to the village, Archie couldn't stifle the disquiet in his mind. He began to think about the path that had led him to that point.

He flashed back to the fight with the Undead that Thord had insisted he join. It wasn't odd for the bully to pick on him like that, but the Illagers generally tried to leave the Undead alone unless they were attacking their camp. After all, it's not like the Undead had anything the Illagers wanted.

But the Undead had been harassing the Illagers quite a lot before that, up to the point that Walda had decided they needed to be eliminated. That made sense, at least to Archie. You couldn't just let the mobs pick at the tribe forever.

What seemed incredibly odd, though, was that the Undead had left Archie alive. At the time, he'd ascribed that to incredible luck—something he'd not had much of before, so he'd not been inclined to question it. As rotten as his life had been up to that point, he'd felt like he might have deserved a good turn of fortune by then.

But what if that hadn't been by chance? What if the Undead had spared his life on purpose?

That seems unlikely.

Archie couldn't disagree. But it had led to him being banished from the Illager camp, which had set him on the road to the hollow mountain.

Although, not directly. First he'd wound up at the village, with Yumi. He might have carved out a life for himself and stayed there forever—if the heroes hadn't arrived. More particularly, if he hadn't run into Smacker again.

That had set him back on the road. But the entire time he'd been on the run, he'd been hounded by the Undead. Every time he'd wanted to relax, they'd been there, groaning and clattering after him, herding him ever farther north.

They'd kept after him, driving him toward the rivers of lava by which he'd fashioned the Fiery Forge. But instead of them surrounding him and killing him, they'd given him room to escape.

Which now seemed like maybe more than lucky.

Why would you question your fortune? It's all part of your destiny.

That narrow escape had led him directly to the hollow mountain. The spiders had chased him there until he'd had to climb to heights that would have otherwise terrified him. He really hadn't had a choice.

And that's what had brought him to the Orb of Dominance. Archie's stomach twisted itself into a gigantic knot.

Once he'd fashioned a staff for the Orb and taken it away from the hollow mountain, much of his life had seemed like it was on rails. He'd created Highblock Keep, and then the Orb had encouraged him to attack the village—just like now.

That had gone poorly, which didn't seem like it could have been part of the plan. Why would his fate be to fail?

Unless it had happened to steer him into the clutches of the Nameless One, the single creature with which the Orb of Dominance needed to negotiate. Without that encounter, Archie wouldn't have gathered the Undead mobs he needed to distract the heroes, and this attack on the village would have been doomed to fail.

It had all come together so well.

Maybe too well.

Just stick to the plan.

Archie shuddered. Even if his suspicions were correct, what could he do about that? If the Orb had plotted out his movements so well, was there any hope that he could alter their course?

Did he even want to?

CHAPTER TWENTY-SIX

The Illager army arrived in the hills overlooking the village late the next day. They rallied at a point an easy march from their target, near a low mountain that offered a view of the area all around. Archie had the Redstone Monstrosity set him down, to make sure that no one in the village below might see it, and climbed to the top alone.

From that vantage, Archie could see the torches being lit. Night would soon fall across the land, and the Villagers were preparing for the darkness to come. They had built some new fortifications around the place, but they weren't much more than low walls. The redstone golems would be able to make quick work of them, Archie thought.

Peering down at the place, he could see Yumi's home, but he didn't spy any sign that she was in it. He hoped that something might have called her out of the village, although he didn't imagine that he could possibly be that lucky.

He gazed up at the Orb of Dominance hovering atop his staff. Finding it had probably used up all of his spare luck for the rest of his life—both good and bad.

He turned his attention to the horizon and spotted exactly what he was looking for: Four dark columns of smoke smudged the edges of the sky.

Walda had done her job well.

Wearing a smile of grim satisfaction, Archie focused once more upon the village, which now stood entirely in shadow. Lots of Villagers roamed about down there, mostly returning to their homes after long hours of whatever they spent the bulk of their days doing. They seemed entirely unconcerned with anything happening outside of their boundaries, as if nothing could touch them while they were together.

As far as Archie could tell, no heroes walked the streets among the Villagers. With luck, the ones whose homes Walda had attacked had brought Smacker along with them to help them out, taking him out of the picture as well. Either way, the place seemed relatively abandoned.

Behind him, a little way down the far side of the slope, the Illagers were growing restless. Archie could hear them starting to chant. They sensed the big fight about to come, and they were spoiling for it.

He realized he didn't feel the same way. As he gazed down at the village, he wondered why he'd ever wanted to attack it in the first place.

Maybe it was part of being an Illager, which meant you weren't generally allowed into villages in the first place. That was, of course, because the Illagers tended to attack the Villagers and pillage whatever they could find. Their way of life was built on that cycle of beating other people up and claiming their things—which the Villagers understandably didn't care for.

It was one thing to raid a village though. Tonight, if all went well, Archie and his army would destroy it. After tonight, the name of the Arch-Illager would be known far and wide, and it would cause those who heard it to tremble in their shoes.

The last time Archie had been here, about to attack the village, the thought of that happening would have delighted him. Now he hesitated.

Could he just walk away from all this? Could he send everyone home and then make his way down to the village and find Yumi's house in the dark? Did he really have to become the legend he was supposedly fated to be?

Yes.

"You're not going to give me a choice?" Archie bristled at the idea that the Orb of Dominance would overtly control him like that. Could it just grab him and use him like a puppet?

You don't want a choice.

To Archie's absolute horror, he realized he didn't. He was comfortable—if not actually happy—about following the path fate had carved out for him. Even if the Orb was the primary instrument of that fate.

After all, he was the Arch-Illager, soon to be the ruler of all the land. That was a position he would never have dreamed of achieving on his own. He hadn't even aspired to becoming the leader of his own tribe before this.

But was that true? Did he really have the ambition to transform himself into the Arch-Illager? Or had the Orb of Dominance simply planted that thought in his mind?

Archie honestly couldn't tell.

Does it really matter?

It bothered him to even admit to confusion about that point. Like it or not, he was fated to be the Arch-Illager.

In fact, he had already become the Arch-Illager. Now all he had to do was play that part the best he could manage.

He turned and walked back down the far side of the slope to where his army was waiting for him. Their chanting had become louder and louder, rising to a fever pitch.

Some of them toted torches to light their way through the darkness. Others carried blue banners that marked them all as members of the Arch-Illager's army. One and all wore faces twisted with ginned-up anger and the lust for battle.

"Arch-Ill-a-ger!" they shouted. "Arch-Ill-a-ger!"

They were ready. There was no need for a speech.

Archie stood on a rock before them and gazed down at them all. He'd never felt such power. Such pride.

He'd melded the Illagers into the greatest fighting force the land had ever seen. Together with his redstone golems and his secret weapon—the Redstone Monstrosity—nothing could stand against them. They had become an insatiable war machine, one that needed constant feeding to grow—and new foes to fight. Without such things, the entire affair would implode and collapse atop Archie's dreams, smashing them flat.

Along with himself.

He almost wished the heroes were hiding in the village, waiting for them. Then he could have crushed them then and there, once and for all.

Instead, he would have to be satisfied with destroying the entire village as a warning to them. One that would keep them away until he was prepared to defeat them all.

Archie held his staff high, the Orb of Dominance glowing like a small sun on top of it. He waited for a moment, savoring the tension in those final seconds before the battle began. Then he thrust the staff forward, toward the village, and his army launched itself on its mission of utter destruction.

The Illagers roared in anticipation of the thrill of the upcoming battle as they charged down the path that would lead them straight into the village. The redstone golems followed in their wake. They moved more slowly than the Illagers—silent but for their booming footsteps—but they stood twice as tall, so their longer legs helped them keep up.

Archie resumed his position on the head of the Redstone Monstrosity. That meant he wound up leading from the rear, but he decided he was okay with that. He could direct the redstone golems and the other Illagers better when he could see where they were heading and what they were up against.

As the army rounded the edge of the hill, Archie was pleased to see that the Villagers still weren't ready for the attack at all. A couple of them were patrolling the perimeter, keeping their eyes peeled for threats, but they were on the opposite side of the village. They wouldn't reach the bells in the center of the village to sound the alarm before the Illagers crashed into the place like a tidal wave.

Archie smiled. He couldn't have planned this any better.

The Illagers reached the village in no time flat. The first of them simply ran around the fortifications the Villagers had slapped up, swarming their way into the streets. The rest of them waited for the redstone golems to arrive moments behind them and begin knocking those defenses to the ground.

By the time Archie and the Redstone Monstrosity caught up

with them, the golems had cracked the defenses in half. Archie pointed the monstrosity straight at the walls, and it shattered them into rubble with a swing of its gigantic fists.

The nearby Illagers roared in triumph as Archie and his redstone creatures stomped into the village. The fleeter-footed Illagers poured past their gigantic compatriots and began the attack in earnest.

Illagers took torches and tossed them into the Villagers' homes, flushing them out with flames. When the Villagers emerged—dazed and confused by the terrifying assault—the Illagers grabbed them and began rounding them up as prisoners. No one was safe.

Archie cackled in triumph as the battle ramped up, the screams of Villagers echoing in his ears. He spotted Salah emerging from his home and glancing all around, astonished at how quickly the village's defenses had fallen. He looked like he might drop dead of surprise alone.

Archie didn't blame him. The previous attack had gone so poorly that the Villagers must have felt themselves relatively safe. If reports of the Undead mobs attacking the heroes' homes had reached the village, Salah had probably figured the village was at least safe from assaults from that corner.

That likely explained why the Villagers on patrol had let their guard down. They were ringing the bells now, alerting the few Villagers who weren't yet aware of the threat to their lives, but they were far too late to do anything to stop it.

Archie pointed the Redstone Monstrosity toward Salah. He wanted to see the look on the Villager's face when he saw who it was that was going to seal his doom.

The Villagers barely put up a fight. They seemed too shocked by the destruction flowing through their streets to be able to do more than either gawk at the invaders or flee before them. One by one, they were swept up by the Illager horde.

"That one is mine!" Archie shouted as he pointed his staff at Salah.

The rest of the Illagers parted before him, giving him plenty of room. The redstone golems went off in search of other targets.

Salah goggled at Archie and the Redstone Monstrosity beneath him with eyes widened by absolute terror. He fell to his knees as his legs gave out beneath him. He looked like he wanted to run, but he couldn't figure out a way to persuade his legs to get started.

As the Redstone Monstrosity towered over Salah, Archie slid down the creature's arm and landed crisply in front of the cowering Villager. He strode up to the shivering man, using his staff as a walking stick, until he was standing right over him.

"Hello," Archie said. "Remember me?"

Salah nodded, unable to get his tongue to work. He looked like he might freeze up and fall over at any second.

Archie leaned over and smirked at him. "Looks like you were right about me after all. I am a danger to the village. I am, in fact, going to take you all and press you into work in my mines."

Salah's lips began trembling. If he had something to say, it was warring with his need to start sobbing instead.

"Archie!" a familiar voice said from somewhere over his shoulder. "What are you doing?"

Archie turned around to see Yumi storming toward him. She had no iron golem with her this time—it must have been destroyed already—but the other Illagers all gave way before her, just as Archie had ordered them to. He might have to destroy the village, but he wasn't about to let her be harmed if he could help it.

"Hello, Yumi. I've missed you."

That bare sentiment expressed in the middle of a raging battle stopped Yumi in her tracks. She stared at him, uncomprehending. "What? After all you've done, you have the gall to talk to me like that?" She gaped in horror at the Redstone Monstrosity behind Archie and then at the destruction happening all around her. "Like we're still friends? Are you insane?"

Archie motioned for the Redstone Monstrosity to move off to give them space and then gave her a helpless shrug. "If you want to blame someone, blame him." He pointed at Salah. "If he hadn't worked so hard to get me kicked out of the village, I might still be here, and the whole place might still be standing come morning."

Yumi gaped at him in dismay. "You can't do this. Please. I beg you. Just leave us alone."

"Look around you." Archie gestured toward the entire village, which was ablaze in more places than it was not. "It's already done."

She looked as if she was about to cry. "I trusted you. I took you in."

Her sense of absolute betrayal tugged at Archie's heart. He wanted nothing more than to call a halt to the entire invasion. To take her away from all this. Or maybe to just make peace with the village—with her in charge of it.

It is too late.

Archie couldn't argue with that. It was too late for the village. But for her?

It's too late for her—and for you.

An agonized grimace creased Archie's face. "Get out of here," he said to Yumi. "Take whoever you can with you. My army has orders not to stop you."

She opened her mouth to protest, but he cut her off.

"Still, accidents can happen. Do your best to not become one."

Yumi started to say something again—to snarl at him, perhaps, to chew him out—but this time she shut herself up. She screwed up her lips in disappointment and dismay and gave him one last disgusted shake of her head.

Then she turned and was gone.

Archie felt the last of his hopes of ever standing up to the influence of the Orb of Dominance flee with her. If the best friend he'd ever had couldn't believe in his inherent goodness after everything he'd done, how could he?

He turned back toward Salah then and saw that the Villager was trying to slink away. "Hold it right there," Archie said to him. "I'm not done with you yet."

"Hey!" an obnoxious voice called out. "*I'm* not done with *you!*"

CHAPTER TWENTY-SEVEN

Archie turned to see Smacker standing in the center of the village, his sword out and ready. The hero had apparently not gone off with the others to see who had attacked their homes. Instead he'd stayed behind, either to protect the village or because he was simply too lazy to leave it.

Smacker stood near a statue of a horse that had been erected atop a stone patio in the main square. Torches on high sconces surrounded him. While they illuminated anything beneath them, Archie knew from experience that the light made it harder to see much beyond them. In fact, he was surprised Smacker had spotted him at all.

"How come I can understand him?" Archie said.

I am translating his language for you.

"Why didn't you do that before?"

He wasn't saying anything you needed to know.

"And he is now?"

Perhaps.

Archie rubbed his chin as he mulled that over for a moment. "Can you make him understand me?"

I'm not inside his head.

Archie nodded his understanding to the Orb. Fair enough.

"You thought you'd catch us unawares!" Smacker called out. "But I would never leave my favorite village unprotected!"

Archie bared his teeth in a vicious grin. "I was hoping for exactly that."

Smacker glared at Archie, unable to understand a word he was saying. The threatening tone of the Arch-Illager's voice, though, must have been unmistakable.

At that moment, a redstone golem swung toward Smacker as it lumbered through town, but rather than attack him, it veered off at the last instant, almost as if it had found something more interesting to destroy. A cluster of Illagers did the same thing, moving away in the other direction rather than charging at the hero.

Smacker tracked them each with his sword, a wide smile on his face as he waited for someone to challenge him directly. "Come on!" he said. "I'm right here! Ready and waiting!"

As he'd done with Yumi, Archie had ordered his people to avoid Smacker, no matter how much the hero taunted them. For one, none of them had the power they would need to stand up to someone as inherently strong as Smacker. As the hero had proved the last time Archie had led an attack on the town, he could take apart even a redstone golem in single combat.

For two, Archie didn't want anyone else to get between him and what he had planned for Smacker. He wanted a front-row seat for when he brought the hero down.

"Come on!" Smacker bellowed as another of the redstone golems swung straight past him without slowing down to confront him. "Bring it on, you cowards!"

Archie waited until Smacker had shouted himself hoarse trying to challenge the others. Then he stepped forward again, just enough to get the hero's attention.

"You!" Smacker stabbed his blade in Archie's direction. "You're not afraid of me, are you? Come here and fight me so I can hand you your head!"

Archie snickered at the hero as he strolled closer to him, just to the edge of the halo of light the torches in the center of town provided. "That's not going to happen," he told the hero. "No matter how much you shout about it."

He still can't understand your words.

"No, but he can get the gist of what I'm saying from my tone," Archie said as he peered at the hero. "Can't you?"

"I recognize you!" Smacker gave Archie a suspicious glare. "You were here the last time, leading these idiots into the village. How'd that go for you then? You got yourself all shot up by those skeletons before I could get to you, didn't you? You ought to count yourself lucky for that!"

"He likes to hear himself talk, doesn't he?"

Clearly.

"Well, you're not going to be so fortunate this time!" Smacker said. "This time, I'm going to put you so far down into the ground they're going to have to dig a mine to find you!"

Archie couldn't help but laugh. He threw back his head and let out a long, loud cackle that seemed to spring from the bottom of his feet and shoot all the way up through his body until it came blaring out between his teeth.

That seemed to give Smacker pause. Archie was sure he'd never had an Illager laugh at him. Certainly not like that.

Rather than charging at Archie, Smacker held his ground. He couldn't seem to make up his mind about the Illager. He just stared at him wide-eyed for a moment instead.

Archie started forward then, but as he did, he beckoned with his staff for the Redstone Monstrosity to return.

The gigantic creature lumbered forward into the light, passing Archie almost instantly with its long, thundering strides. Before Smacker could even properly see it, his bravado began to waver.

He could tell right away that it was a huge mob. At first he probably thought it was a redstone golem, which would have been a challenge, but one that he'd beaten before. Then he might have realized the ground was shaking too much for it to be that, and he could have thought that two or three of the creatures were coming at him at once.

Then he saw the actual Redstone Monstrosity. The whole of it. The towering figure of glowing-red rock, complete with its arms as wide as trees and the horns stabbing out from its head, each of which was as long as his sword.

Smacker took one long, entirely horrified look at that mob—and he turned and ran.

Archie crowed in triumph as the Redstone Monstrosity chased Smacker out of the village and into the hills beyond. The creature was under orders not to stop until the hero had vanished from its sight.

While the monstrosity wasn't as fast as the hero, it didn't get tired. Archie suspected that Smacker was in for a very long night.

Eventually the Redstone Monstrosity would return to him—unless something unbelievable happened to it. In the meanwhile,

Archie decided to enjoy the screams of terror still echoing throughout the village and the glow of the fires burning the buildings there to the already scorched ground.

While he waited for the rest of his army to rally to him, he stood there in the center of the village and began to plot his next steps for conquering the land. He might need more soldiers, but he'd have to wait to see how many of the Undead mobs returned to Highblock Keep with Walda. Either way, he should set up a team at the Fiery Forge to build him as many inert redstone golems and monstrosities for him to animate as they could manage.

With those kinds of forces behind him, who would ever dare to challenge him? There was the matter of those four other heroes roaming around, but with luck they'd make the same decision as Smacker, leave the land, and put it as far behind them as fast as they could.

Perhaps they'd come after him for revenge—if they could figure out who had damaged their homes. If they did, he'd be ready for them. He'd give out orders to hinder them every step they took, all the way from the Squid Coast to Highblock Keep.

And if they somehow persisted through all of that, he would take care of them personally.

He and the Orb of Dominance. Between them, nothing could hope to stop them.

There might have been a part of Archie that still wished he could get away and live quietly and alone, far from the troubles that came with becoming the overlord of a land. But apparently that was not his fate . . .

Wise Illager. Once you're on a ride that can't be stopped, it's best to figure out a way to enjoy it.

Archie seethed at the Orb's words. He knew that he wasn't in full control of the Orb anymore—if he had ever been. Worse yet, he was no longer sure he was in full control of himself either. The artifact had wormed its way into his mind and taken root there like a vicious cancer he could not remove.

Would this be the way he lived until he died? Unsure of who was making his decisions? Himself or the Orb of Dominance?

Yes.

Of course.

And how long would that be? Would he age and grow old? Or would the Orb keep him alive long beyond his natural years? Would he ever be free of it?

Not of your own accord.

Archie realized that he should have known this from the start. He was not the sort of Illager who just stumbled into success—especially not the kind of success that gave him unbridled power and the ability to conquer the entire land.

He'd secretly craved power his whole life—if only to keep others from hurting him—but he'd never dreamed of attaining it like this. Or of the bargain he would have to make for it.

He'd been so stupid.

He should have seen the warning signs. One of them had been right there in the name: the Orb of *Dominance*.

From the moment he picked up the Orb, Archie had thought it would give him the power to dominate everything around him. Instead, it had dominated him.

Still, there were worse problems to have. Even if Archie was secretly the Orb's servant—rather than the other way around—his job gave him not just power but prestige.

No one had ever united so many Illagers like this. Or forged an alliance with the Undead mobs.

No one had built a fortress like Highblock Keep.

No one had ever conquered the entire land.

Archie wondered if someone else had laid claim to the Orb of Dominance before. Had they become its servant as well? If so, how had they managed to free themselves from it? Could he hope to do the same?

No.

Of course it would say that. The real question, he supposed, was this: Once they'd gotten free, why hadn't they destroyed it?

It is impossible.

One thing Archie had learned about the Orb: Sometimes it lied—and maybe it was lying now.

He could hope. The Orb couldn't stop that.

Meanwhile, Archie decided—at least he hoped *he* decided—to embrace his new life. He still had a land to conquer. Mobs to make his own. Heroes to defeat.

If he had to rule the land, then he might as well play that role to the hilt.

He would be the Arch-Illager, and no one would ever stop him.

Right?

EPILOGUE

The heroes didn't mind the destruction of their houses. Not really.

Sure, they had spent a lot of time on getting them just the way they wanted. They'd mined the things they needed and crafted them into the things they required. But they'd enjoyed the process as much as the results, and these were all things they could do again if they wanted.

But what had happened to the village? That was awful.

"It was the work of that Illager we saw being bullied in the village," Adriene—the hero Karl had nicknamed Pinky—said as they gazed down from atop a nearby hill at what remained of the village. Parts of it still stood burning. "Remember him?"

"That squirrelly little guy?" Hal (whom Karl had called Stache) said with a deep frown as they surveyed the heartbreaking damage done to their favorite settlement in all the land. "Seriously? He didn't look like he could lift an axe much less raise an army."

"It doesn't matter if it was him or someone else," Hex—Karl had known them as Scarface—said in a bitter tone. "This was a coordinated attack, and we need to put a stop to it. This may look like it's over—the village certainly does—but take it from me. This is just starting."

Valorie—known to Karl as Red—nodded in agreement. "Conquerors like that never stop with a single place. You don't gather an army like that to destroy a single village and go home. They keep going and going until they grind down everything whole and good under their force's boots."

"So what can we do about it?" Adriene said. "You saw Karl fleeing through the forest. I don't think I've ever seen anyone run that fast. He's not going to stop until he hits the sea."

"If then," Hal laughed despite the seriousness of the moment. They all knew that Karl was a bully, and they had barely been able to tolerate him and his antics. Some of them had even discussed having to banish him from the land themselves.

If there was an upside to all this, it was that the attack on the village had done that for them. All told, Karl had been pretty useless as a hero. They'd left him behind to protect the village while they checked out the fires that had been set at their houses, for instance, and look how that had turned out. And that had just been the latest in a long line of failures by him.

Either way, with Karl gone, they were the only heroes left in the land. No one else could hope to stand against this threat. No one else could possibly protect the innocent.

Hex coughed. "I hate to say this, but for all his clear and awful faults, Karl knew how to fight. If he couldn't deal with this new threat, what sort of chance do we have?"

"Well, for one, there are four of us," Valorie said. "Even if the numbers aren't exactly on our side, that has to count for something."

"And together, as a team, we're far better than the sum of our parts," said Adriene. "That's how this attack managed to destroy the village. They divided us. They drew us away from the village and sent us off to our respective homes. If we'd kept together instead, do you think they would have stood a chance?"

"It wasn't like they beat Karl either," Hal pointed out. "Like most bullies, he's a coward at heart. He finally had someone with enough power stand up to him, and he just turned and ran. We're not going to do that, right?"

"We're not cowards," Hex said. "But bravery on its own isn't enough. Those were Undead mobs that attacked our homes last night. If they did that to draw us away from the village—and it seemed pretty clear they did—that means the Illagers and the Undead are working together. That's a kind of alliance of evil this land has never seen."

"That's why we have to stick together and fight to stop it," Valorie said. "The alternative is too horrible to contemplate. To leave the people of this land on their own against such a force? Unthinkable!"

"So we're agreed?" Adriene asked. Even though it was clear what the answer would be, Adriene needed to hear it. "We're banding together to fight this new threat and rid it from the land?"

They all knew what Karl would tell them. *You're all fools! They're too powerful! Did you see that monstrosity? You're all going to be killed!*

And then he'd probably cackle about the fact that he'd been smart enough to run away rather than stay behind, fight, and risk being killed.

Hal gave the rest of them a grim nod. "Count me in. Just as long as you all swear never to say, 'The real treasure we found was the friendships we made along the way.' Okay?"

The rest of them laughed in agreement. From what they could tell, this wasn't going to be some soul-searching journey that taught them something about themselves. It would be a brutal battle to defeat the greatest threat they'd ever seen. And they were all ready for it.

"Of course," Hex said with a wolfish grin. "I never liked the rest of you anyway."

Valorie shook their head at the others. This adventure was sure to test far more than their friendship. They'd be lucky if they all survived it. Still, there was no doubt what their answer to this call to action would be. "I'm in. Let's get to work."

ACKNOWLEDGMENTS

While my name may be on the cover, a lot of people spend a tremendous amount of time putting a book like this together. First and foremost, I need to thank my editor, Alex Davis, whose unflagging enthusiasm and constant support always spurred me to make this story the best I could manage. You were a joy to work with every step of the way.

On top of that, I want to thank my copy editor, Liz Carbonell, who helped polish the book's text to a gleaming shine.

Also at Del Rey, I'd like to thank Keith Clayton, Tom Hoeler, Julie Leung, Sarah Peed, Elizabeth Schaefer, and Dennis R. Shealy, both for getting this book rolling and for their ongoing help.

M. S. Corley deserves huge praise for the wonderful cover art. I adore it so much I've had it staring back at me from my computer's desktop for months.

Thanks also to Dan Bittner for narrating the audiobook. I love listening to Archie's story being told in a whole new voice that's even better than the one in my head.

Of course, not a bit of this book would have been possible without the entire team at Mojang who works hard to make Minecraft so much fun. Special thanks should go to the whole Mine-craft Dungeon team—especially the leads, David Nisshagen and Måns Olson—for concocting such a vibrant new adventure for us all to play in.

On top of that, I want to recognize Agnes Larsson and the rest of the amazing Mojang team I met when I was a guest last year at the Nordsken games conference in beautiful Skellefteå, Sweden, a wonderful little city that sits just shy of the Arctic circle. Joining you at the dinner before the inaugural White Reindeer Award was one of the highlights of the week.

I'd also like to thank Jennifer Hammervald, Max Herngren, Alex Wiltshire, and Kelsey Howard at Mojang for all their help, plus their fantastic partners at Microsoft, including Vanessa Dagnino, Kevin Grace, and Dennis Ries. You are the unsung he-roes of these Minecraft stories.

In addition, I want to give a shout-out to my fellow Minecraft novelists, who blazed such a glowing trail before me: Max Brooks, Tracey Baptiste, Catherynne M. Valente, Jason Fry, and espe-cially my friend Mur Lafferty, who gave me invaluable insight as I embarked on this story. You set high bars for me to measure up to.

Of course, I can't end this without expressing my gratitude to you, the reader. Stories really only come to life when they have heads to live in, and I'm thrilled you've chosen to invite this one into yours. Thanks.

ABOUT THE AUTHOR

MATT FORBECK is an award-winning and *New York Times* bestselling author and game designer with over thirty novels and countless games published to date, which have won dozens of honors. His recent work includes the new Dungeons & Dragons: Endless Quest books, *Halo: Bad Blood,* and *Life Is Strange: Welcome to Blackwell,* plus work on the Rage 2 videogame and the Shotguns & Sorcery role-playing game based on his novels. He lives in Beloit, Wisconsin, with his wife and five children, including a set of quadruplets.

forbeck.com

ABOUT THE TYPE

This book was set in Electra, a typeface designed for Linotype by renowned type designer W. A. Dwiggins (1880–1956). Electra is a fluid typeface, avoiding the contrasts of thick and thin strokes that are prevalent in most modern typefaces.